BEYOND

by

BRUCE McLACHLAN

CHIMERA

Beyond Charybdis first published in 2002 by
Chimera Publishing Ltd
PO Box 152
Waterlooville
Hants
PO8 9FS

Printed and bound in Great Britain by
Cox & Wyman Ltd, Reading.

BEYOND CHARYBDIS

Bruce McLachlan

This novel is fiction – in real life practice safe sex

Oceanus was the first to pull back. 'Ready, slave?' he asked, his free hand resting on Tethys's hip as he flexed the other in preparation.

'Yes, master, I am your slave to do with as you will,' she whispered, closing her eyes and bracing herself.

He brought his palm down hard on her bottom, clapping the flesh with a loud smacking sound. She gasped from the pleasure, rapture spawning inside at the thought of being punished by her owners as she hung defenceless before their eyes. He concentrated on one buttock to make it glow with its own internal fire, until it was hot and prickly with sensation, and then he paused, leaving her panting and heart racing, her body quaking slightly as though an invisible force was fucking her.

Chapter One

It could have been months or years since she was sent into the ocean as a helpless slave, hidden from view by the machinations of a vengeful Titan. Mina's mind was numb, her thoughts dull and indistinct. Her visage now that of a lowly beast it was as if her psyche had decided to follow suit and adopt a lower form of sentience.

Each day forced the same repetitive trauma on her mind. She swam amongst the lowest reaches of the coral travelling to the various valves whose locations she had memorised to receive her bodily sustenance. The valves were frugal suppliers, refusing to grant a refill for at least an hour. When she stumbled upon a port recently used by another of her eel sisters, she had to quickly rush to a different site before her paltry supply of air ran out.

Sleep was impossible except for brief, light naps. The beeping always woke her and prompted her to slither to a valve in order to prolong her miserable existence. The constant deprivation of prolonged rest speeded her descent into a bestial mentality, robbing her of all motivation except survival. The need to find her owners became a distant memory only half recalled when she caught sight of the fish swimming freely above or stumbled upon a Titan playing with Nymphs amongst the rocks.

Mina swiftly discovered that such recreation was not for her because all the eel women were of the electrified breed. Should they be handled they, and the person trying to access them, would be subjected to vivid shocks channelled through subtle circuits located both inside

5

and outside their secondary skins. No one dared touch them, depriving them of all contact and denying them any sensual pleasure save the endless steady but feeble rocking of their dildo as they swung their legs against the currents.

Yet strangely enough, the absence of sensation and the unrelenting bondage did not trouble Mina, but instead afforded her a sense of security. The endless routine never wavered, never offered any surprises, and she could soothe herself with the arousing notion that somewhere some mysterious Titan was thinking of her, titillating himself with the knowledge that she was suffering for her crimes.

She missed the lack of carnal pain and pleasure, but her severe bondage almost made up for it. The one thing she truly missed was the weather, for the seasons of the abyssal deep never altered. She often dwelt on what it would be like to feel the elements again, to feel rain on her face and the wind in her hair and the sun on her naked skin. She longed to see the sky and the clouds.

At some point in the uncertain longevity of her rubber imprisonment and its resulting mental and physical devolution, Mina spied something never before seen in the oceans. In the distance, she spotted a dark shape moving beyond the perimeter of the lights as she skirted the farthest reaches of the garden. After finding several used valves, her quest for air was diverted outwards, sending her places into which few other eels had ventured.

Mina found herself in an area where the plants and the coral thinned and gave way to shadows, broken areas of dark rock and grey sand, the wall of utter blackness beyond them a most ominous sight. Only a few of the most hardy and monstrous species managed to thrive there, little fiends of the deep that kept well away from the garden as light was a terrible blight to their crushed

6

and frozen anatomies.

Spotting a valve, she slotted herself onto it and gained a full measure of air before lifting away and peering more leisurely at the large shape hanging in the distance touched by only a few weak rays of stray light. Risking a closer look, she paddled forward, leaving the flourishing garden behind her. The waters began getting colder as the temperature plummeted towards sub zero hell.

Suddenly, she spotted the broken outline of a floating submersible. The deep-sea pod was a crooked contraption made up of mechanical arms, pipes, tanks and bulbous windows, a steel beast that came to life abruptly as she watched. Several soft lights rose to brilliance along its sides as its propellers gave sudden flurries of motion, gouging at the waters and turning it about towards her.

With a startled squeal, she jerked around and rushed away, only to cry out against her gag again as the headlights of the sub flashed to their full brilliance, paining her eyes and filling her world with a pure white sheet. Incapacitated, she lurched unevenly, her equilibrium lost, her sense of direction completely compromised. She flung her legs against her costume, trying to get away while hoping she was not heading deeper out to sea. If she went too far she would not be able to get back before her air ran out and hypothermia set in.

A metal fist closed twin pincers around her calves. With a desperate wriggle she slipped away from them, but they caught her ankles next, compressing them and taking firm hold of her. Flinging herself frantically against her suit and the anchor, she was suddenly plunged back into darkness as the sub cut off its lights while towing her away. The lights of the garden dimmed as the vessel banked and ducked into a series of outlying trenches. Panicked, she continued fighting to free herself, fearful she would be held until she perished, her body left floating in black waters where no one would ever find her.

Something snapped to her faceplate, locking to the valve that fed her, and the waters began getting warmer as she found herself thrashing inside some sort of container. The clamps at her ankles gave way then, and a moment later she heard the sound of something closing and locking into place as once more a sudden bright light blinded her eyes. Blinking wildly, she discerned a globe just slightly wider than her body surrounding her; a transparent shell reinforced from without by riveted bands. A heavy articulated cable had been set to her faceplate, reaching down into the steel base of the golden fish bowl, where small vents regulated the water level and temperature. She was inside the craft as a detachable part of it, but she could not see into the vessel for her bubble was like a cargo container located halfway down its spine.

Circling impotently within her new claustrophobic world, Mina watched the ocean floor fall away as their ascent carried them out of the trenches, allowing them to travel far from the complex. All about her was darkness; she could see and hear nothing. She did not know if she was being stolen or liberated or being taken in for questioning by someone intent on exposing the Charybdis Project. A thousand possibilities rushed through her mind, none of them helping to soothe her frayed nerves.

Then light began filling the waters around them and she glimpsed the ocean life characteristic of the upper reaches of the Pacific. Horrifying visions of explosive decompression plagued her as she continued upwards, but she could feel no change in the water pressure. The bubble in which she floated was clearly protecting.

Sunlight dazzled her eyes, and she sobbed with joy as its golden aura exploded into thousands of brilliant stars as the sub broke through the surface of the waves. Water poured down her sealed dome through which she glimpsed the light-blue vault of the sky with a few white clouds scattered by the wind. It was the most beautiful thing she had ever seen. Then she saw the large ship, and when the sub reached it several men in dark overalls dropped down and began fastening the hook of a crane to the craft. They signalled to the operator and she was lifted from the water, swung round and placed gently on the deck.

Mina felt horribly embarrassed and exposed as the crew stared at her with a mixture of awe and bewilderment – a latex-bound woman swimming inside a bowl sent to gather specimens from the deep.

Unable to hear them, she watched as her cell was quickly drawn over to a chute in the deck. The seal was locked to the base of her prison, and suddenly the bottom of the dome opened up. Bubbles launched from the floor and the water level began falling rapidly, robbing Mina of the realm in which she could move. She flapped helplessly against the bottom of the bowl as her head emerged from water for the first time in what felt like forever. Struggling to move she felt a tremendous weight descend on her, the return to gravity making her realise just how dependent she had become on her fluid environment.

Once the waters were gone, the base of the bowl opened completely and she slipped down into the small chute, her latex form sliding smoothly against the steel. The cable detached from her faceplate as she began her descent and she flowed down the slender pathway, traversing the long slide until she eventually came to a stop at a slight angle and rested against a hatch.

The lowest part of the chute was slightly wider than the rest of it, and she soon realised why when four panels opened and mechanised arms emerged. The dull teeth tore through her latex shell, but only brushed her skin with a tickling sensation. The saws cut through her prison as a set of steel hands took hold of her and, with some awkward motions, managed to turn her over so her back could be exposed. Her tank was extracted and her latex cocoon slid away from her.

Mina gurgled and sobbed as her arms came free, her numb limbs dropping uselessly to her sides, condemned to immobility for too long to be of any immediate use to her. She tried to pull them up to her face to haul her gag free, but they refused to respond to her mental commands.

The dildo slithered from her tracts and the collar vanished, whereupon her head lolled weakly. Laying slack across the floor, her legs and torso the only working parts of her, the mechanical hands grabbed her gag and drew it away, the hoses paying out of her nostrils and mouth finally popping free. She coughed and nearly retched before sucking down a breath of genuine fresh air. It felt cold and sharp and hurt her lungs, which had been force-fed for so long that they were taken aback by what real air tasted like.

The hatch beneath her head suddenly opened with a hydraulic growl and she tumbled out onto steel deck plates.

Looking around with her eyes wide, she found herself in a decompression chamber. The small room contained a single bunk bed, a basin and a toilet, and the steel walls offered one small, reinforced porthole.

Fighting to move, Mina slowly managed to haul her wet form up using the bed frame as a handhold and support. Her shoulder-length hair hung in moist strands past her shoulders, revealing just how long she had been imprisoned as an eel.

Pulling herself up onto the bed, she collapsed across the sheets with a groan of rapture. She had forgotten how good it was to smell something as she inhaled the delicious scent of fresh cotton sheets.

Giggling weakly with joy, she drifted into a deep and contented sleep.

Chapter Two

With a cry of terror, she hurled herself against the smothering arms of latex transforming her into an eel... and woke to find herself covered in perspiration and lying across a bed, naked and free.

Yet now she was lying comfortably across a bed, her previous incarceration felt like a treasure to be held and revered. Pulling the sheet over her she closed her eyes and let her hand drift between her legs. The slight pressure of her fingertips against her clitoris had it erupting with long denied sensation, and her climax was strong and succulent, making her shudder against the mattress.

Afterwards she managed to sit up and explore her small world. A pair of white panties and a vest she had failed to notice before lay at the foot of the bed. She slid into them slowly, and the tight cotton clung to her, emphasising her curves in an erotic fashion.

Then she managed to stand up and found a hot meal in the airlock hatch. Her throat felt chafed by the passage of solid sustenance as opposed to the nutrient sludge she had lived on for so long, but her tongue was in ecstasy.

After eating, and both struggling with and relishing every bite, she began trying to exercise her limbs back into shape. It riled her to find herself so feeble in comparison to how strong she had been before her imprisonment as an eel.

With nothing else to occupy her, she applied herself to the task of reconditioning her body. She exercised and worked out constantly, stopping only to eat and sleep.

She washed in the basin and devoted herself single-mindedly to the regime of muscle development. She practiced old moves, trying to recapture her lightning reflexes and killer instincts, but her skills were rusty.

She thought often of Atlas and her owners, of Charybdis and the Titans and the various acts she had been forced to perform. It kept her in a constant state of sexual arousal, which was only intensified by the anxiety of wondering who had fished her out of the depths and what they planned to do with her.

Mina knew she had a masochistic streak and more than a casual taste for fetishism, but she had assumed her tastes had been influenced by her surroundings. She had believed that if she left the complex and returned to the real world she could wean herself back to normalcy. Clearly, she had underestimated the profound level of the indoctrination visited upon her. The project had branded new lusts deep into her soul where she could not expel them.

She tried to fill her mind with more banal fantasies, but every time she pictured normal lovemaking with a man or woman they invariably became vengeful dominants clad in latex or vinyl tying her down and whipping her before pleasuring their gagged and struggling slave.

The religious rebuilding of her physique was the only stabilising force in her life, helping to keep her from dwelling too much on the past. Yet every day and night when she was not exercising herself into exhaustion, even in her dreams she wallowed in memories of her subjugation to others. The remembered blend of pain and pleasure was a potent narcotic, and she had been rendered a hapless addict who craved it more and more with every passing moment. She would not know what to do with herself if she had been rescued by some normal agency. She now longed for a life of bondage,

13

and Charybdis was the only person who could give it to her. She could not betray his secrets. But if the complex had been discovered and was under surveillance, surely its end was approaching.

Sitting on the edge of the bed, Mina rested her elbows on her knees, leaning over and staring blankly at the deck plates as she let her latest meal digest. Her body felt much better; her limbs had become true extensions of her willpower rather than awkward appendages over which she had little influence.

She jerked around when she heard heavy clunking sounds coming from the door. Remaining where she was, she adopted an indifferent façade, feigning apathy so she might more easily unleash a surprise attack should it be required. She did not tense her body, for that might betray her intentions. Instead, she regulated her breathing and let the cold clinical wall of a fighting trance embrace her.

The click of a heel against metal sounded like a judgement trump in her heart, and she melted, all notion of combat vanishing like a morning mist as submissive fires raged through her body, burning away even the concept of resistance.

Tethys stood tall and defiant on the threshold, a smile on her ebony lips. She was clad in latex leggings in a garment with a black zip crotch. The polished jet fabric followed her delicious curves and flowed almost imperceptibly into knee-high riding boots with wicked heels and silver spurs. The waistband of her leggings was surrounded by a studded belt, from which hung a leather sheath. A purple riding crop with a black leather handle and a ringed tip was slung into the holster, reaching down to her knees. A rubber bra clung to her breasts and offered her cleavage to Mina's adoring stare, its slender straps draped over her elegant shoulders. A spiked rubber choker encircled her throat, and wrist-high gloves of the same clinging fabric encased her hands, leaving her fingers free, her long black nails curved like pointed daggers.

'How is my slave?' she asked happily. 'Did she miss me?'

Mina plunged off the bed and sank to her knees to embrace the lower half of the woman's body, her cheek resting against her naked belly. Tears flooded her eyes and spilled down her face as she wept with joy upon seeing her beloved dominatrix once more.

'I'll take that as a "yes",' she said wryly, stroking Mina's hair. 'But don't forget to thank my boots, slave.'

Without even thinking about it, Mina collapsed and kissed them in adoration. She curled her tongue around the heel, her body shaking with pleasure at once more performing this humble task.

Tethys crouched down as Mina worked, the sound of creaking rubber bliss to Mina's ears as her mistress's sharpened digits ran through her hair, and then lodged beneath her chin to draw her face upward so their eyes met. For the first time Mina saw the woman's true eyes with her coloured contacts removed. The cool blue irises were flecked with streaks of light green, a marked contrast to the consuming featureless black Mina was accustomed to.

'How do you feel, slave?' Tethys asked, affirming that nothing had changed between them.

'I'm fine,' she replied calmly, trying to hide how elated she was to have been rescued by those she loved, and who loved her.

'Here you call me *mistress*, slave.' She tapped a finger lightly to the tip of Mina's nose in token chastisement.

'Yes, mistress, but…' she began, looking around her cautiously.

'Yes, slave?'

15

'Where is *here*, and is Oceanus with you, mistress?'

'Come and see,' Tethys offered, rising to her full impressive height over Mina's cowering form. She walked out into the corridor, her heels sounding dark notes against the metal floor like a heartbeat that captured Mina and lured her forward.

Following her mistress across the cold floor, she could not take her eyes off the bottom so beautifully presented by the skin-tight leggings, the fabric delving into the sweet valley between her cheeks, her high-heels tautening the muscles of her buttocks in their mouth-watering rubber skin.

Walking up a flight of steps they emerged onto the deck, and the sudden flood of sunlight made Mina bow her head and shield her eyes with a forearm. She hesitated a moment, afraid of the light's intensity after her long gloomy life in the depths of the ocean.

'Come on, little slave, there's nothing to fear here,' Tethys assured her, her black-clad figure exquisitely silhouetted against the luminous air.

Mina walked after her, and the feel of the sun upon her skin was a delight she had not experienced for a long time.

'Oh my, I'd forgotten what it felt like,' she murmured, caressing herself and tossing her head back to feel the full force of the sun on her face.

'It's been a while, hasn't it, slave?' enquired a familiar male voice.

Mina's lips curved up in a smile of joy. Using her hand as a visor, she gained enough shade by which to scan the deck.

Oceanus was dressed in a similar riding style as his wife, except the trousers hugging his legs were white, flowing into polished black boots fitted with spurs. A studded belt encircled his waist and served to tuck in a black silk shirt. In his hand he held a riding crop that was a twin to Tethys's, but for its deep sapphire-blue colour. He wore mirrored sunglasses, and his hair spilled down his back as he smiled down at Mina's greeting. She had run over to him and dropped to her knees to hug him as she had Tethys, overjoyed to see him.

'I take it she remembers us,' he commented to his wife.

'How could I ever forget you, master?' Mina blurted, assuming the change of title extended to him as well.

'Such a sweet slave,' he laughed.

'What happened?' Mina begged to know. 'How did you find me? Where am I?' She held on to him tightly, unwilling to ever let him go again.

Tethys stepped behind her and ran the tip of her crop down her back, rolling the leather against the wrinkles in her vest. 'Once you were kidnapped, we used every resource to try and find you again,' she began, setting the weapon aside and kneeling down behind her. Mina leaned back a little, raising her arms so her mistress could pull off her vest. 'We looked everywhere,' Tethys went on. 'We called in favours to have others use their contacts to try and locate you.'

'Nothing worked though,' Oceanus announced, sinking to his knees before Mina, who shuddered when Tethys tossed her vest away and ran her nails down the inside of her arms and then over her breasts.

'Eventually, however, Poseidon came to be deeply in our debt,' Tethys took up the tale, 'and offered us a way to erase it. When we accepted, he told us you had been taken by Atlas on someone's behalf. He had sent you to Hephaestus to be concealed until such time as we had given up on you.' She paused to kiss Mina's neck, who was panting in delight as Oceanus pinched both her nipples, squeezing them softly and rotating them in his grasp.

'We've had dealings with Hephaestus before, so we

17

could guess he would get a perverse joy from hiding you right under our very noses,' he explained. 'Once we saw him launch his eel project into the oceans, we knew you would be amongst them, at some point.'

Mina's lips drifted around to meet those of Tethys, and the two of them exchanged a deep and lust-filled kiss, their tongues dancing around each other's, tasting and devouring with gusto.

Tethys pulled back. 'We waited until the eel population had stabilised and then began checking the bodies of the Nymphs until we were certain which one was you. It took a while, because even though you have a very distinct and luscious form, little slave, it's hard to tell who's who in those suits, and even harder to keep track of the possible candidates.'

Oceanus lowered his head to suckle her teats, his hands massaging her sex and causing her panties to grow damp with desire for them. 'A little assistance from Poseidon, in exchange for a favour, allowed us to manipulate the valves,' he murmured against her breast, 'and draw you to where a submersible could snatch you back to us.'

'Didn't Charybdis see?' she gasped, with physical and emotional pleasure.

'We told him secretly, in advance, informing him we intended to take back our slave,' Tethys replied, letting a finger reach into the cleft of Mina's bottom cheeks, pushing her panties in and then hooking a digit around them to drag the bunched cloth and pull it up against her pussy. Oceanus did the same, turning the cotton underwear into a version of a crotch-rope the two of them played against her, the fabric chafing against her clitoris and parting her vulva as it dug against her anus.

'What did Poseidon want?' Mina asked breathlessly, overwhelmed by sensations, the warm sun penetrating her skin as she surrendered to the hot joy of their combined touch.

'His one stipulation for rescuing you and for arranging your escape,' Tethys answered her, 'was a return to the surface so you could come to his ranch. We were invited as his guests, and so here we are. Take a look at your new home,' she urged, rising in tandem with her husband.

Wincing slightly but still possessed by a heady bliss, Mina let the improvised crotch-rope force her back up to her feet, and her eyes were sufficiently accustomed to the intense tropical light to let her see the deck, littered with comfortable lounge chairs, and a pair of maids, naked save for their chastity belts and a slick coating of sun-block, holding trays at the ready to serve the needs of the nobles on board.

The ship was moving slowly along the perimeter of what Mina recognised as the territorial waters of China. The strange collection of misshapen islands extended to the starboard side, filling the sea with sporadic clumps of overgrown rocks, the isolated mountains coated in luscious green vegetation. They seemed to be heading for a fair-sized peak surrounded by a maze of smaller islands, many of them barely clearing the ocean surface.

'What's going on, mistress?' she asked, marvelling at the gorgeous view.

'We're about to arrive on Poseidon's island, where we're going to train you as a pony, Mina.'

'Does that sound intriguing, slave?' Oceanus asked her kindly.

'Oh yes, master,' she replied, mulling over the concept of being harnessed and bridled as a beast of burden and transport. It would be massively different from her position as a hapless fish, for as a pony she would be expected to obey commands. As a fish she had nothing to do save meander and perpetuate her own existence. As a pony she would be looked after and subject to

19

intense training. It was a far more attractive fate, and she was eager to embark upon it.

A third servant walked out onto the bow where they stood gazing out at the sparkling blue-green sea lapping against golden beaches or crashing against rocks to create areas of snow-white surf.

'Lord Oceanus, Lady Tethys, the captain wishes me to inform you that the landing craft is ready for launch,' the girl said meekly. 'Your baggage has been placed onboard and they await your arrival.' 'Excellent,' Oceanus declared. 'Shall we go, my love?'

'Yes, indeed,' his wife replied. 'We don't want to keep our host waiting. Our slow boat to China has been fun, but I'm eager to feel dry land beneath my feet again.' Smiling, she turned and led Mina down the starboard side of the ship to where a large dingy with an outboard was waiting for them.

The three of them climbed into the yielding craft, and the crew lowered it to the water. A stern haul brought the motor to chugging life, a puff of acrid grey smoke rising into the air as it began churning the sea with its small blades. Once freed of the cranes, the small craft cruised effortlessly away from the side of the ship, making straight for the island weaving deftly amongst the jagged rocks protecting it from any larger vessels.

Mina leaned against the soft sides of the boat, her two beloved owners sitting opposite her arm-in-arm, watching the island looming closer. She looked around her, bouncing slightly as the small vessel rode the waves. The sun was beginning its descent towards the horizon, and long shadows were stretching across the sea while the far side of the island was sheathed in twilight. A warm breeze caressed her hair as she gazed up at the towering dagger of stone forming the centre of the island. A few sporadic ledges provided veins for life on the massive, lifeless fang, which was flanked on one side by jungle and on the other by the golden crescent of a beach that continued all the way around the island. Small rock outcroppings on which Mina could spy figures rose from the ocean a few yards offshore dressed in barnacles and devoid of plants. At first she thought the figures of the women were merely standing still, but as they drew closer she discerned they were made of stone and were representations of classic mermaids. The statues stood to attention facing the sea like sentinels guarding the island.

The scent of the sea overwhelmed Mina's starved senses as she traced her fingertips along the edges of the boat, feeling the smooth fabric and taking the opportunity to be thankful for her freedom of movement, savouring it while she could, because she had no idea how much longer she would possess such a gift.

As they approached the beach, she noticed people moving about or reclining beneath colourful umbrellas, iceboxes and other luxuries surrounding them. Just before the tree line sat a small primitive hut with log walls and a straw roof, apparently a bar manned by two naked, dark-skinned women. Another small group of females in chastity belts wandered the beach and served the needs of the guests, while still more young women played in the sand or the surf, chasing each other and swimming in the crystal waters wearing only steel bands about their loins and around their throats.

Passing the first of the rocks rising from the water, Mina saw the statues were alive; women had been encased in stone shells and set as trophies upon the rocks. Their eyes were visible inside small ovals permitting them a view of the sea, their stone cells penetrated by internal hoses, enabling them to remain inside their immobile tombs for lengthy periods of time.

The sand grated against the yielding hull of the craft with a scraping hiss as the motor forced them up out of

21

the waves onto the beach. Two Hispanic looking women promptly paddled over and took hold of the bow as other slaves hurried down the beach from a paved road leading into the trees. Wading into the water, they took the suitcases from the boat and headed back up the trail with them.

'Well, here we are,' Oceanus declared, jumping out onto the sand and extending a helping hand to Tethys, whose heels sank into the soft surface, forcing her to walk on her toes until she reached more solid ground.

'Come on, Mina, let's go,' he called over his shoulder, waving her out of the boat where she still sat staring dreamily out at the tranquil, lovely island.

The sand clung stimulatingly to her feet as she followed her masters, the feel of the particles shifting beneath her bare toes and tickling her soles making her giggle like a child. The euphoria gripping her heart and mind in those moments was like nothing she had ever experienced before. She felt completely at peace, her life full of new promise and wonder.

Crossing the beach, the couple waved to a few shadowy forms lounging beneath umbrellas, their features hidden by sunglasses. Most of them were either naked or wearing only token garments.

The delicate chirping of birds and the music of leaves rustling in a gentle breeze gradually replaced the sound of waves breaking against the sand. The slender road wound between the trees, the shaded air of the forest cool and moist and saturated with all the heady scents of untamed nature. Then the trees gave way to a large meadow so lush it resembled an emerald carpet. A sizeable mansion rose from its heart, built entirely of wood and dotted with individual balconies accessed by sliding doors. Mina could see people relaxing on these vantage points being tended by slaves as they enjoyed the sunshine and the temperate climate. The main doors were fronted by a sizeable portion of pavement into which had been secured whipping posts, gallows, stocks and other heavy engines of restraint, some of them currently occupied, some not. In the rapidly dying light, a woman was lighting torches set in iron shafts approximately five feet high that supported metal braziers forged in the shape of flames. The jagged fangs rose up to mimic the genuine article as the woman placed a flame in the interior of each one, the small pyres flinging up a cascade of flickering yellow and orange light and banishing the gathering darkness.

To the right of the house sat a squat and windowless oval building, the purpose of which was impossible to determine from its façade. Then whinnies and neighs reached Mina's ears, distracting her from her contemplation of the strange building and drawing her attention to what she assumed to be an ordinary stable shaped like an L to the left of the mansion. The wooden barracks encompassed a courtyard where metal fences divided the area into individual pens and training grounds. The occupants of these were the source of the sounds, but there was no normal beast in evidence.

Human ponies were undergoing their regime of indoctrination – women sealed in a variety of costumes and prancing about at the command of whip and crop, their hoofed feet pounding the rich soil beneath them. Taller torches were being lit in this area as well, that were slightly more dense in construction, the wider bases providing more support, apparently for safety reasons, so they could not fall and harm a helplessly bound slave.

The slaves carrying their luggage entered the house while Oceanus and Tethys paused in the courtyard to wait for Mina to catch up. As she arrived between them, they smiled and indicated a set of gallows.

'We shall be leaving you in bondage for the night, slave, to prepare you for tomorrow,' Tethys informed her, one hand on her hip, the other running down the polished wood of the main support beam.

'You still want to be trained as our pony?' Oceanus asked soberly.

Mina looked up into his eyes and nodded fervently. 'Yes, master, I do.'

His smile deepened as he kissed his wife before preparing the gallows for Mina's bondage. They looked ordinary, except there was no noose at the end of the rope, from which hung a heavy set of leg-spreaders. A cluster of three hoops were sealed to each end of the iron bar, and onto these had been clipped a set of sturdy leather fetters. A collection of riveted straps was configured to create a funnel-shape for the foot, with other bands for the ankles made of soft padded leather to ease the strain of suspension. The rope holding the contrivance ran through hoops set in the wood and connected to a winch placed at the side, making lifting a slave a vastly less taxing feat.

'Lay down on your back,' Tethys commanded.

Mina swiftly spread herself across the cold stones, her lowly position leaving the gallows and her owners towering over her, emphasising her feeling of servility as they each took hold of one of her ankles and lifted it, slotting her feet into the awaiting straps and tightening them to an exact fit, the cushioned interior clamping gently to her extremities. Once she was secured, Tethys turned the crank and the mechanism quickly gathered the rope, lifting Mina's buttocks into the air and then her back, her shoulders and finally her head, leaving her swinging gently to and fro, her legs splayed wide by her confinement.

Her wrists were drawn before her and locked into a set of matching shackles. The padded leather enclosed her joints and the D-rings that lay on either side were all captured by a single padlock, so she could not remove them from her wrists or even part her hands. Rope was fed around and joined her elbows, pulling them together behind her. Her cuffs were then dragged to her belly as her elbows were hauled closer in a familiar pose, depriving her of the use of her arms.

Left hanging in the cool air of early evening, Mina watched impotently as her two owners looked her over lustfully, clearly fighting the urge to succumb to their carnal passions.

'Is our slave happy?' Tethys asked with a purr in her voice, running her hand down Mina's thighs and squeezing the firm flesh.

'Yes, mistress, I am glad to be yours again,' she replied truthfully.

'Such delightfully pert mounds… they just scream for abuse, don't they, Oceanus?' his wife mused, tracing a finger across Mina's buttocks. She then thrust her digit through the cleft in her bottom cheeks, riding down the tight valley and across the fabric covering her pudenda. 'So desperately in need of discipline, and so hungry for it,' she went on dreamily, and pulling Mina's panties aside she shoved a finger into her moist sex.

'Oh, mistress,' Mina gasped, her hands clawing at her bonds as she shuddered with ecstasy, feeling the finger swirling insider her in lazy circles.

'Would our slave like a sound spanking before we retire?' Tethys offered. 'Would our slave relish such attention, or revile it?' Her other hand reached down and cupped one of Mina's inverted buttocks.

'Oh yes, please, mistress,' she begged, keen to feel such chastisement, her long exile from sensations leaving her desperately hungry to taste what she had missed so much.

'Shall we give our little pet what she wants?' Tethys asked her husband.

'How could we resist such a tempting sight?' he

replied, stepping up beside his wife, who abandoned Mina to embrace him. The two nobles kissed passionately, stoking the fires of their libido, their hands wandering sensually over each other's bodies.

Oceanus was the first to pull back. 'Ready, slave?' he asked, his free hand resting on Tethys's hip as he flexed the other in preparation.

'Yes, master, I am your slave to do with as you will,' she whispered, closing her eyes and bracing herself.

He brought his palm down hard on her bottom, clapping the flesh with a loud smacking sound. She gasped from the pleasure, rapture spawning inside at the thought of being punished by her owners as she hung defenceless before their eyes. He concentrated on one buttock to make it glow with its own internal fire, until it was hot and prickly with sensation, and then he paused, leaving her panting and heart racing, her body quaking slightly as though an invisible force was fucking her.

After a moment of contemplative silence, Tethys applied her hand to Mina's other buttock, repeating the treatment with her virgin cheek, her hand ringing applause against Mina's tender flesh, flesh unaccustomed to maltreatment and yet so desperately in need of it.

After tenderising their slave's skin and making it hypersensitive to the slightest touch, Tethys and Oceanus began spanking her together at a more leisurely pace. Their palms slapped against her bottom, and lingered there to relish the feel of the abused skin, sometimes pinching or squeezing it to make her groan. On occasion they assailed her inner thighs to increase her havoc, and once or twice slapped her between the legs, cruelly smacking her damp sex.

In a stupor of exquisite delight, Mina trembled and moaned beneath each new impact, her body writhing against the immobilising bonds.

'Would our slave like something more substantial?'

Tethys asked, and slapped the tender area where Mina's thighs merged into her bottom.

'Oh yes, mistress, yes,' she groaned wantonly.

'You have to earn it, slave.'

'Anything, mistress,' she promised. 'I'll do anything.'

'You would have to service us both, slave,' Tethys explained, lifting Mina's head by the hair so her scalp resounded with distress.

Mina clenched her teeth, yet the pain only added to her willingness to do whatever her owners said. 'I will, anything for you, mistress,' she whimpered, the roots of her hair protesting vehemently at being pulled.

'Good slave,' Tethys purred, releasing and permitting her to swing back into her upside down position, her legs spread wide, her buttocks and thighs turgid with heat. 'Ready, slave?' She stepped in front of Mina's face, one hand dropping to take hold of the zipper at her loins and lower it slowly.

'Yes, mistress,' she whispered, her eyes wide with anticipation as she watched the latex-clad body of her beautiful owner close in, the dark fabric shining in the torch lit tropical evening.

Taking hold of the back of Mina's head, Tethys forced her face into the leggings, and Mina's tongue spilled through the aperture to fawn on a hot wet clitoris. The taste of her mistress was like nectar to her palate, the flavour of another woman's pudenda a delight she had not enjoyed for what felt like an eternity. The feel of the soft, slick tracts sliding against her tongue was pure bliss.

'Oh, that's it slave... good slave... I can see you haven't lost any of your old skills,' Tethys commented breathlessly as she rode Mina's face. The gorgeous dominatrix tossed her head back and exhaled deep, rhythmic breaths into the cool twilight.

Buried amidst intimate flesh and latex, Mina was in heaven, lavishing her devout attentions on the swollen

27

clitoris between her lips.

In mere moments Tethys was crying out with pleasure, emitting heady moans as she rejoiced in Mina's skilled cunnilingus. Once she had ridden the spires of an orgasm, she gently released her slave's head and stepped back, leaning into the arms of her husband for support, her features slack and her body languid with prurient intoxication.

'That was quite something,' she muttered, kissing Oceanus as he gazed at Mina with ravenous desire in his eyes. 'And now it's your turn, my love.' She kissed him as her hand fell to his open breeches and pulled out his swelling member. 'But first let me get her into a better position for you.'

Mina's elbows and wrists were set free and her arms dragged behind her, the shackles used to lift her as the rope was attached to and thrown over the spreader bar. Hauled over the metal beam, the woven coil was drawn in, bending her around, hoisting her up by her arms so she was doubled back, her spine aching a little from the contortion. With her features brought almost upright by the cruel position, she tried not to resist the bondage knowing she would only make it worse for herself if she struggled. Groaning softly, her jaw trembled as the pain in her back and arms grew worse, punishing her relentlessly as she was forced to maintain the unnatural position.

'There, all set,' Tethys decreed. Mina's face was now upright and able to service Oceanus much more readily despite the vicious impositions of her current position.

He stepped forward with celerity and fed his rigid length into his slave's gaping mouth.

Mina swallowed the engorged flesh and locked her lips to it. Recalling her training under Atlas, she employed all the skills she had learned from his stringent lessons, rocking her head back and forth and attending to her owner's pleasure with as much skill and devotion as she could muster in her constraining bondage. Her growing discomfort only seemed to add to her enthusiasm, magnifying her diligence and her skill as her body ached and her mouth watered from the wonderful taste of him.

'She has improved with age, that's for certain,' he remarked softly as she lapped and sucked his stiff organ while he clung to her thighs for support.

'Someone's been tutoring her, I'll wager,' his wife suggested, painting small whirls of sensation around Mina's clitoris with her fingertips, tracing a slow, methodical route that made Mina sob with delight around the phallus filling her mouth and nudging her throat.

Shuddering with the rising ecstasy of being masturbated by one of her owners while she pleasured another, Mina hauled at Oceanus with her tongue and lips and mouth, drawing out his orgasm and feasting on his murmurs of delight. Then, with a low growl, he poured his seed down her throat, baptising her tongue as she drank all he was able to give, milking his climax for all it was worth, her own rabid pleasure driving her on.

The noble stepped back finally, pulling free of her mouth and leaving her constrained and twisted in her bonds licking her lips, her chest having as she gasped with mingled pleasure and pain.

'I can see how close you are, slave,' Tethys whispered in her ear. 'Soon you'll be dancing for us again, but don't you dare come until I give you permission. Yet perhaps I should stop and leave you hanging on the edge of release. Would you like that, slave?'

'Oh, please don't mistress!' Mina was livid with distress at the mere prospect. 'I've done as you asked!' Her rising plume of pleasure was too hot to resist; she simply could not cope with denial, not after her long captivity and period of isolation. To be inverted and bound, restrained and forced to service both her owners before being masturbated by one of them was so acutely arousing she felt she would explode if she did not give vent to the need raging inside her.

'I don't recall this being part of the bargain,' Tethys said cruelly. 'I offered to crop you if you serviced us, is that not so?' She slowed the rhythm of her fingertips, threatening to stop if the answer failed to satisfy her.

Mina's pleasure began stalling, kept at a crucial point by Tethys's experienced ministrations but moving no closer to the heavenly goal of a climax. 'Yes, mistress, but please, it's been so long and I've missed you both so much, please don't deprive me. Desperation saturated every syllable of her plea.

'Maybe, maybe not, I'll decide in a moment.' She drew Mina closer and closer, making her fight to stop herself from coming. But battling the will of her body was more than she could handle at the moment; she was simply too aroused to be able to hold off. She needed permission right now or she would end up disobeying her mistress's command through no fault of her own.

'Mistress, please!'

'No, not yet,' Tethys snapped, working her fingers with skill and making Mina's mind boil as her synapses burned with the effort of mentally resisting an orgasm, every second a brutal war she barely won.

'Okay, you have permission, slave,' Tethys said at last. It took a moment for Mina to realise she was being allowed to climax. 'Come on slave, let's see you come.' She accelerated her ministrations.

Mina's features contorted in a silent frozen cry as every fibre of her being tensed, and the shattering joy that flooded her made all her muscles ripple beneath it.

'That's it, slave,' Tethys said contentedly as Mina thrashed against her bonds.

'Thank me, slave,' she commanded. 'Thank your

mistress.'

'Oh thank you, thank you, mistress! Thank you for letting your slave come!' She sagged in her bondage, wheezing softly.

'Good girl,' Tethys murmured, lifting her wet fingers away and presenting them to Mina so she might take them into her mouth and clean them of her own juices.

Sucking her mistress's skin and the cut off latex fabric, Mina's mind reeled from the intensity of the ordeal as her limbs continued to release the occasional fit against her bonds.

'You've earned your reward, slave,' Oceanus told her. 'Are you ready?'

Mina had all but forgotten the beating she had begged to receive after being spanked. 'Yes, master, I am,' she said softly, closing her eyes and readying herself for the imminent trial.

The couple retrieved their crops and stepped behind her once more, each one targeting a cheek. The crops hummed their sibilant songs as they cut the air and applied their ferocious tips to a bottom already smouldering from a recent chastisement. The leather hoops etched hot welts into her skin, the flesh rising in trenches that burned like the sun, each stroke adding to the general fury suffusing her buttocks. Wailing and pulling against her bonds, Mina sobbed and begged for mercy.

Launching the implements against her flesh, the couple marked its property with welts of love, each one a terrible blessing to Mina as she endured them, reviling and revelling in each scorching kiss of the stinging black leather. Afterwards, they gathered close to her and offered the tips of their weapons to her lips, and shuddering from her trial and feeling purged by its savagery, Mina kissed them reverently.

'Thank you, master, thank you, mistress,' she sobbed,

tears streaming down her face as a mysteriously numbing euphoria washed through her burning form in the wake of the torment. Her body was charged with bliss, with a sense of utter and complete satisfaction, having been adored by the riding crops of her owners.

'Good slave,' Oceanus said quietly, loosening the rope around her arms and letting her straighten again.

She grimaced as her back protested, and still weeping with exquisite happiness, she hung in her bonds and watched as her beloved owners walked away, leaving her alone to treasure the ferocious ache in her buttocks.

Chapter Three

Fingers of early morning sunlight reached across the tops of the trees and caressed Mina's bound form. The night had been cool, but not cold enough to cause her any serious discomfort. Relaxed in her bondage, she had managed to sleep for long periods of time, her dreams infected with lustful images of being whipped, bound and made to serve others sexually. The intense prurient lust ignited by her escape from the depths was almost more painful than the ropes binding her. Fortunately, she had eaten before leaving the ship. The only thing that disturbed her slumber was the excitement she experienced wondering what dawn would bring, her enthusiasm to be trained by her owners making her heart race and filling her mind with hopes and possibilities.

The warm touch of sunlight stirred her from sleep as it travelled gradually across her suspended body. When it reached her face she was brought fully awake. Stretching as much as she could in her confined state, she yawned and sighed, feeling content and refreshed, the addition of suspension to her existence an uncomfortable but welcome treat.

Tethys and Oceanus were spry of step as they emerged from the manor house, the first of the nobility to exit the building this morning. Both had donned riding attire for the day's events, indicating they truly did intend to train her as their pony. Knee-high polished boots with silver spurs rested over tight white breeches adorned by a studded belt. Other than that they wore nothing else except short leather gloves. Tethys's breasts were fully exposed to Mina's hungry gaze, perhaps to tease her all the more. Both carried the same crops they had wielded last night. They quickly lowered Mina to the ground and untied her.

'Did our slave sleep well?' Oceanus asked her, running his hand down her spine. The soft leather brushing against her skin left goose bumps in its wake as she nodded weakly, her eyes narrowing beneath the exquisite sensation as she inhaled the crisp morning air.

'We're going to take you to the stables and get you dressed, and then we'll start your training, slave,' Tethys informed her, and Mina stood to attention, ready to obey any order they gave. A furtive glance over her shoulder showed the angry imprints left by the pair of crops across her buttocks, the vivid welts distinct and vibrant against her pale skin, criss-crossing in an intricate web of purple strips.

'Follow us, slave,' her mistress commanded, and she and her husband led Mina towards the stables.

They passed through a pair of large doors at one end of the curved building. To the right lay a series of closed doors, plain portals hiding secret interiors from view. To the left were the individual stables, box rooms strewn with hay furnished with a trough of food and water and equipped with metal rings set in the walls. Some rooms had the saddle of its occupant placed on a beam, waiting for a rider to fasten it on his or her chosen mount. The two sections of the doors leading out of the stalls were located on the outer wall, the simple latches beyond the ability of the bound female ponies to operate. Some of these doors were open as Mina was led down the central path, the closed lower half serving to prevent exit while the open top half allowed passing nobles to see the ponies within.

The pony-women were bound in a number of different ways. Some were relatively free while others were terribly incarcerated, their extreme bondage tantalising

Mina's penchant for claustrophobic entrapment. Some rested on their 'hooves' with their arms twisted up behind their backs, their figures encased in latex, their bridled features connected to the wall via a chain. Others were stooped over, their arms locked within artificial forelegs, the weighted constructs rendering them quadrupeds, and the influence of the rest of their uniform preventing them from rising. And in case they attempted to do so, devious additions had been set into place to punish them for their effort.

Still more pony-women were joined together so the features of one were bound to another's rear end, thereby creating a form of centaur. Numerous different examples were on display, some with their flesh exposed and others locked within a bodysuit moulded to fit like a black second skin hiding them from view. The most amazing centaurs, however, were those created from one woman. They stood bound and adorned as their owners had seen fit, their bridled faces connected to their stable to prevent easy movement, and from the base of their spines their bodies and legs were that of a pony. Some of these girls were full-figured and covered by an artificial skin to add to the realism, others were thin and revealed more of the intricate core of the mechanism controlling the artificial animal legs.

The level of technology involved was impressive, but Mina knew it was possible. The toys she had used in the corporate world she'd been a part of had been many years ahead of what was ordinarily available. The most powerful people in the world were greedy hoarders of technology, keeping the latest refinements and breakthroughs to themselves to gain an edge over the competition. Once upon a time, secret agencies had possessed the money and the power to attract the finest minds, now multi-national corporations owned them.

They turned a corner and continued down the corridor

to the door at the end. Tethys opened the portal, and Mina found herself in a chamber devoted to turning women into beasts.

The walls were lined with hundreds of outfits, and coils of chain emerged from openings in the floor and ceiling, the slender lines fixed to the restraints in which a slave was obviously placed during the process of bestial transmogrification.

Mina's owners led her to a set of restraints and snapped leather cuffs around her wrists. A few touches to a pad of buttons on the wall and a cranking rattle of mechanised motion sounded from above, lifting Mina's arms high over her head while spreading them, forcing her to balance on tiptoe. Then her feet left the ground and she was hanging in midair, the restraints digging into her flesh as she was racked by the suspension. She groaned with pleasure at her elevation, the prospect of what was to follow spicing her excitement.

A spinning purr of motion showed her hair strippers, the drum-like heads whirling with clasping sets of internal tweezers. 'Time to be smooth again, slave,' warned Oceanus, lifting the device and looking over her helpless legs with a flicker of amusement in his eyes.

Mina jerked in her bonds as the weapons swept across her skin, tugging hairs free at the root and stripping her legs bare. The machines worked swiftly, running in steady lines, and she occasionally struggled to move her legs away from the devices when the effects of their plucking teeth became too much for her to handle. But she was spanked mercilessly until she settled down again, making any period of reprieve from the implements a session of equally painful chastisement. Finally, the surface of her limbs was left feeling soft and smooth as satin and Mina was left panting and light-headed from the excruciating ordeal.

'There, that's all for now,' Tethys said.

'You took that well, slave,' Oceanus praised her while running his hand over her bottom. 'Now we can start getting you into your outfit.'

Tethys brought over a delicate nylon garment. 'Help me get our slave into this,' she petitioned her husband, holding up an open crotch cat-suit. Pulling down the zip in the back, they manoeuvred Mina into the sleeveless garment, caressing the sheer weave across her limbs and erasing the wrinkles as she squirmed slightly with pleasure at being handled by both her beloved owners.

Thigh-high boots were then slipped onto her feet, moulding them into a smooth curve from toe to ankle, where the customized footwear fanned out into the appearance of a hoof concealing a stiletto heel. The entire area above the sole was fitted with a studded band of silver metal, and a matching metallic circlet gripped her thighs. Half of a buckled strap hung from the outermost side at the top of each boot, a dense suspender that could be attached to a belt and deny her any hope of kicking off the weighty footwear. The heavy boots placed more strain on her wrists, making her paw at them feebly.

'There, you now have your hooves,' Tethys smiled, 'and you'll get used to the weight soon enough.' 'But first we have to pull in that salacious waist a little more and fill these wanton holes,' Oceanus, chuckled patting Mina's sex, and the soft spanks made her quiver with pleasure and ache for something more substantial.

A stern leather corset was selected, the front an unbroken sheet of leather, the back sections joined by a dense wall of laces. Two buckles hung from the front and back hems awaiting a crotch-piece. The belt that would mate with her boots hung from the corresponding sides of the bodice. Two fat silver rings had also been riveted to the sides of the garment at the level of her waist, which could serve as sturdy anchors.

'This should look quite fetching on you,' Tethys remarked. 'I can't wait to see the finished product.'

'Our little slave always looks wonderful,' her husband commented. 'I expect as a pony she'll shine even more brightly, especially once she's fully trained.'

'It's well worth losing a sexual pet for such a vaulted cause,' agreed his wife. 'To have this delightful physique proud and obedient, guided by the whip as she tows us wherever we wish... Mm, I cannot wait.' Her eyes sparkled as she pictured what Mina was going to look like as a pony-girl.

The stiff bodice was wrapped around Mina's torso and the laces tightened as much as possible, and then fetters were applied to her ankles. A push of a button had the floor chains retreating and drawing her legs apart, splaying her wide and applying more havoc to her stretched and suspended body. Mina's head fell back and she stared up at the ceiling as she whimpered in distress, stabs of pain flashing through her strained limbs as the leather jaws of the corset ground against her ribs and made it hard for her to breathe.

'We'd best finish off before we add the rest,' Oceanus decreed.

'Hold on, let me just grab my trimmer,' Tethys replied, moving away.

Riding endorphins set loose by the stress of enduring the process of being stripped and suspended, shaved, dressed and bound, Mina shook with apprehension as the hair strippers were once again taken up and activated, her exposed crotch obviously their next target. They began nipping at her pubes and her perverse need for excruciating discipline enabled her to relish what would ordinarily be considered an unbearable experience. Whimpering and groaning and jerking in her bonds, Mina's head lolled as she drifted off in a masochistic haze, reviling the pain even as it saturated her flesh with a terrible delight. The heads bit across her mound, delving into her bottom crack to remove every hair, leaving her utterly smooth. Her owners caressed her, and sighed with satisfaction.

'Perfect,' Tethys said. 'Just perfect.'

Her ribs gloriously squeezed by the corset's leather hourglass, Mina panted meekly, revelling in the painful constriction that seemed to crush any thoughts of resisting whatever her owners had planned for her. The matching crotch-piece was brought over, the triangular front buckled to the corset and the pair of ridged jelly dildos attached to it carefully pushed up into her loins. As the pliant lengths filled her hungry orifices she stiffened and moaned with rapture as the unnaturally large organs expanded her tracts to their delicious limits. And from the thong back of the crotch-piece, a conical leather stem sprouted and spilled a great plume of black hair – a tail that hung down to the backs of her knees.

'That's it, slave, let it out,' Oceanus urged, 'we want to see you express what you're feeling.'

The two dildos pressed deep into her pussy and her bottom and the slender strap at the back slid tightly between her buttocks as it was buckled into place.

'I bet they feel wonderful, don't they, slave,' Tethys purred, 'those big rods shoved all the way into you?'

'They are there by our will, slave,' Oceanus told her firmly, 'and they will stay there all the time to remind you that you belong to us.'

Mina quivered with pleasure as she shifted her loins against the soft intruders. Then he grabbed her tail and gave it a few tugs and she whimpered as the action played the crotch strap and moved the jelly lengths inside her to a minimal but intense degree due to their monstrous size, their ridges plundering her depths. With a contended smile, her master made her cavort against her trammels by exploiting the plugging toys, and then the thick leather suspenders at her sides were connected and tugged to a thrumming tension before being buckled into place. A dense studded collar with a strap hanging from one side was placed around her throat, the metal ring in front resting against her collarbone as its width forced her head up to perky attention.

The chains suspending her were finally given some slack, lowering her to the floor as the chains at her feet pulled back, forcing her down to her knees, at which point two more chains were brought up from the floor and attached to her collar, keeping her where she was, unable to rise, her arms still stretched straight up over her head.

Tethys said, 'Let's sort out her hair before we finish off.'

'Shall we go with a mane, or a single tail?' her husband enquired.

'I prefer the tail, and it looks better with the bridle we'll be using.'

'Very well, I agree.'

A set of rechargeable hair clippers released their purring hum into the air as Oceanus brought the implement over. The buzzing head rolled along Mina's skull, shearing away her hair in great tufts, the amputated strands falling to the floor in lush piles. Her head was completely shaved except for a single plume of hair high on her crown, a makeshift mane held in place with a tight black latex ribbon.

'Shall I apply the bridle now?' Oceanus asked eagerly.

'Hold on a minute,' Tethys muttered, 'just let me get rid of these loose strands.' The soft bristles of a brush tossed aside the few lingering particles of hair on Mina's head, and then the bridle was brought over.

'There, she's all yours,' Tethys said with satisfaction, stepping back.

The thick rubber bit was forced into Mina's willing

mouth, the rings at the sides pressing against her cheeks. The straps affixed to the circle were set in place with precise motions, the band at the sides fastened about her head and pulling the wide bar deeper against the corners of her mouth, her teeth grinding against the slightly yielding but still relentless bit. From the lower portion of the ring another strap descended below her chin to cup her jaw and press it to the invasive strut. Another pair of straps rose to connect at her brow and ran across her head to grab the belt at the back, a slit in the leather allowing her ponytail to emerge from the band. Secondary straps ascended at her cheeks, rising up to the slit at her crown. They added no real additional strength to the bridle, but they did hold a set of blinkers that deprived her of her lateral vision, leaving her with a restricted forward facing view.

'Right,' Oceanus crowed with delight, 'that just leaves her arms, and we're ready to begin.'

'You get the first one out and I'll get the glove,' Tethys said briskly, and one of Mina's arms was promptly set free as Oceanus held her tightly. The strength of his grip was not necessary; the brawn he applied to keeping her subdued Mina knew was intended to stoke her lecherous desires. She was aware that her beloved owners were considerate of all their slaves, always incorporating actions they knew would please them, acting not only to indulge their own passion for domination but also to ensure the submissives they used gained as much pleasure as possible from their service. Mina felt proud to be owned by such a beautiful and considerate couple as they gently forced her arm into a leather opera glove fitted with a metal band at the top and a dense manacle at the wrist. The mitten at the end bore no accommodations for her fingers, leaving her digits bunched together and useless within its close confines. The restraints were tightened to a more secure fit and padlocked to the rings of her corset, leaving her arms mobile but unable to break free of the corset and anchored to her waist. The strap at her collar met the strap at the top of the opera gloves, running down her shoulder and connecting to ensure she could not struggle free of the tubular restraints. Then her other arm was identically bound, completing her transformation from young woman to pony.

Chewing on her bit, Mina wriggled upon the dildos and waited while the chains holding her in place were snapped free.

'Stand up, pony, and let's have a look at you,' Tethys commanded, stepping back with her husband to admire their work, smiling and holding hands as they beheld the final product.

Mina lifted a leg, and her hoof clopped against the stone floor. The sound made her smile even though it was a strain to force herself upright and stand on her new equine feet. She felt wonderfully constricted, her transformed appearance acting as an intense aphrodisiac.

'Utterly delightful,' Tethys declared as she moved forward to caress Mina's nylon-smothered assets and tease her nipples through the suit's gossamer weave.

'Definitely,' her husband agreed fervently. 'I hope her persona as a pony is as pleasing as her appearance.'

'Oh, I'm sure our little slave won't disappoint us,' Tethys assured him, spanking Mina's taut bottom.

Mina stiffened, her arms straining against the fastenings, her fingers making the slim gloves ripple as they fought to move. The casual smack sent heat coursing through her fresh welts, reviving them and making them burn afresh for a few tormenting seconds.

Removing reins from the wall, Oceanus clipped them to the rings against her cheeks, and using them to tow her along, her hooves clattering against the stone floor with each step she took in her new bizarre footwear. As she walked, Mina told herself she was now an animal. Owned and controlled by the beautiful couple, she was a pony in their care tottering forward with the awkward gait of a newborn foal. She pondered what effects her training would have on her. She vaguely recalled her loss of sentience during her stint as an eel, brought on by extreme sensory deprivation, and wondered if behaving like a pony day in and day out would produce similar results as time passed.

Chapter Four

Led out of the dressing room, Mina was taken through one of the stalls and out into the open courtyard. Other nobles had risen by now and were working on their chosen fillies. Dressed in varying modes of riding attire, nobles trained their mounts to trot properly, to perform tricks or simply to obey verbal commands if they were particularly recalcitrant or unused to their new uniform.

Tethys stepped past Mina holding two dressage whips, the lengthy slender struts of punishment fitted with a thin, dangling cord at the tip and handles made of silver and ivory. She lifted a simple bolt to open the metal gate of a pen, and let Oceanus lead Mina into it. The soft dirt gave slightly beneath her hooves, leaving behind then U-shaped footprints. He moved to the centre of the arena, letting his hands slip through the reins and giving Mina more slack.

'Okay, pony-girl, time for some exercise,' Tethys announced, shifting one of the whips to her other hand and tossing it to her husband.

Mina looked across at the other pens until the soft hiss of a whip cut the air and she felt it sting her bottom, the long stem cutting into her sensitive cheeks with a searing heat that made her toss her head back with a cry of shock the sensation was so unexpectedly savage.

'Come on, pony, get those hooves moving,' Oceanus ordered, lifting the weapon again and preparing to repeat the lesson if she failed to learn from it.

Pulling unconsciously against her wrist shackles, Mina turned and broke into a steady romp around the pen, the welt he had given her pulsating distinctly across her already well marked buttocks. The vicious stroke had drastically increased her willingness to obey, the flare of pain melting her own willpower with its dark seductiveness.

'Legs up, pony-girl!' Tethys snapped, her whip singing out as Mina skipped past her. The length crossed both her bottom cheeks, the lithe tip flicking around to paint an even more stern mark across her hip through the fine suit.

Mina staggered and swayed beneath the impact, jerking against her reins as she doubled up with a croaking wail of anguish. The weal throbbed, the fresh mark caused by the whip's mordant tip scorching her drastically, the sheer havoc it roused in her flesh for a moment crippling her ability to respond to commands. Yet straightening up, she managed to swallow the torment as though it was the sweetest candy as she launched herself back into a swift trot. Lifting her legs she continued at the limit of the reins, keeping her head high and tilted slightly back as the collar required. It was a strangely satisfying experience to be casually treated like a beast, her sentience ignored as the whip became her persuasive instructor.

'Higher,' Oceanus demanded, giving a slight tug to her reins and pulling on the harness encompassing her head. The whip arched around, making her tense the moment she heard the telltale sound of its passage through the air, but awareness of its pending impact across her buttocks did little to assuage the excruciating agony of the woven stalk's cruel kiss. Croaking against the bit, her eyes moist with tears of hopelessly mingled resentment and satisfaction, Mina continued her prancing motions with even more gusto, pushing her body to its limits as she pranced in the exaggerated fashion her owners demanded.

The dildos within her shifted with each bounding cavort

of her hooves against the soil, the raked dirt increasingly marked with the circular imprints of her hooves. Mina was glad she had filled her time of decompression on the ship with intense exercise, for otherwise behaving like a pony would have left her a wheezing and enervated wreck after only a few laps. With her current level of fitness she was at least free to enjoy her training as the whips continued goading her on.

'That's it, pony-girl, keep those legs up!' Tethys shouted with gusto. 'And head back!' She gave Mina another capricious lick with the whip as she trotted by.

'Now a little faster,' Oceanus urged. 'After all, we want to get our pony nice and fit.' He applied a trio of gentle flicks from his whip across her straining buttocks that served to aggravate the ache of her existing welts without causing her any fresh trauma.

Marching round and round at the limit of her reins, Mina listened to her owners' commands and did as she was told, the dressage whips falling constantly to keep her mind and her submission strong and focused. Rhythmic stings from the whips were her constant companion, the more stern flavour of the wicked weapons only becoming evident when she slowed her pace or let her rigid prancing posture grow slack. Of course, on numerous occasions she deliberately failed to keep pace and to hold her back straight, letting her performance slip a little in quality so she could suffer the exhilarating scourge meted out by her masters that made her feel wonderfully owned and debased.

It was pure bliss to be steered around and totally controlled in a pen made for an animal, her eyes staring intently out from between her blinkers in an effort to catch sight of her beautiful owners whenever she passed them. Her prurient lusts fed on the image of their perfect bodies, presented to her in the arousing role of implacable trainers of submissively sensual creatures like her. Her tail swept against her legs, brushing her bottom cheeks as her ponytail, all that remained of her hair, caressed her shoulders. Her breasts bounced inside the sheer top, a slippery sheen of perspiration making it shine as she performed the rigorous and monotonous exercise of trotting around the pen.

The sun crept up into the blue sky, pouring its golden bounty across the island and warming the air. At first the stables and trees provided a decent amount of cooling shade, but eventually the sun rose above them all, leaving the pony-girls to toil and serve beneath its penetrating rays. It would be a good few hours before the mountain afforded them some protective shade again, but the stables were arranged so the holding pens only admitted a small amount of light, shielding the human fillies and mares within from the full force of the sun's harsh eye.

Fully exposed, her nylon cat-suit growing moist with her perspiration, Mina continued exercising for her owners. Her muscles ached, and her buttocks smouldered as the blood rushed into her sensitive welts. But her previous life before she became a slave in Charybdis had taught her all too well how to resist fatigue and push her body beyond what it would ordinarily be able to tolerate, her stamina and determination brooking no defeat.

Finally, the couple stopped urging Mina on with their whips and wiped the sweat from their own brows as they rubbed their weary arms. 'I think she deserves a break,' Tethys sighed.

'I don't know about our pony,' Oceanus stretched his back and flicked the whip across Mina's rump one last time, 'but I certainly need one. *Whoa* girl,' he commanded, and brought Mina to a halt with a soft swipe of the whip across the front of her thighs.

She stood to attention, panting, her chest rising and falling against the oppressive corset, her limbs seeming to burn from within.

'Let's get something to drink, hose down this filly and take a rest,' Tethys proposed, opening the gate as Oceanus gathered in Mina's reins, capturing them near her face and leading her out by them.

Immediately behind the stables was a courtyard accessed solely by metal shutters placed along the outer wall of the stable. A single road led into the forest, its paved line vanishing amidst the trees. An expanse of grass divided the courtyard from the side and back of the main building, where Mina discovered there was a large patio, the flagstones strewn with chairs, lounges, tables and brightly patterned umbrellas. Slaves, naked except for collars and chastity belts, attended the Nobles enjoying this area, while other slaves provided comfort in the form of human footrests and tables.

Mina was taken to the edge of the patio where a standpipe bore a coil of green hose. Oceanus handed his wife the reins and slid into a seat nearby, taking refuge in the shade and beckoning to one of the serving slaves. A tanned Hispanic girl carrying a serving tray promptly wandered over to him, her buxom form sauntering against her chastity belt.

Tethys led Mina onto the grass and paid out her reins, taking the hose with her as she went to join her husband.

'Bring us the usual, slave,' Oceanus smiled up at the girl as she straightened up from her respectful bow, 'and some lunch.' He subjected her to a flick of his whip to send her scampering back into the building.

Tethys squeezed the pistol-like nozzle of the hose, and a spray of cool water streamed from it that splashed across Mina's body, making her gasp with shock and tense against her bonds. The sensation was overwhelming, the cold water in such stark contrast to her hot flesh that she shuddered from head to toe beneath the chilling cascade. The leather corset became saturated as the water seeped beneath it, cleansing her smothered skin.

Tethys ensured Mina was completely refreshed by the powerful stream, and then angled the hose so she could soothe her parched throat by gulping down mouthfuls of water before letting it wash across her flushed face. Then the dominatrix took great delight in playfully teasing Mina by shifting the waters aside to make her totter after them, trying to keep up with the cool flow so she could continue quenching her thirst.

The serving slave returned and laid down a tray laden with sandwiches and two colourful cocktails adorned with extravagant plumage. Then rather than dismissing her, Oceanus gestured for her to kneel at his side so he might stroke her lovely figure while chatting idly with his wife.

Tethys shut off the hose, leaving Mina standing in a puddle of water on the grass, her breathing deep and steady and her body shivering slightly as sunlight caught the water droplets covering her and began warming her up while also making her sparkle as if covered with gems.

'Come here, little pony,' Tethys commanded, pulling at her reins as she tossed the hose back towards the standpipe.

Mina obeyed at once, her hooves clapping onto the stone patio as she was led in close and then tugged down to her knees beside her mistress. Kneeling to attention, her blinkered eyes were facing the field behind the main building, a smooth expanse of grass stretching out to the trees.

'So, what'll we do next to our little filly?' Tethys asked her husband, running a hand over Mina's shaven head and down her plume of moist hair.

'We should probably opt to run her for the rest of the day,' he suggested, idly caressing the serving slave

49

kneeling obediently beside him. 'This fitness training will be good for her.' He raised his drink, took a deep sip, and sighed contentedly as he leaned further back in his padded chair. 'Ah, that's the stuff. This island is unmatched anywhere. Poseidon certainly knows how to treat his guests.'

'Did I hear my name?' a familiar voice enquired. Mina heard footsteps approaching from behind, but obedient to her beloved owners, she resisted the urge to turn around and look. Instead she remained still and tense, chewing softly on her bit.

'Poseidon!' Tethys exclaimed with what sounded like genuine pleasure. 'Please do join us. We were just commenting on your wonderful retreat here.' She sipped her own drink contentedly.

'Thank you,' Poseidon replied, 'I believe I shall.'

'How *did* you come by it?' asked Oceanus, his words muffled slightly as he chewed a bite of his sandwich.

'I have friends here and there,' the Titan replied amiably. 'A few illicit favours provided to a certain government and it was more than willing to let me create my own little empire out here. In fact, a few high-ranking officials make this their favoured vacation spot.' He chuckled as a serving slave appeared as if by magic to pull out a chair for him.

'Are these slaves from Scylla?' Tethys wondered as she reached down and presented a piece of fruit to her pony's lips. Mina leaned forward and nuzzled her face into her owner's palm, experiencing some difficulty in getting to the juicy fragment over the bit. Once it was in her mouth, she mulled it over and swallowed carefully, her tongue doing most of the work of softening it up and breaking it down since she could not use her teeth. Stretching her jaws wide, she slipped her tongue out around the bit and lapped up the trace of juice lingering on her lips as best she could, savouring her humiliating

50

position as much as the taste of the fruit.

'No, so far I have recruited all my slaves myself,' Poseidon replied proudly. 'They are all willing and genuine submissives saved from humdrum lives and given purpose and direction by their tenure here.'

'Not bad.' Tethys nodded, glancing at the slave her husband was still idly caressing. 'Not bad at all.'

'How many Titans are here at the moment?' Oceanus asked languidly.

'Not many,' their host informed them, owner of the island and Mina's personal saviour. 'Most are probably still blowing down from the complex trying to make it to the party on time. Everyone else is from the other sects.'

'I don't see much identification.' Tethys's seat creaked as she glanced over her shoulders at the other nobles enjoying the island's decadent lifestyle.

'It's one of my unwritten insistences,' Poseidon explained. 'I don't like the obvious means of sect membership here; there's too much factionalism in Cabal. Getting rid of such trinkets helps keep things more amicable.'

Listening intently, Mina abruptly realised her owners were not wearing their rings, which fit in with their altered titles.

'It's gotten that bad?' Oceanus sounded concerned. 'I had no idea.'

'Being on the complex severely limits our awareness of the outside world,' his wife reminded him in a disgruntled whisper, clearly none too pleased with Charybdis's blackout on information.

'It's not *that* bad,' Poseidon assured him. 'It's rare, but it does happen. I mean, the Parisian sect and the sect from Berlin constantly bicker and moan about each other's presence. Getting rid of their markings tends to make them a little more tolerant of each other. There's plenty of other sects that don't mix well, but that's as good an example as any.'

'I've heard some rumours of it,' Oceanus admitted, 'I reckon they're both just playing for extra power by getting rid of a neighbouring rival.'

'There's an underlying animosity between all the European sects. It's just one of those things spawned by territory and proximity, and emphasised by the unification occurring there. The borders are dissolving and people are getting paranoid of losing their identity.'

'Good point, I suppose it's natural,' Oceanus sniffed disdainfully.

'Human nature,' Tethys chuckled.

'So, how is the pet you wanted me to help you rescue from her doomed fate?' Poseidon changed the subject.

'She's fine now,' Tethys replied merrily, 'and glad to be back with us, where she belongs.' She reached down and yanked Mina's tail, making the jelly dildos rub their ridged surfaces against her tracts. She moaned and tightened her inner muscles around them, straining to maintain her required pose amidst the playful rocking of the strap against her crotch and the resultant shift of the pliant interlopers inside her.

'I saw her in the pens.' Poseidon regarded Mina lustfully. 'She looks exquisite as a filly. How long did you have her as a pony in the complex?'

'We didn't, today is her first day,' Tethys replied proudly, wiggling Mina's tail and making her grit her teeth against the bit as her belly succumbed to a delightful swelling of sensation.

'Really?' The Titan seemed genuinely surprised. 'Well, congratulations. She performs wonderfully for someone so inexperienced. New ponies are normally dropping from exhaustion after a few hours at a good trot. She must be exceptionally fit.'

'There's that, but there's more to it. Remember, she's been an eel for months,' Oceanus reminded his host.

'She's got stamina, then. More than I've seen in a newborn filly for a long time.' Poseidon's voice was deep with admiration.

'Now you see why we were so eager to get her back,' Tethys purred. 'She's quite something. She adapts well, she's devoted, skilled, eager and flawlessly loyal, once you've won her over.' She continued playing with Mina's tail, making her shiver and causing her breathing to quicken as the plugs began sliding more freely inside her and her belly grew warm and her pussy moist with desire.

'Well, I've got to get back to my duties,' Poseidon sighed, pushing his chair back and rising. 'I've a few projects I'm working on for the party and I want to make sure they work properly.'

'Anything you'd care to reveal?' Oceanus grinned.

'Sorry.' He shook his head. 'I love my surprises. You'll just have to wait.' His eyes shone with a teasing mirth.

'Damn!' Oceanus indulged his host with an exaggerated exclamation of disappointment.

'Intrigue and curiosity will keep you on the island, won't they? After all, I'd hate to lose your company.' He kissed Tethys's hand as she held it up to him.

'As if we would leave so soon anyway, my dear Poseidon,' she said sultrily.

'See you at the beach tonight?' Oceanus asked.

'Count on it.' The two men clasped hands and then the Titan wandered back towards the house, occasionally pausing to speak to some of his guests.

'He seems a bit better,' Tethys observed, releasing Mina's tail and letting her settle back down, aroused and starved for more sensations.

'Those projects are getting him down, I think,' Oceanus mused out loud. 'Perhaps they haven't been going as smoothly as he'd like to make out.'

'He's a bit of a perfectionist. I reckon he just wants

everything to be wonderful for his party.' Tethys took up Mina's reins and drew her closer, turning her around so she might lay her head upon her lap.

Nuzzling her face against the tight white trousers, Mina caressed them with her cheek as Tethys's nails drifted along her bare upper arms and onto her nylon cat-suit. On a whim, Mina turned her face towards the other slave and found the girl's eyes on her. She looked away instantly, and her furtive embarrassment at being discovered staring at her made Mina smile.

'No matter what, it'll be some event, that's for certain,' Oceanus declared. 'How could you do anything here and not have it be spectacular?' He indicated the fields with a sweep of his nearly empty glass.

'That's true enough,' his wife agreed. 'Well, shall we finish up and head back to continue the training of our sweet pony?' She offered the last bite of a sandwich to Mina's lips, and she devoured the food as best she could, the loss of her thirst having been replaced by an intense hunger.

'Lay on your belly in front of the pony, slave,' Oceanus commanded the serving slave, and the girl promptly stretched herself out before Mina. Oceanus dropped bits of sandwich meat along the girl's back, following her spine down to the gentle slopes of her lovely bottom. 'There you go, pony-girl, a trough for you to feast from.' He chuckled and leaned back in his chair, a sparkle in his eyes as he watched Mina intently.

Draping herself forward, she started feeding off the girl, her lips brushing the soft skin making her sigh and shiver with sensual pleasure. She devoured all she could, sucking the bits of meat in with a motion of her constrained tongue and then swallowing against the demands of the bit. Once she had cleared her living plate she ran her tongue along the girl's silky skin, gathering up any residual flavour, evoking soft moans

54

from the prostrate slave's throat as she delighted in her lot, aching for relief as her sexual frustrations were magnified by Mina's oral caresses.

'There, isn't that better?' Tethys asked rhetorically; she did not really expect a reply from Mina.

'To the pens?' Oceanus rose with a slightly disgruntled growl, having grown comfortable in his chair, but equally enthused to see Mina being trained again.

'Come on, pony-girl,' Tethys ordered, pulling on the reins as she stood up. The leather straps tugged at Mina's face, moving her away from her sentient dining table and forcing her back onto her hooves. Her belly was comfortably full, and she had just adored the sweet flesh of another slave girl. The lunch break had put her in considerably high spirits.

She was taken back to the pen and set at the end of Tethys's grip, while Oceanus hovered around her and applied his whip to her forcibly as she trotted around the pen. The sun soon slipped behind the cathedral of stone towering over the island, spreading a cool and welcome blanket of shade across the perspiring pony-girls. But the heat remained aggravated by Mina's exertions as she exercised and pushed herself to her physical limits for the pleasure of her owners.

On and on she trotted, the dildos shifting slightly with every step she took, her exhaustion fighting a constant, rising arousal as the tiniest movement began lifting her towards a lethargic climax. The strap was too tight to actually let her gain relief, but it teased her relentlessly, making her relish her status of slave all the more fervently as she enjoyed being whipped around the pen at the reins of her owners. Many times she slacked her pace somewhat to relish the mordant caress of the implements plugging her and to gasp with perverse joy beneath the searing kiss of the whip.

Finally, shadows began gathering around the pen as a

wild and angry series of red and orange stripes decorated the western horizon like welts inflicted by a divine whip, the fierce glow of colour visible through the trees as the sun battled for every last second of dominance before submitting to the softly falling darkness.

'Whoa, girl!' Tethys said at last, yanking on the reins and slapping her whip across Mina's breasts, stinging them painfully to make her skid to a halt. She gasped for breath after the long run, her body aching and soaked with perspiration again. Her throat was painfully dry and her loins chafed from riding the dildos for hours on end. 'I think we can call it a day,' Tethys sighed, running her bare forearm over her brow and brushing back some loose strands of her short hair.

'Let's get her cleaned and in her stall, then find a slave to freshen us up and help us get changed for tonight's beach party,' Oceanus said briskly, leaning against the fence as a centaur on the other side caught his eye.

The woman who formed the front of the latex-sheathed beast was watching Mina's training, as the other woman's face remained hidden where it was pressed between the cheeks of her partner's bottom. Clomping together in unison without their owner, the head of the practiced pair had been watching Mina on and off all day. It seemed the slender dominatrix who had been training them to trot more effectively was a fickle tutor who was easily distracted by other pleasures and spent much of her time elsewhere.

Staring over the moulded characterisation of a pony's snout, the woman yelped as Oceanus's whip swept out and caught her assets, causing her arms to thrash against the sleeves folding them up her spine. She turned to try and escape the whip as it sang through the air again and struck the fronts of her shapely thighs, the cutting weapon easily sending its effects through the dense layer of rubber. The added swipe made the pony's head turn more rapidly than the rear, exposing it to the chastising device as it continued assaulting the interlocked couple. The plug in the centaur's tail shook its plume of hair as her rubber-cocooned buttocks were abused, her legs tensing and rippling the rubber shell encasing them as she kicked into the dirt. The muffled wails of the hidden woman emerged from the buttocks of the leader as her legs fought to push her partner on and get her out of the whip's range. Finally gaining unity, the beast swiftly galloped to the other side of the pen and moved in irate circles, pawing the ground with its hooves as it endured the lingering throb of the whip.

Still panting from her own exertions, Mina studied the delicious vision of the centaur, mentally projecting herself into such a transformed state with her face pressed between another girl's buttocks, nuzzling the sphincter as she was locked in darkness to serve as the hindquarters of a beast...

A yank to the reins distracted her from her titillating fantasy as Tethys walked out of the pen and took Mina with her. She was led back into the stalls and to one of the anonymous doors on the right. Oceanus threw it open and revealed a shower room, the white tiled interior equipped a drain in the centre where a telescopic metal pole waited with open metal fetters at its base. The tip of the device was a two-pronged pair of rounded nozzles, each with a series of small holes flecking them. A shower nozzle hung directly over this device, with several poles fixed to the wall, the heads armed with a variety of sponges and brushes near a shelf lined with bottles of coloured liquid soaps. Next to the cleansing poles were three faucets, each with a temperature dial set above it.

'Come on, girl, nothing to be afraid of.' Tethys urged Mina in, her hooves clattering loudly across the shower room's polished tiles. Oceanus closed the door and helped Tethys unfasten Mina's crotch-piece, snapping open the buckles and drawing it free.

The flight of the ribbed shafts literally made Mina shake in her boots and gasp from the delicious sensation of their rampant retreat from her tracts. Sagging slightly from their loss, she was led closer over the pole. Her ankles were locked in place, the metal gripping her feet to prevent escape, and as they touched the base of the instrument the hydraulic spear began rising beneath her.

'Just relax and let them in, pony-girl,' Oceanus murmured, taking hold of her hips to help steer her onto the rising shafts.

Her eyes widened with shock as she felt the cold tips touch and begin gathering more force against her. She mewled and wriggled in protest as the steel devices demanded entry into her body.

'Easy, girl,' Tethys said soothingly, stroking her ponytail.

Mina's legs fought their bonds as she tried to lift them and grant herself a few more seconds' reprieve from the dreaded penetration. She responded to the entry of the cold shafts with a gurgling hiss as her orifices expanded around the unforgiving lengths, allowing them to slide up and sheathe themselves deep inside her, until the bar connecting them was pressed against her crotch.

'There, that's better, isn't it?' Tethys asked, smiling. 'Now we can get you clean.' She and her husband moved over to the wall and gathered up a set of poles armed with sponges. Squeezing soap onto the honeycombed balls, they turned the temperature dials to their required settings and turned on the taps. The showerhead above Mina churned with sound, and released a warm sparkling deluge over her, the myriad small jets directing streams of water all over her. She arched her back above the shafts impaling her and turned her face up to accept the gloriously refreshing rain on her flushed features.

The warm water trickled down her body, making her skin shiver with delight as the sponges closed in and began rubbing themselves across her form, the long poles to which they were attached permitting her owners to remain outside the shower's steaming flow. Shuddering and groaning deep in her throat, Mina swayed as she was treated like a beast and scrubbed clean by her owners, the two of them working together to ensure she was purified of the day's accumulated dirt and perspiration.

Stepping back, husband and wife replaced the sponges and left Mina under the shower's cleansing waterfall as they manned a series of other taps.

Watching them with a sense of apprehension, Mina stiffened and cried out against her bit, sinking her teeth into it as water suddenly emerged from the rods imbedded in her pussy and anus. The tight jets pummelled her membranes, sending a swell of churning fluid through her. Her arms battled their restraints and her ankles struggled against their fetters, the sensations were so incredibly potent as small whirlpools and eddies beat against her insides. Gurgling and whinnying, she shook and struggled against the deep and powerful enema as her owners manipulated the faucets, changing the pressure and sometimes making her wail with mingled stress and ecstasy as the streams of water penetrated her with vicious force.

By the time they finished washing her insides, Mina felt weak and light-headed. The couple turned off all the taps and approached her, and she held herself perfectly still as they retracted the internal nozzles and lowered the pole as the fetters around her ankles clicked open.

Her legs quaking beneath her, Mina was only half conscious as they led her back out into the corridor and past several stalls before one opening one and ushering her into it.

'Sleep well, pony-girl,' Tethys said. 'We'll see you tomorrow for more training.' She locked Mina's reins to a wall ring as Oceanus hung her crotch strap on a hook, ready for the morning.

'Sweet dreams,' he added, and without even bothering to take in her surroundings, Mina slumped to the soft hay and fell asleep instantly.

Chapter Five

The sound of movement nearby and a pressure against her body made Mina's eyes flit open. It took her a moment to focus, and realise that a woman was resting her head on her thigh.

Mina discovered herself lying on her side in the hay, the hand she had fallen asleep on completely numb. Her legs were spread open and the other pony-girl was using one of her thighs as a pillow. The woman was nestled adoringly against her, her uniform identical to hers.

Looking up, Mina saw another crotch band hanging beside hers, and she followed the woman's reins to the other side of the room where they were locked opposite her own tethers.

Had she been so exhausted that she had remained utterly oblivious as another pony was brought in and stationed with her? It was still dark out, the chirp of nocturnal insects filling the air and merging with the tune of dozens of pony-girls slumbering soundly in their stalls.

She calmed her racing pulse and laid her head back down on the straw. If the girl was as worn out as she had been, then she was not going to disturb her. Besides, it felt pleasant to have a companion, and she wondered if the newcomer was one of Tethys and Oceanus's slaves as well, or if she belonged to someone else.

She closed her eyes and shook her sleeping hand until prickly influxes of feeling began flowing back into it. The girl's head remained on her thigh as she shifted slightly into a more comfortable position and drifted back into a deep and dreamless sleep.

The weak rays of dawn appeared and made both pony-girls stir beneath their light caress. Mina sat up as her partner also dragged herself onto her knees, fully revealing herself.

She was young, perhaps in her early twenties, with bleached-white curls of hair spilling from her crown in the requisite form of a tail. She did not appear to be as tall as Mina, but she was lithe and slender, her breasts small and pert and inviting caresses where they pressed against her nylon sheath. Her face was angular, almost severe in appearance, but her eyes helped soften the almost fierce cast of her features with their calm blue innocence.

The two pony-girls stared at each other for a long moment, and then Mina completely took in her surroundings for the first time.

The stall they were sharing looked like all the others. Locked to the wall was a small trough of water and another containing nutrient pellets, and that was all. She had already seen the hay strewing the floor and the hooks holding their crotch straps. The two-panelled door was shut from the outside, as was the interior exit to the corridor.

Rather than attempting to communicate around their bits, they stared silently into each other's eyes. Then the other pony smiled, leaning towards Mina so they could nudge noses in greeting, and she steered into a new position with a series of snorting prompts.

Complying mainly out of curiosity, Mina fell back across the hay with her legs spread and raised. She assumed her companion was going to try and pleasure her, a favour she was eager to receive and more than willing to reciprocate. But then the girl started dragging her reins beneath Mina's left side, and the pull of the leather straps against her shins made her lift them so it slipped between her legs. The girl then shuffled aside and pulled up, causing the straps to fall against Mina's crotch and cleavage with a soft slap. With a gasp of astonishment, she squirmed against the hay as the pony-girl began rocking her head back and forth and pulling at the reins so the leather rode against Mina's sex. The taut strip caressed her clit, slithering between her sex lips and quickly becoming moist as she groaned softly, sinking her teeth into her bit as she shuddered with pleasure. The reins rode up over her chest and between her breasts to emerge at her collar, from which they stretched to the other pony.

Melting with rapture, Mina pushed against the girl until she was squatting against the wall, her legs spread as she balanced her haunches on her hooves. Still playing the reins against Mina, she emitted soft mews of delight as Mina stretched her tongue over the bit and began lapping her exposed sex. She shivered against the wall, her operation of the strap momentarily lapsing as she relished Mina's oral attention. And as the pleasure between them mounted, they settled into a fervent rhythm of leather and flesh slapping against moist pudendas.

Mina could not have been happier with her lot as a pony-girl. She had the discipline and control she craved, the bondage, the attention, and now she had a comrade, a secret partner to share her existence with, the two of them able to revel in their degradation and conduct an illicit affair as they did so.

The straw scratched and tickled her breasts as she thrust her tongue determinedly through her bit to lick the other pony-girl's pussy as she in turn worked the strap faster and harder, drawing Mina towards orgasm. She flitted her tongue with gusto, fawning upon the juicing loins before the crotch straps once more sealed them away from each other. The sense of iniquity and misbehaviour was a strong and potent aphrodisiac, forcing them to keep utterly quiet lest they reveal their crime. The feeling of danger spiced the exchange, making it all the sweeter for both of them.

The detailed attention of her tongue proved a swifter encouragement than the caressing strap. The nameless pony-girl's body shook as she was beset by a powerful orgasm, soft croaks of rhapsody escaping her bit in response to Mina's energetic cunnilingus. Once she could take no more pleasure she pulled aside, closing her legs tightly while remaining on her knees, recovering from Mina's devastating devotions. Then hauling the strap up, she made Mina sob and bury her face in the straw, her thoughts drifting as her fingers pawed at the fabric entombing them as a climax exploded between her legs and made her fight to keep mute as every cell in her body begged to be allowed to scream her pleasure to heaven.

The pony responsible for her ecstasy continued her ministrations fervently, delighted to see Mina dancing upon her reins, groaning softly, the rocking tethers stealing her strength with joy and making her sag across the floor.

Removing the reins, the pony-girl nestled closer to Mina, brushing their breasts together and teasing each other's nipples. Mina was delighted by the improvised play, which bypassed the use of their bound hands, and realised she would need to work in ways she would never have considered before. Not being able to use their fingers was forcing them to become more imaginative in their passion for each other, forcing them to come up with unique ways to find sensual fulfilment before the day's training began.

Their lips touched, brushing against each other's around the bits in a delectable kiss whose pleasure was perversely augmented by the bondage hampering it. They were fighting the will of their owners and the restraints that transformed them into ponies and garnering a little pleasure for themselves, giving in to the animal lust that seemed so totally appropriate for them. The girl shuffled down as Mina rolled onto her back, and plunged the tip of her tongue into Mina's pussy, devoting herself to paying back her companion's skilled cunnilingus with the same fervent currency.

Mina's back arched and she whimpered softly with pleasure, lifting her booted leg between the girl's raised buttocks. Using her shin, she rubbed the pony-girl's polished hide as she rode her, treating Mina to another long session of intense delight. It was not long before soul-churning spires of pure bliss carried her away, shaking and snorting in an effort not to shriek with joy, her teeth chewing upon the bit as she weathered a second climax.

Panting, Mina sat up and pushed the girl back, urging her to her feet by nudging her breasts with her bit. Then she stood up and pinned the girl against the wall as she adored her sharp nipples as best she could, the tip of her tongue doing most of the work. She raised her leg, pressing her thigh into place against the girl's crotch.

The pony-girl strained upwards as she gasped with rapture, rocking her hips so her sex shifted along the smooth field of Mina's thigh. Her hooves scratched into the hay as her neck tensed with stress and she moaned softly, biting down on her cries as Mina dragged her helplessly through another climax teasing her nipples the whole time.

Afterwards, she rested her head on Mina's shoulder, nuzzling up to her, her warm breath spilling across Mina's skin.

Mina supported her for a moment and then eased back, letting them both sink slowly down into the hay. Relaxing, their minds at peace, they fell asleep again awaiting the return of their respective owners.

Chapter Six

When their stall opened, the pony-girls found a nurse standing before them. She was an Asian woman who looked to be somewhere in her mid or early thirties. She was wearing subtly applied make-up, and her jet-black hair was pulled back into a stern bun pierced by two spires of dark lacquered wood. She wore a plain white nurse's uniform, the bleached white material protected by a latex apron. Her limbs were also encased in latex beneath the short sleeves and skirt, rising above the plunging cleavage of the dress, sheathing her entire body in tight and shiny rubber. The unnatural cocoon flowed into gloves and knee-high patent leather boots, the seam between the two fabrics almost imperceptible.

Stepping forward on wicked heels, the nurse looked them over with a surgical intensity, apparently seeking signs of physical distress in the two human fillies.

'Up we get,' the woman stated brusquely, her accent thick. 'Now, let's have a look at you both,' she muttered to herself once both pony-girls had risen to attention before her. She looked them over closely, examining their welts.

'Humph, naughty ponies,' she remarked, detecting the gynaecological signs that gave away their wild sensual exchange in the stall. 'Okay, you're both fine,' she concluded. 'Time for your morning cleansing.' She stepped back and kicked some of the hay away from a hidden trapdoor. Grasping the latch, she lifted the small metal sheet and fished inside the interior.

Mina craned her head forward to try and get a better look, wondering what the woman meant, for she had already been comprehensively cleaned the night before. She sincerely hoped the procedure would not be repeated twice a day.

A funnel of moulded black plastic appeared in the nurse's hand, the slightly oval object fitted with a thick articulated metal hose at its smallest end, while several straps hung from the padded and flared lip. Mina's companion stepped forward, apparently well versed in the morning's routine ablutions. Bending at the waist as far as her corset would permit she offered her hindquarters to the nurse.

The woman promptly pressed the crotch-spanning funnel against the pony-girl's bottom and belly, using her fingers to pull her buttocks apart even more, thereby ensuring that the padded rim was airtight against the girl's anus. The attached straps were then wrapped around her upper thighs and her waist, fixing the funnel firmly to her so she could not dislodge it. The pony-girl then straightened up, scowling slightly as the hose was pushed forward and delved into her anus.

'Now it's your turn,' the nurse informed Mina, removing another funnel from the storage compartment hidden in the floor and stepping before her. Obediently mimicking the other pony-girl's actions, Mina turned around and offered her bottom to the woman's attentions. The funnel was pushed against her, the yielding rim clinging to her flesh and creating a hermetic seal as the straps were set in place to ensure the device's integrity. There was a push to the hose, and her sphincter was breached, the cable feeding into her insides a short way before stopping. Squeezing her muscles to it, Mina found she could not shift the intruder, which left her completely helpless to the forthcoming douche.

The nurse moved back to the pit and turned on two hidden faucets, making the hoses shudder and gurgle as water began flowing through them. She then straightened up and leaned idly against the wall, watching the two pony-girls as they shivered around the swelling force spreading through their innards. Mina grimaced even as the other girl smiled, taking pleasure in the feeling of being flushed out for the day, and taking the opportunity to urinate. Unsure whether she would have another chance, Mina dropped her barriers and allowed herself to be fully purged of all waste.

The nurse turned away, apparently satisfied that her charges were secure and the automated system would attend to them in full.

Left alone in the stall, the pony-girls tolerated the enemas sloshing around inside them, the hose increasing the force of the jet before retracting of its own accord, slipping out of their anuses as the funnel suddenly fired sharp streams of water at them. Both fillies jumped and wriggled against their bonds as the tickling spray pounded their rears and their sex, washing away all leakage. Mina sagged against the wall with her eyes tightly closed as she ground her teeth against the bit, sobbing with pleasure. She pressed her legs tightly together, her thighs clamped to the funnel as she struggled to endure the unbearable teasing influence of the intimate sprays as they pummelled her loins and clitoris. Despite her recent orgasms, she was being worked back towards yet another climax, her body unable to resist such a concentrated method of stimulation, the enema having once more roused her profound sexual appetite. And she was not alone in how she felt, for the other girl was shaking with ecstasy too, her eyes closed as she braced herself against the wall, lost to animal passions and instinct.

Finally the funnel finished its work, leaving Mina and her companion panting for breath as they slowly recovered from the strange ordeal. The nurse appeared a short time later to remove the straps and funnels and set them back in the storage compartment beneath the trapdoor, which she closed until the next morning. Then taking up their crotch-pieces, she buckled the fronts to the two pony-girls and steered the attached dildos back into them, their wet orifices allowing the soft shafts to plunge in effortlessly as the ribbed surfaces made them jolt and quiver.

The nurse bowed in respectful acknowledgement suddenly and retreated as Tethys and Oceanus strode into the stall, dressed as the day before in seductively modified riding attire.

'And how are our little beasts this morning?' Tethys asked brightly, twirling a short crop in one hand.

'We've got a somewhat gruelling day in store for both of you,' Oceanus decreed, running the leather hoop of his own weapon across Mina's nylon-coated assets, 'but you'll benefit in the long run.'

'Today will be devoted to physical training to help get you fully into shape so you can be the best fillies ever,' Tethys elaborated. 'It will also help break you into your new existence.' She removed Mina's reins from the wall as Oceanus grabbed her companion's, and together the two pony-girls were led from the stall and down the corridor.

Another door opened, and they stepped into a rectangular hall, the long sides of the room lined with treadmills. The exercise machines had been fitted with the necessary additions to ensure that those destined to use them did not slacken their pace or jump off, the various restraints and harnesses fixed into place and immobile. They resembled individual cells more than treadmills, for instead of the usual guardrail, the front and sides rose to the ceiling, the polished steel panels affixed with a single weak light to illuminate the interior, accessed by an open door at the back.

'First let's get our little Mina in place, and then sweet

Trisha,' Tethys said, leaving Oceanus to knot the other girl's reins upon the neighbouring machine so he might follow and assist her.

Mina was brought over to one of the machines and delivered onto the thick rubber belt, her reins removed and cast away first. A small aperture in the ceiling allowed a harness to descend on some dense cables, the formation of straps falling across her chest and tightening to a snug fit, the cables fixed to the shoulder straps. Another cable was then lifted from the wall before her, the metal weave bearing spiralling coils of insulated wire. The cable clipped to the front of her collar, and the wires were brought down to reveal a small black tube with four hooked metal arms. The clamps were attached to her nipples and pulled back. Their grip was relatively weak compared to the other forms of nipple clamps she had endured, and she guessed they were more of a conduit than the actual source of the distress themselves. These token additions to her body completed, the door to the chamber was closed, leaving her standing alone in the dim light of the tall and narrow space.

Listening to the faint sounds of Trisha being similarly confined, Mina was glad she at least now knew her peer's name. Then suddenly the floor broke into movement, passing slowly under her hooves and dragging her back towards the door. Stepping forward she gave a yelp of distress as the cable to her collar snapped taut, instantly pumping biting shocks down the wires and through the clamps. The voltage chewed upon her nipples, the sensation intense and distressing, making her yelp with surprise and break into a swift trot. And no sooner had the cable gone limp between her collar and the wall than the electrical attack stopped.

Mina continued walking briskly upon the belt. Looking up, she lowered her body a little, placing some tension on the overhead cable. Again her teats suffered the charged retribution of the sensors, demanding that she stand erect and remain in her place. The small nips were a spiteful and effective discipline, but they were also intriguingly pleasurable.

Locked in this small cell, she was being forcibly coerced to do as she was told, and the level of mindless automated control her owners had placed upon her filled her submissive soul with a warm and comfortable glow.

The day wore on as the belt slowly and steadily increased its pace, accelerating and forcing Mina into a swift trot, and then a steady run. Her muscles were still raw from the previous day's workout, and numerous times she was shocked into making more of an effort to keep up. Yet it felt good to exercise, to run and feel her body coursing with strength and health, her heart pumping against her leather-squeezed ribs, her lungs burning.

At regular intervals the belt slowed to a lethargic walking pace, keeping her moving slightly so her muscles would not seize up during the small breaks permitted her. Sucking in deep breaths, she steadied her pulse and with a sly smile allowed herself to drift back and enjoy the shock to her nipples. Groaning softly upon her bit, she endured a few more electrical nips before picking up her pace to stop once she had her fill of the excruciating sensation. And yet almost immediately she longed to subject herself to it again, which made her wonder if this was also part of her training. She wondered if her masochistic streak was being fed and nurtured even as her body was strengthened and her physique refined.

Staring blankly at the misty, distorted reflection of herself in the polished metal wall before her, she wondered how Trisha was faring. The other girl was clearly a more experienced pony than she.

Trotting along, Mina closed her eyes and fantasised

71

about being ravaged by fatigue as she let her legs trail to once more experience the painful shocks to her nipples. She imagined them stripping her feet from under her and leaving her dangling, her hooves dragging against the belt as the shocks grew more and more potent, demanding that she resume her run. Quivering and gasping, she pictured herself hanging there for a few seconds before the intensity of the heat in her breasts eclipsed her ability to find pleasure in it. Gaining her feet in her mind's eye, she commenced the required gait and eased the strain on her form, smiling to herself, for in reality her body was more than fit enough to meet the parameters the machine required.

Untold hours passed as her body grew slick with perspiration and her idle mind fished back through her memories, hooking onto scenes and reeling them in to re-experience. She drifted back through her times with Atlas and with Jupiter, with Charybdis and the Pleiades, dwelling on them with fond enthusiasm. Even the impossible bondage during her time as an eel was a favoured trinket to mull over in her mind now. She had hated it, but recalling her utterly helpless stint in the dark waters was more exciting than the tedious period of confinement and exercise she was being subjected to now.

Her body weary and aching, Mina at last heard the door behind her open, and light flooded her monotonous cell. Tethys's voice asked, 'Has our pony had a good run?'

'I think she's done better than poor little Trisha,' Oceanus replied. 'Our Mina has a far more demanding temperament.'

The belt slowed to a halt and she felt hands removing the bonds securing her to her fate.

'I think they'll both sleep well tonight,' Tethys remarked, clipping Mina's reins back on and leading her out of the sadistic treadmill. Standing still, but slightly wobbly from the lengthy period of physical exertion, Mina watched as the couple entered the neighbouring cell and released Trisha.

'It's okay, little Trisha, it's all over for today,' Oceanus murmured soothingly, stroking her ponytail as she emerged. 'You did well to last as long as you did.'

Trisha was sobbing quietly and breathlessly, clearly overjoyed to be free of her torment, her gratitude to those who had released her knowing no bounds despite the fact that it was they who had instigated her bondage. She had obviously suffered considerably more than Mina. She may have been a more experienced pony, but the training programme required of her was beyond her current physical prowess. She had been shocked into exertion time and time again by the clamps affixed to her nipples, and her mind and body appeared to have been left dazed by the rigorous trial.

'Come on, girls, we'll get you cleaned up and fed and then you can have a nice long sleep,' Tethys promised. 'Then tomorrow we do this again.'

Trisha sagged and wept more loudly.

'I don't think Trisha is too happy about that,' Oceanus commented lightly.

'She'll be okay,' Tethys pronounced, tugging the girl's reins as she started to lag behind. 'Once she starts becoming more fit, it'll be easier on her.'

'You'd think a girl who's been a pony for so long would be accustomed to the odd marathon run,' Oceanus remarked more sternly.

'Perhaps we should lower the demands of her programme?' Tethys suggested.

'That will not help get her into shape,' Oceanus disagreed, drawing Mina towards the door.

'You think we should increase them?' his wife asked, and the query made Trisha visibly tremble with dread.

'No, just increase the intensity of the shocks for them both. It's only fair they follow the same schedule.'

With stiff movements, Trisha was led out of the exercise barn with Mina trotting beside her. Mina felt pity for her, but also envy, as she would have liked to be pushed beyond her physical endurance; to be hauled out onto complete exhaustion and shocked repeatedly. But Mina knew that when she was under duress, when the impossible was demanded of her, she always managed to push her body past its limits and succeed magnificently in whatever she was doing. In her old line of work winning had meant surviving, and the dire consequences of defeat in her old vocation had branded her psyche with the need to succeed in everything she did.

Led down the corridor, the two pony-girls were once more delivered to the shower room. Mina was the first to be attended, leaving Trisha sagging against the wall, half-unconscious. The rods were sheathed in her tracts and the waters flushed her clean as the overhead nozzle poured a warm soothing flood across her sweat-soaked form.

Trisha was cleaned next and drawn from the room, and then they were both placed in their communal stall. Their reins were locked into place on the walls and their crotch-pieces removed. The second their owners retreated and shut the doors behind them, the two ponies placed their faces cheek-to-cheek and blinker-to-blinker to drink greedily from the water trough before filling their bellies with the soft bland nutrient pellets filling the adjoining basin.

Collapsing across the hay, the two pony-girls were asleep in seconds, Mina curling up to help cradle Trisha's tortured form.

Chapter Seven

For the next week the two pony-girls were served up to the fate of being run until they were utterly exhausted. Mina's body quickly adapted to the routine, her toned muscles making the constant exercise not only easier on her, but enjoyable too. Trisha, however, was constantly kept in a state of turmoil as her body sought to keep up with the increasing demands of her training, but never quiet succeeded in pushing itself far enough to catch up with Mina.

Every evening they collapsed in their stall, soaked from their shower and drained of all vitality by the day's run. They used the last shreds of energy they possessed to feed themselves and to drink heartily from the water trough before falling asleep in the hay. A night of deep and dreamless sleep always ended with the arrival of the nurse, and robbed them of any chance to exploit the short period during which they had enough energy to try and assuage their increasing sexual frustration. Even the morning douche failed to satisfy them, their bodies too weary to rise to the exquisite demands of an orgasm, too slow to respond to the teasing jets.

After seven days of severe and seemingly endless toil, after the nurse had finished cleaning them and left the stall, Mina was surprised when the main doors were unlatched and opened to reveal the stable's main pens, a marked deviation from the relentless training routine.

Tethys and Oceanus stood out in the early morning sunlight, the soft light catching their polished cat-suits, the shimmering rubber cocoons flowing into matching boots and gloves.

'Good morning, pony-girls,' Tethys called out to them, smiling. 'I trust you slept well?' She leaned against the doorway, her curvaceous form straining against the tight confines of the suit and inspiring the appetite of her two equine slaves.

Cursing her crotch band, Mina's eyes locked on the fetish-clad forms of her owners, her loins aflame with longing after a week spent fantasising and recalling all her previous ordeals and experiences.

'We have a treat for you today,' Oceanus announced, slipping an arm around his wife's waist.

'Seeing as you've both run so well all week long and shown definite improvement, I think you deserve this reward,' Tethys stated, and turning her head kissed her husband's cheek fondly as his hand wandered up and cupped one of her breasts. She in turn assessed him through his latex suit, following the hard outlines of his body with admiring eyes and rubbing herself against him, aroused by the scene and eager to play.

'For the whole day you are free to run around the island as you wish,' Oceanus revealed the surprise. 'You're wild ponies for a while, so enjoy it.'

'But make sure you get back here by nightfall,' Tethys warned, making it clear that she would not tolerate tardiness in their return.

'Okay, off you go,' Oceanus snapped, unclipping their reins and slapping their bottoms as they tottered out onto the soft dirt. Then breaking into a sprint, they dashed through the weave of pens, almost literally skipping with jubilation.

Giggling, Mina led the way and Trisha followed close behind as they ran out into the field and headed for the trees. With a wild leap, Mina launched herself into the foliage, the leaves brushing across her suit as she wove between the trunks and crashed through the lush vegetation, her hooves crunching over fallen twigs as

76

she ran, relishing her token freedom. The undergrowth sought to snag her, but her powerful strides sloughed it off, her nylon and leather-clad limbs immune to nature's scratching fingers. Rays of golden light poured down through the canopy of leaves, creating streaming cascades of warm radiance that washed over the happily prancing human ponies. Pausing, Mina turned to watch Trisha catching up with her. She was running more carefully, and she did not possess the same level of stamina.

Mina drunk deep of the jungle warmth and scents, drawing a deep breath to let the lush smells course through her lungs. She felt like a true animal, wild and free.

Trisha stepped beside her and looked Mina up and down lustfully, her mouth watering against her bit as she moved closer, trembling with excitement. Catching her breath, Mina approached her in turn, and let her breasts graze the other girl's through the sheer body stockings. With a sigh of rapture, Trisha brushed her lips against those of her partner in slavery.

Spinning away playfully, Mina dashed recklessly into the woods, the joy of being able to run free and head wherever she wished intoxicating her. Skidding to a halt, she adopted a petulant pose and wiggled her tail in Trisha's direction, teasing her before starting to run again, encouraging her to give chase and follow her lead.

Together the two pony-girls scampered through the forest, weaving through the maze of trees, their hooves pounding the ground, their bodies honed for speed by a week of relentless exercise. Now they were free to exploit their strengthened physiques however they saw fit, the act of running no longer a punishing chore because they were dashing madly through the wilderness not trapped in a machine, which made physical exertion a delightful blessing, recreation rather than torture.

Mina vaulted over a fallen trunk, her body soaring and then landing in a tense crouch, her supple form doubling over with an animal's protective instincts as she found herself exposed in the heart of a small clearing. The ceiling of interlaced leaves gave way above, letting her drink in a dazzling view of clear blue sky.

Trisha jumped into the clearing and sashayed forward, and Mina spread herself across the grass as the girl padded softly over and knelt down beside her. She leaned over and grazed Mina's nipples, brushing them with the tip of her tongue through her bit and making her sigh and gasp with pleasure.

Bending one of her legs, she ran the top of her boot against Trisha's loins, rubbing the crotch strap to move her dildos. The girl stiffened and her tongue grew livelier against Mina's stiff peaks before moving up over her nylon-encased mounds, placing kisses over her breasts as she sought her mouth. The two pony-girls let their lips touch, and kissed as best they could through the impediment of their bits, the implements feeling as much a part of them now as their own tongues.

Lying beside each other resting on their sides, they continued their passionate, hampered exchange, their bound hands reaching out to paw at each other's crotch bands. They lacked the manual dexterity to pluck open the buckles, but they could still slip the point of their gloves beneath the tight strap and pull at it, creating the most subtle of rocking motions, which caused the ridged shafts inside them to rub back and forth and in and out to a minor degree. Their plugged tracts increasingly damp with lust, they kissed wildly, the slow and painstaking process of gaining satisfaction making them wriggle and sob with frustrated pleasure. They lay in the sun manipulating each other's belts, helping each other towards the heady peaks of bliss they so badly craved. Mina was burning with need from her week of diligent fantasising while exercising, while Trisha undoubtedly needed an orgasm to help her forget the pain of her enforced training.

Mina tossed her head back, her cheek slipping against the tickling blades of grass as she howled through her bit, her mouth open as she screwed her eyes shut and shouted with pleasure. Her vaginal muscles contracting around the jelly dildo penetrating her, she was hauled slowly through her orgasm. She was desperate to make it quicker and more intense, but the straps were misers and allowed only a gradual savouring of bliss. Weakened by the drawn out ecstasy, she continued operating Trisha's belt as best she could, and moments later the girl was shrieking wildly into the forest air, her rapture echoing between the trees as she was finally granted orgasmic relief.

The two pony-girls remained huddled together, kissing each other, running their tongues over leather and nylon and exposed flesh, dedicated to the sensual banquet of exploring one another in the cosy afterglow of climax.

With a strain Mina lifted herself up, raising her arms over her head and arching her back as best she could in the confining corset in a luxurious stretch. Then she looked around and listened in an effort to determine what direction lay closest to the ocean, for she was on a small island and would come upon it soon enough no matter which way she went.

Trisha regained her feet and looked to Mina for guidance, clearly willing to follow her anywhere.

On a whim Mina began jogging to her right, out of the clearing and back into the jungle. The cool shade of the trees enveloped them, an occasional stray ray of sunshine winking across their polished figures.

A short run brought them closer and closer to the thunderous sound of waves breaking on a beach, and finally the pair of ponies stepped off dirt and grass onto soft sand. The particular area of beach onto which they emerged was fairly deserted, a few rocks facing out to sea carved in the form of mermaids imprisoning slaves who watched the horizon but never saw freedom until Poseidon decreed it.

Padding across the sand, their hooves sinking silently into the yielding surface, the pony-girls slowly approached the rolling waves. Then Mina chuckled and broke into a run, dashing along the water's edge and splashing through the crashing and ebbing waves. Pearls of salty water lashed her as she trotted at the edge of the sea, sometimes forced to lift her legs high even as her watertight boots kept her dry.

Trisha did not wade in as far as Mina, opting instead to run on the firmer sand left behind by the waves as they flowed back out in the ocean, her hoof marks creating two wavering lines behind her.

Then just as abruptly as she'd headed for the ocean, Mina ran back towards the trees, and merged again with the deep shade of the wilderness where she looked around wondering how she could amuse herself next. Spying a broken branch, she walked over to it and lifted her foot. Running her hoof along the stem, she trimmed off a few dead sprouts and crouched down to examine it more closely.

Trisha trotted over and watched Mina with bewilderment, as placing the branch between her thighs, she threaded it beneath her crotch strap. With the leather band locked over the wood, she started pulling her body forward and back, riding against it. The anchor to her crotch strap proved to be an admirable device, allowing her to haul the plugs further out of her passages, almost bringing them to the point of full departure from her. Then she relaxed and let the elasticity of the straining belt shove them back in, filling her with pleasure. She groaned, the exquisite feeling of penetration filling her belly and sphincter with flashes of rapturous heat. She gasped around her bit as she rode the branch, wildly thrusting the plugs in and out of her pussy and her bottom with increasing speed while praying the branch would not snap until she climaxed.

Trisha stepped in front of her, kissing Mina all over as she pounded her sex and her buttocks with the trespassers. Kisses across her breasts were a delectable treat combined with the thrusts of her intimate companions, and her legs shook as she cried out onto the warm tropical air, beset by a shockingly intense orgasm.

Climbing down from the plateau of bliss, she unfastened herself from the branch and arched her back as the strap shoved the rods back into her, her hypersensitive membranes lighting up with fresh waves of feeling as they plunged. Staggering, she tried to regain her composure, but overwhelmed by the full presence of the dildos she collapsed across the grass, her hooves kicking the ground as she rode the intense experience.

Unable to resist what she had seen, Trisha threaded her crotch strap onto the branch and began rocking back and forth towards her own satisfaction. It took Mina some time to recover from the event, and by the time she was able to lift herself up, Trisha was squealing and bucking like a wild beast. The girl was barely able to keep going against the fierceness of her pleasure, fighting to push her body onward until she had exhausted the full supply of ecstasy the experience could provide. Then her wail resounded through the forest as she came free of the branch and the plugs jammed themselves back into place deep inside her, felling her with sensation and leaving her twitching spasmodically on the ground beside Mina.

Looking up, Mina found that the day had darkened somewhat, a sheet of clouds having emerged from the horizon and drifted across the sky to blot out the sun. The atmosphere was pregnant with rain, holding onto vast bellyfuls that could drop at any moment. She indicated the ominous sight to Trisha once the other girl had recovered from her elaborate masturbation, and together they began walking slowly back towards the beach. The moment they stepped out from beneath the shelter of the trees, the heavens opened with a torrential assault, throwing down heavy droplets that slapped against them and punched small craters in the sand.

Standing perfectly still, Mina threw her head back and drank in the feel of the cool deluge lashing her, pummelling her bound body, drumming on her skin-tight uniform. Her hair was a slick tail down her back, the water crept beneath her attire, and her nylon cat-suit stuck to her body shimmering like plastic from the moisture linking and filling very tiny hole of its weave.

After permitting herself a prolonged communion with the elemental forces of nature, Mina turned to Trisha and looked her up and down. Soaked through and streaming with water, her ponytail flat against her back, her black-clad body reflecting light like a dark mirror, she was an even more tantalising vision than before.

With a nod of her head Mina indicated the cliffs of the mountain peak towering at the centre of the island, and began walking towards them, hoping to find shelter amidst the monumental spire of stone. There had to be caves there; such a rocky façade would have been honeycombed with caves either by volcanic activity or the endless assault of the eroding sea.

Walking the path of sand between the ocean and the piercing pinnacle of stone, Mina soon spied an aperture and headed for it, eager to be out of the rain. Wandering into the shadows of the rock, Mina was surprised to see light emanating from deep within the craggy passage. Meandering between the boulders, they emerged into a large cavern, where they discovered the smouldering remains of a fire and several blankets spread out across the soft sand, the imprint of people's bodies still upon them.

The fire would have poured smoke through an angled blowhole forged by the waves, which provided a natural chimney while keeping the interior of the sea cave warm and dry by protecting it from wind and rain alike. The pile of logs had burnt down almost to ashes, but extra fuel was piled nearby, apparently left behind by the noble or nobles who had entered this place to play.

Mina sat down beside the dying fire and used her hooves to clamp hold of a log. She lifted it up in a scissor grip and placed it carefully on the fading embers. She added another log, and then another, and was gratified as the weakening flames began feasting on the fresh wood, curling around it and hungrily devouring the new sustenance, their flames dancing strongly up into the air again.

Warmth spread out from the fire, caressing their tightly bound forms, and Trisha, shivering with cold, moved closer, spreading herself out on her side and cuddling up on the blanket. Mina spooned up behind her, helping to warm the cold pony-girl, and the two of them huddled close, their bodies releasing faint trails of steam as they dried. They lay together watching the flames lick and spit, the soothing crackle of the logs echoing through the cave. Mesmerised by the sight of the flames, they found solace and comfort lying by the fire pressed together, their helplessly bound forms as one.

Content and lazy, they dozed off, relishing this meagre time together and enjoying it to the full. But they knew they had to return to the stables, and as the fire once more began dying, they lifted themselves up and wandered back towards the mouth of the cave. The rain was still coming down hard outside, descending as an obscuring sheet, rendering the world a variety of grey shadows and erasing the horizon. The tide was beginning to come in, creeping up the slender beach, giving them only a little time before their way out of the sea cave was cut off. Mina was tempted to deliberately become stuck in there, which would give her and Trisha more lovely time together. People would search for them and find them, but their disobedience would be exonerated by the tide. She did not wish to upset her owners, however, for she loved them passionately, and for that reason, not out of fear, she obeyed them now, as always. Although it was tempting to gain punishment for the crime of tardiness, she was more eager to have them be proud of her obedience and loyalty.

Turning to Trisha, Mina smiled warmly and kissed the girl before she walked out into the rain. The water rolled over their forms once more, banishing the cosy warmth the fire had ignited in their flesh. Moving onto the sodden sand with Trisha close behind her, Mina headed back towards the trees and entered the forest, walking in a straight line hoping to come across the main house while the canopy of leaves provided a little more protection from the deluge. The pitter-patter of droplets overhead was almost deafening in its intensity as streams of water wound down the trunks and through breaks in the ceiling of leaves and branches.

The open field around Poseidon's mansion finally came into view between the trees, and together the two pony-girls stepped out onto the well tended grass, walking slowly and calmly back to the stables through the storm's onslaught. They found their stall open and waiting, and a single maid manning the door in expectation of their return. The girl was young, perhaps in her late teens, her long red hair tied into a plait that hung down to her chastity belt. She was short and slender, her eyes dark and full of a passion that reminded Mina of the smouldering fire she had helped stoke back to life.

'Welcome back,' she said with a slight English accent, giving them a smile as she let them into their stall and applied their reins. She clipped them back to their rings and locked them to the wall, making Mina sigh with anticipation as rain played a soft drum roll across the roof of her new home.

'Mm, you two look so beautiful together all tied up and helpless and bound into beasts,' the maid commented, her nipples tickling Mina's body as she placed both hands on Mina's hips and smoothed her palms over her corseted waist, feeling the tightness of her bondage and seemingly envying it. 'Oh, I'd so love to be a pony like you some day, but they say I'm too young still.' She rose up on tiptoe so she could kiss Mina's chin. Her fingers tweaked Mina's nipples, clasping the erect teats through her suit to pinch them softly, rubbing the constricting nylon. 'But I'm seventeen and I think that's plenty old enough, don't you?' she asked, pouting. 'Yet they won't even let me have sex yet, not until I've proved myself in some way. It doesn't seem fair, does it?' She moved behind Mina and sank to her knees as she took hold of Mina's buttocks. 'I've heard about you, Mina. Everyone talks about you. No slave has ever prompted the sort of actions you have incited in your owners and in others. Some say you used to be an assassin. Is that true?'

Mina did not respond, only continued to stand still and tense as she felt the young lips brushing her bottom, skimming the soft pelt, her words sending warm exhales across her rounded cheeks.

'You must be skilled in so many things. I am too, and I'll prove it. I'll show you I'm good enough, just to prove a point between us.'

Mina knew the girl wanted to prove her erotic skills to someone, anyone, be it a Nymph or a Titan, or even a slave everyone regarded so highly. She felt the buckles of her crotch-piece being removed, and then the girl's fingers pulling the plugging dildos free, making her gasp and sway beneath their flight after their long companionship. The small hands then reached between her legs and grabbed her reins, pulling down on them to bend Mina at the waist as she steered her over to a corner. With her head pressed into the space where two walls met, Mina was held at the required angle as the girl sought access to her bottom. Her soft features nestled between Mina's buttocks, her lips grazing her sphincter as her tongue slithered in. She started fervently suckling and kissing the pony-girl's dark orifice, thrusting her tongue deep in the style of penetration, the soft, slippery organ darting back and forth tasting as deeply of Mina as she could manage.

'That's it… let me in,' she muttered, using a finger to plunge into the slick sphincter. 'Mm, I'm good, aren't I?'

Mina gave a breathless whinny of affirmation as the digit curled and wriggled inside her before slipping out and allowing the tongue to thrust back in. The girl possessed a strong, deft organ, and her enthusiasm and hunger more than made up for her lack of experience. Rising, she trailed her young breasts through the cleft of Mina's buttocks before turning her around, and pressing her back against the wall as she sank to her knees and shoved her face into Mina's sex, driving forward so her nose slid through her vulva, rubbing against her clitoris as she drank deeply of her juices and her rich sexual scent. Gasping with arousal, the girl plunged her tongue into Mina's pussy, making her mewl with delight. The pleasure of the dildos had been good, but in her opinion nothing surpassed or even rivalled a good session of cunnilingus. She closed her eyes, losing herself to the feel of the young English girl's flitting tongue as it thrashed against her clitoris and drove as far as it could into her pussy, probing and exploring.

'Come on, Mina, I want to see you come,' the girl gasped. 'I want to see the body everyone wants quivering because of what I've done to it. Prove I'm good, Mina,' she urged softly, rubbing her sex lips with fervent adoration before running her fingers across her tongue and lapping up the salty juices coating them as she smiled up at Mina's bound body. Then her tongue slithered back in, fawning upon her, bringing her to a sudden and incredibly intense climax. And as Mina's body thrashed against the wall in the throes of bliss, the girl's tongue worked faster and more diligently, the famous slave's response enticing and exciting her, making her wild with vivacious passion.

'Now that I've serviced you, Mina,' she looked up at her worshipfully as she spoke, clearly idolising her, 'will you do the same for me? I'll handle your friend if you do.' She rose and turned around to reveal that her belt was of the kind that broke into two chains at the back, rising to the waistband so her bottom was left open for bodily functions.

Mina looked down and then up at the clearly frustrated Trisha. The other pony-girl was hopping from hoof to hoof in response to the erotic display before her, yearning to experience the same herself. Smiling at her, Mina looked back at the eager girl, and nodded her consent.

With a wild grin the girl moved to Trisha, her fingers fumbling on the buckles of her crotch strap as she opened it and removed the plugging lengths of the dildos from her. Upon witnessing the sheen of moisture coating the vaginal shaft, she gobbled up the rod, rolling her tongue around it as an appetiser and a precursor to the taste of Trisha herself. Then she spread herself back across the hay with Trisha by her head and Mina at her feet. 'Someone as good as you should be able to work even over the bit, eh?' she teased Mina, ignorant of the fact that she had already performed oral sex with this impediment.

Trisha set her legs astride the girl's face and lowered in for her ride, smothering lovely face with her vulva and sighing as the tongue flicked energetically up between her sex lips and into her pussy.

Mina knelt down as the girl lifted her legs, throwing them up so she could slot them into the crook of Trisha's bound arms, the extreme contortion offering her anus more openly than any other position could have. Shuffling forward, Mina gazed lustfully at the young and supple flesh before eagerly lowering her face into position, the tip of her tongue working against the girl's tender bud, and slipping in as deep as she could work it between the girl's nether lips, working her pleasure with detailed precision. The young slave gurgled and moaned into Trisha's smothering loins as the pony-girl rocked over the face attending her, and enjoyed the feel of the girl's hands stroking the body towering over her. The muscles in her thighs rippled inside her boots as she shuddered upon the girl's face, absorbing her passionate attentions with small gasps and hisses of pleasure. Then she rose and spread herself on her side in the hay, and the girl swiftly moved back away from Mina, the loss of one playmate and her inability to have her own pudenda attended to obviously a frustration she could not tolerate. The savaging of her anus by Mina's agile tongue had fanned her need for relief all the more and she was quivering with denial, trying to overcome the effects of the rimming but finding herself unable to accept any more lest she burst with need.

'Oh, that was wonderful,' she groaned, wrapping her arms around herself and letting her hands travel upon her own slender body, her eyes half closed with a gloating lust. 'I just have to get you to do that when I'm not wearing this damned belt,' she added, fondly caressing Mina's face around her bit. Then she stood up and moved to the door, her steps slightly unsteady after the intensity of their play and from her own hot and frustratingly plugged up needs. Mina could understand her insane hunger, for she herself had been similarly starved before. The belt was a curse that boiled in the mind, making the wearer more and more depraved in an effort to try and find satisfaction. It was a cunning way to forge a slave willing to perform the most perverse sensual acts.

The latch was thrown and Mina spread herself across the hay, sidling up against Trisha as the other pony-girl breathed softly and contentedly, resting and recovering after their wonderful day of freedom. Lulled by the sound of the rain drumming across the roof, the two pony-girls drifted into a deep and comfortable sleep.

Chapter Eight

Dropping them neatly back into the normal routine to which they had become accustomed, the nurse entered Mina and Trisha's stall in the morning and began the daily process of cleansing them internally. The two ponies complied with her wishes actually enjoying the process as the woman strapped them to the hoses, penetrating and bestowing upon them both a debilitating orgasm with the powerful jets issuing from the hoses into both their orifices.

There was something innately gratifying about being treated in such a way, of being effectively stripped of sentience and importance and their every action regulated and controlled. They had freedom to rebel and buck and fight as did any domesticated beast, and even though they knew they would be punished for it, the option was there and always tantalising their masochistic need for discipline.

The nurse finished her chores and departed, leaving the pony-girls plugged once more as they awaited the arrival of their owners.

Tethys and Oceanus appeared a few minutes later, once again clad in seductively modified riding outfits. Both wore tight white breeches with tall leather boots and a close-fitting leather vest with matching gloves. Riding crops and helmets tucked beneath their arms, they preceded a pair of slaves carrying saddles. The leather seats were of a far different configuration to those used for normal equestrian riding, for they were crafted in such a way that they could rest across the shoulders of a human.

'Today we'll be going out for a ride, slaves,' Tethys informed them, 'with both of you providing the transport, of course.' She pushing open the far doors to expose the pens, where already several Nobles had risen to begin the task of training their mounts. There seemed to be more activity than usual, no doubt as preparations for the big party began in earnest, and those with private steeds sought to have their behaviour fully modified before the critical eyes of fellow guests fell upon the pony-girls they had created.

'Saddle them,' commanded Oceanus, putting on his helmet and adjusting it on his head as he wandered out into the warm sunlight. The smell of moisture was heavy in the air, the rains having ended some time during the night. The warm and sunny morning was coaxing a soft mist into the air from the wet grass, the shifting luminous veil skimming across the fields carried on a languid, pollen-scented breeze.

The saddle bearing slaves moved forward together, and set the leather seats across the shoulders of the pony-girls. Mina did not resist as the soft interior settled over her, running around the back of her neck and falling into place as a harness of straps was wrapped tightly around her body, affixing to her corset and bridle to ensure it did not come loose. A set of stirrups fell from the front, ready for the boots of whichever noble decided to mount her. Mina was tingling with excitement. This was the culmination of her transformation into an animal. She was going to be used as a steed, used to carry a dominant owner. Another human being was going to swing up into the saddle and ride her as though she were no better than a pony. The concept made her stomach flutter with excitement and her mind swim with libidinous desires.

The maids stepped back and Tethys grabbed her reins as her husband took hold of Trisha's. The two pony-girls were then led out into the open air, their hooves sinking into the wet soil as their owners conducted a brief but thorough check of the various straps holding the saddles on them, pulling on a few to ensure all was in place and secure.

'Down girl,' Tethys ordered, pulling on the leashes so Mina wilted before her into a tight crouch. The dominatrix then swung a leg over her slave and settled into the sculpted arms of the seat, taking up her hat and setting it upon her head before getting a more effective grip on her crop. 'Okay, *up!*' she cried, hauling at the reins.

With a hiss of exertion, Mina pushed up with her legs, bringing herself erect and accepting the full burden of Tethys's weight. The saddle made it much easier to carry her mistress on her shoulders, the soft leather soothing the areas on which the curvaceous form rested. It was a strain but also a distinct pleasure to bear her beautiful owner in such a way. The stretch cotton breeches clinging to the magnificent legs around her rubbed gently against her cheeks, the warm thighs entering her vision after clearing her blinkers. Her smooth crotch was against the back of her head, resting in the nape of her collared neck, pressed to her by the demands of the saddle. With every movement Mina made, she felt the satin folds of taut fabric brush against her, causing her to sigh with pleasure, her mind filled with the lingering image of her mistress swinging up and straddling her just like a pony, transforming her into a lowly beast.

Tethys's boots were marked with soft spiralling lines of lingering moisture from the tongue that had cleaned them this morning, making Mina a little envious that she herself had not been able to perform the task. With a small shuffle, they caught the metal stirrups and stretched into them, pushing down to drag at Mina and ensure that she was kept properly under control.

'Come on, slave, let's see what you can do.' She flicked her heels back to nudge her spurs into her pony's hips. The sharp flash of pain made Mina squawk and pound her hooves against the soil. She bolted forward as the crop swung down in long arcs to savagely kiss her buttocks, smacking soundly against her cheeks as she ran. Yet Tethys's weight upon her was a burden she willingly revelled in, the feel of being forced to support her mistress as she punished her goading her on, the harsh swipes to her bottom encouraging her lively trot.

With her world blinkered, the reins served to guide her more effectively, the pulls to the corners of her mouth steering her though the maze of pens and onto the grass. Mina could hear a second set of hoof beats behind her as Oceanus rode Trisha.

'Come on, husband, you're lagging behind,' Tethys laughed, slamming the leather tip of the crop against Mina's buttocks with more force, the hot lines being burning into the pony-girl's bottom as she increased her efforts, forcing her body onwards. Her chest heaved against the corset, her breaths pouring over the bit as she gurgled with effort. Her legs were hot, the muscles taxed to their very limits as she continued to meet the demands of her owner.

'I'll beat you to the beach yet!' Oceanus retorted with a merry shout, the sounds of the scourging crops and the pounding of artificial hooves nearly drowning out his words.

'Maybe you're getting fat!' his wife taunted him. 'Your laziness is putting too much of a burden on that poor sweet pony you're riding and slowing her down!' She steered Mina into the trees and towards a narrow path. The dirt track was occasionally obstructed by lush foliage, the vegetation creeping furtively back over it, stretching its green fingers to slap against the pony-girl's leather-bound legs as she thundered past.

Mina gave up trying to negotiate her own route and placed herself totally at the whim of her rider. Turning her head, she let her eyes soak up the vision of Tethys's white legs. Her hungry eyes devoured the image of taut material stretched over shapely limbs, and of polished boots brushing their sharp spurs against her flanks when she required a sterner means of being steered.

'And Oceanus the Great takes the lead!' he proclaimed with a jubilant shout.

Mina forced her head against the reins, defying Tethys's wish that she not catch a glimpse of her left side where Trisha was being whipped past her, her nubile form diverted from the path and forced into the brush to overtake Mina. Oceanus's crop danced back and forth, clapping against the girl's bottom, driving her on towards victory. The undergrowth snapped and broke beneath her hooves as she negotiated the uneven terrain at a wild pace, desperate to meet the demands her rider was placing upon her.

A yank to the reins hauled at her bit, making the strut dig into the corners of her mouth. Mina emitted a whinnying sound of discomfort as control was once more taken from her, and Tethys's crop became even more energetic in its lambasting of her bottom.

'Come on, girl!' Tethys barked, her arm bringing the weapon down with force and sending blasts of agony into Mina's straining bottom cheeks. 'Faster! Faster!'

Oceanus turned Trisha and drove her back onto the path ahead of Mina, her slender form running beneath the weight of her owner, her buttocks quivering in front of Mina's eyes as she struggled to stay ahead of her rival. Squeaking beneath each cruel stroke of the crop, incensed that she was possibly going to lose, Mina fired her legs into motion, accelerating her pace with a groan of strain.

'That's it, girl!' Tethys shouted ebulliently, overjoyed

as her mount once more gathered fresh speed and began galloping even faster. 'Come on, faster! You can do it!'

'See you at the beach!' Oceanus laughed, thrashing his hapless mount, demanding she keep up the mad sprint he required to stay ahead of Mina and his wife.

'Come on, pony, you can go faster than this!' Tethys growled, applying her own weapon with more celerity, fuelling Mina's strength and stamina with lucid streaks of suffering.

With a mewling cry Mina threw herself forward, her body awash with intense sensations from her own efforts and from the rhythmic beating applied by her mistress. Defying the reins, she wove briefly into the undergrowth, half running on the path, half careening into the dense foliage seeking to snag her hooves and topple her and her rider to the ground. Ignoring the branches trying to bar her way, she drew level with Trisha and nudged her fellow pony's shoulder. She adored Trisha, but there was no way she was going to lose this race. With another resentful nudge Mina started capturing more space on the path, running neck-to-neck with Trisha and demanding access to the path's smoother terrain. The crops continued pummelling their bottoms, making them gasp and moan as they struggled to catch their breath.

'You bloody cheat!' Oceanus declared angrily, but there was an edge of amusement in his voice.

'Out of the way, slowcoach!' Tethys retorted, allowing Mina to fight for position by barging against Trisha and forcing the girl deeper into the vegetation lining the narrow path.

'Come on, girl, move those hooves!' he demanded, trying to force his struggling mount back against Mina's aggressive physique, but the brief diversion into the undergrowth had pulled and dragged at Trisha's boots, slowing her down a crucial fraction and letting Mina streak ahead.

Trisha jumped back onto the path and tried to keep up, chasing after her fellow pony as she furrowed her brow and chewed on her bit, applying her full fury and strength to the task of running as fast as possible with a man's weight straddling her shoulders.

Mina flew down the trail, the feeling of being driven to such extremes making her giddy with satisfaction, her pleasure and pride accentuated by the torrents of adrenaline and endorphins pumping through her raging veins. With a growl of exertion and triumph she fired herself forward, pushing further and further ahead of Trisha, who was unable to keep up with her. Oceanus eased his use of the riding crop, obviously realising there was no hope of beating Mina.

The hard dirt of the trail suddenly gave way to soft sand, her hooves giving slightly against the new environment. The sun's light glinted on the ocean's rolling waves, the beach gleaming beneath the luminous rays. Trotting nimbly across the sand Mina was driven towards the sea, where the salt spray splashed her legs and belly, soothing the heat in them as Tethys finally allowed her steed to slow down.

Her heart thumping against her ribs, Mina walked through the surf and let herself be steered around towards a set of beach umbrellas and lounge chairs placed near the tree line. Her legs trembled beneath her, and exposed to the sun she felt her leather hide warming up fast as the waters of the ocean evaporated along with her perspiration. Her hair was damp against the back of her neck, and jewels of perspiration glimmered on her eyelashes.

Several men and women were relaxing in the sun, served by the chaste submissive slaves. Other slaves were bound with straps and applying themselves in different capacities to the pleasuring of the dominant caste. Some were curled up in tight balls on the sand so they might bear the feet of their owners, while some had a circle of glass on their backs upon which drinks and plates of food were arrayed, along with implements of correction.

Closing in on the hedonistic scene, Mina was driven aside by her rider towards a pair of empty lounge chairs. Two maids stood a step behind the reclining seats, and another pair knelt to attention before them, ready to accept the boots of the approaching noble couple.

A wooden post had been driven into the sand with steel eyelets placed around the top. The apparatus had been set near the chairs with a small trough running around the base of the post, the circular vessel currently empty.

'Down,' Tethys commanded, pulling at the reins until Mina lowered herself to the ground. The dominatrix dismounted, easing herself off the modified saddle with a subtle and elegant creaking of leather. She flicked the crop across her steed's smouldering buttocks and drew her towards the post, where she then threaded the reins through the eyelets and tied a swift knot to secure them. A child could have picked the simple weave, but denied use of her hands, and unable to even lift her arms, the elementary knot constituted an insurmountable barrier to Mina.

Standing beside the hitching post, Tethys ran her hands down her pony's heaving chest, delighting in her mount's tightly bound curves. 'You performed admirably, slave, I'm proud of you,' she whispered, her finger pulling at Mina's crotch strap and manipulating the plugs a little, making them rock gently back and forth. The sedate shuffling of her ribbed dildos caused Mina to stiffen and groan softly, relishing this slim but welcome reward for her efforts.

'Such a sweet filly,' Tethys crooned, continuing to play

with the strap, making Mina moan, her eyes closing as pleasure flooded her. The soft pull of the intruders against her sex dissolved her thoughts and left only the growing need for physical relief.

'But a vicious one,' commented Oceanus as he led Trisha up to the same hitching post. The girl looked exhausted, her body quaking from the stresses she had endured in a useless bid to defeat Mina.

'You're just pissed I beat you,' Tethys rebuked him fondly, continuing to toy Mina's crotch strap as a reward for her victory.

'And I suppose you think it was all due to your superior equestrian skills?' Oceanus sneered as he tethered Trisha to the other side of the post.

'Of course.' Tethys raised her nose and waved her crop in a regal manner. 'What else could it have been save my superlative riding ability?'

'Well, next time we'll trade ponies and then we'll see who's the better rider.' He walked over to one of the inanimate tables, and taking up a tall glass of water quickly drained it.

'Don't pout, lover.' Tethys let go of Mina's crotch strap, and sidling up beside her husband, caressed his body with hers while he stood rigid and defiant. 'I'll let you have Mina on the way back if you really want her,' she smiled, kissing his neck and then blowing softly against his earlobe.

Oceanus wriggled and laughed softly, giving away the fact that his dour temperament had only been an act as he turned and embraced his wife. They kissed lovingly, their hands wandering over each other's alluring bodies as their steeds watched hungrily, increasingly aroused and frustrated by the fact that they were powerless to sate their desires.

The couple reclined in separate chairs holding hands, their fingers interlaced as they set down their riding crops and accepted drinks from the serving slaves. Putting their feet up on the living footstools that obediently crouched before them, they sipped the extravagant cocktails on offer.

'Water our mounts,' ordered Oceanus, indicating Mina and Trisha, and a dark-skinned female procured a plastic container of water and carried it over to the post. Unscrewing the nozzle, she poured the contents into the trough, filling it to the brim before returning to see if the noble couple needed anything else.

Mina and Trisha sank to their knees and began lapping up the crystal-clear water, which flowed cool and refreshing down their parched throats, a wonderful soothing delight. They drank as much as they wished over the obscuring bits, and then sat back and rested their weary bodies, lounged in the shade of the trees as their breathing gradually slowed and returned to normal.

Mina watched her owners relaxing beneath the umbrellas and folded a leg beneath her. Resting on her own shin, she slowly drew herself along it, rocking the crotch strap and shifting the dildos inside her. She could not gain enough motion to grant herself release, but she could enjoy this hesitant pleasure.

A serving slave clipped the ends off a pair of cigars, and once the two Nobles accepted them, she lit them, Oceanus's first and then Tethys's.

Smoking cigars, the couple talked idly, running over the events of the past week in low voices, relaxed and content.

Mina moved closer to Trisha, but the girl shuffled away from her with a sullen look, clearly still upset by Mina's aggressive behaviour during the race. Feeling a little guilty, Mina pursued her, moving over and brushing up against her, but Trisha kept her back turned, refusing to meet her apologetic stare. Mina tried to offer her regrets, running her features across Trisha's shoulders and pressing them gently against the back of her neck, trying to draw her out of her brooding mood. Making an effort to speak around her bit would have been more trouble than it was worth, the garbled outpouring inevitably requiring constant repetition to be understood. So instead Mina moved around and tried to assuage Trisha's anger with her body language even as the pony-girl continued to ignore her.

Finally, she started succumbing to Mina's efforts at reconciliation, and slowly turning back towards her stable mate, nestled against her nylon-coated cleavage, her eyes looking up at her with meek solicitation.

Trisha's flickering smile made Mina's heart leap with joy, and she straightened up to press her lips against those of her fellow pony. Exchanging their hampered kiss, they leaned together in the shade, feeling comforted by the presence of another body. They were partners in slavery, there for each other when they were not being made to compete, emotionally united by their submissive caste. Kneeling together, they marvelled at the beauty of the sea and of the tropical paradise nurturing them.

Chapter Nine

The sun was beginning to set, the mountain spreading its shadow across the island. The umbrellas and trees ceased to provide shade as the sun's lowering rays slipped beneath their canopies, and a slight chill crept into the warm ocean breeze.

Two of the slaves knelt before Oceanus and Tethys, drew open the Nobles' breeches and serviced each of them slowly and diligently. The orally skilled young women drew out the couple's pleasure, making it last for nearly an hour as they savoured a relaxing ascent towards orgasm whilst enjoying the sensual beauty of their environment.

Finally, the couple broke free of the lapping tongues and sucking lips of the slaves and fell into each other's arms, their mouths locked together as their tongues circled each other's, their passion raging. Dropping onto the sand, Tethys bent over and allowed her husband to slide into her pussy from behind as he ran his hands up and down her back. Driving into her with murmuring growls of delight, he held her hips and ran his fingers across her bared and inviting bottom. The two ponies and the serving slaves watched with gnawing frustration as the two Nobles made wild love on the beach, indulging themselves freely before those who had no such option. Kept chaste and obedient, the serving slaves would have to earn their relief through subservience, while Mina and Trisha would have to wait until they were alone in their stall and free of the crotch straps before they could satisfy the heat of their lust.

Tethys tossed her head back, her mouth gaping as

she groaned wantonly, feeling her lover swelling potently inside her as he approached his climax. Reaching down for her breasts, he cradled them in his palms and massaged them, his features tightening as his body stiffened and he drove deep into his wife as he climaxed, eliciting cries of delight from her.

He rested across her back for a moment, pressing her cheek to the sand, and then slipped out of her. The two Nobles held each other for a moment, then a wave of his hand beckoned forth the forgotten serving slaves.

The two young women eagerly crawled back towards the couple to resume their oral devotions and cleanse the sated Nobles, the act making them shiver with wanton ecstasy. Once they completed their task, they were brushed aside to await further orders as the couple rose and refastened their clothing, exchanging a final kiss before walking over to their mounts. Trisha and Mina promptly rose onto their hoofed feet as their owners approached.

The setting sun touched the horizon in a dazzling riot of gold and red, casting a purple glow across sea and island as rubies sparkled on the crests of the waves.

'Down girl,' commanded Oceanus, as he removed Mina's rein from the post.

Settling into a crouch, she accepted the weight of the Noble as he swung into the saddle and drew on her reins to make her rise.

'Do you want to race back?' Tethys asked as Trisha strained to regain her feet, her eyes flashing with dismay at the prospect of another fight to try and beat the physically superior Mina.

'No, it's okay, let's just take a nice wander, I'm in a lazy mood,' Oceanus replied, his competitive nature seemingly put away for the day. His spurs nudged Mina's hips and a flick of the reins urged her into a steady trot back towards the trees and the narrow trail.

As they made for the house and stables, Mina saw other serving slaves emerging from another trail to gather up the day's leftovers. She could see the hunger on their faces, not for food but for the sexual release each prayed would come as a reward for having served well all day. Of course, she knew some would be receiving punishment for inadequate work, a treat that would be as welcome to them as the joy of climax.

The walk back to the stables was uneventful and pleasant as the forest darkened around them. Through the chinks in the armour of the forest canopy, Mina saw the first stars sparkling into view, and gathering strength as the blue vault of the sky faded to a deep and impenetrable black.

Their stables were opened and the nobles dismounted, patting the rumps of their respective steeds before departing and leaving them to the care of an anonymous slave who entered the stall holding a black tackle box.

'See to them as we specified, slave,' Oceanus told the girl as he tied Mina's reins to the wall.

'You both did well today, and you'll find tomorrow easier as we'll be taking a gig out for a spin,' Tethys said. 'Sleep well, ponies.' She finished securing Trisha's reins and followed her husband out of the stall, leaving the pony-girls alone with the serving slave, a tall, shapely young woman whose golden curls were pulled back in a chaotic ponytail. The lids of her cool grey eyes were rimmed with coal and her lips were painted a striking red that matched her long nails. Perched atop ankle-high boots, she walked easily on the stiletto heels wearing shiny black gloves that rose all the way to her biceps. Her chastity belt was polished to a mirror sheen that matched her collar, and she moved with a regal and easy grace, at one with her position on Poseidon's pleasure island. And as she drew closer, Mina noticed a small fixture at the front of her belt, the inch-round socket raised slightly from the surface of the steel band.

Unfastening Mina's reins the woman pulled them in, drawing her towards the wall until her collar touched the heavy metal band. A looped knot fastened Mina in place, keeping her on her feet and unable to bend over or sit down. Her crotch strap was then opened and pulled free, and the swift extraction of the dildos made her gasp.

The same ritual was performed on Trisha, leaving the two pony-girls trapped on either side of the stable, unable to reach one another, let alone grant the relief each so fervently craved after the evening's arousing displays of passion.

The woman then opened the metal latch on the box she had brought and raised the lid. She extracted a set of surgical gloves and slid her painted fingernails into them, snapping the sheaths efficiently in place and interlacing her fingers to ensure they were fully stretched.

Next she took a glass pot from within the box, unscrewed the lid and scooped out a generous portion of a white gel. She turned Mina so her face was pressed to the wall, and working the slippery substance across both her hands applied the viscous ointment to Mina's bottom. The cool touch of the thin latex gloves combined with the warmth of the gel simultaneously irked and soothed Mina's burning buttocks as her welts rebelled against being disturbed but accepted the calming effects of the curative gel. The woman continued to smear the slippery substance across her contusions, causing Mina to lean against the wall for support as her grateful discomfort beneath the soothing ministrations lulled her into a hedonistic stupor. Then the skilled fingers began working the greasy substance more forcefully into the crease between her bottom cheeks, driving through her buttocks to rub it against her sphincter. Mina lowered her defences, unclenching the muscles of her anus to permit ingress, and the fingers instantly slithered into her.

At first only one digit slid into her bottom, making her sigh with contentment. Then it withdrew and was joined by another, and then another. The bunched digits rocked into her as one, diving almost to the knuckles. Mina pressed her breasts against the wall, sighing with pleasure as the forceful hand penetrated her.

The extremities emerged and moved a little, locating her vulva and passing the gel across the moist lips of her sex. A moment later a pair of fingers thrust, eliciting a whimper of joy from Mina as two more fingers joined them. The slave rammed her hand up into Mina, making her ride the firm cone of her bunched digits, inflicting flashes of duress along with a warm, deep pleasure. Mina's blissful sighs grew deeper, and were interspersed with soft groans of rapture. Murmuring and moaning wantonly, Mina felt herself being worked gradually towards orgasm, the piston-like action between her legs gathering potency and making her giddy with expectation.

The hand withdrew abruptly, cruelly deserting her. Mina cried out with disappointment and writhed against the wall, her final release slipping through her fingers even though she clenched her legs together in an effort to catch it and make herself come.

The woman returned to her ordinary chore of soothing the havoc in Mina's welt-striped bottom, and then she gathered up a fresh handful of gel and moved over to Trisha. Applying her medicinal remedy, she began penetrating the pony-girl's well-flogged buttocks. Mina turned around to watch the show as Trisha rode the bunched fingers of the slave, her lithe body jiggling softly as she was forced to endure the delightful purgatory of a hand plunging into her rectum. The woman continued teasing her for a while before finally switching to a different orifice, and Trisha literally sobbed with rapture as she was worked towards orgasm, unable to resist the allure of it despite the awful foreknowledge that she would be deprived of a climax in the end.

She mewled miserably when the woman retracted her latex-sheathed fingers and moved away. Garbled pleas for her not to stop spilled over her bit, the gagging implement rendering her desperate words all but incoherent. Mina suspected Trisha had fallen into a trap instigated by their owners. The woman was probably there to tease them and test them on how well ingrained they were into the pony caste.

'Ponies do not speak,' the woman declared. 'They perform and do as they are told, without question, always.' She smirked, overjoyed to see one of them fail so she could exercise a little dominance; Trisha murmured something in her defence, further compounding her offence.

'You continue to speak, pony-girl? I was ordered to punish anyone who tried to speak, and I can see I have ample justification in applying the full discipline to you both. Yes, I'm going to make your fellow pony suffer with you. She was good, she didn't speak, but because of you she'll suffer just as terribly as you will.' Leaning down, the woman removed a leaden orb the size of a tennis ball from the box. The globe had a single hoop set upon its surface from which ran a long, slender chain. The links extended for a few yards and then broke into two shorter lengths, both of which culminated in a clover clamp.

'Now, little pony, I'll escort you to a discipline chamber where you'll be taught the price of disobedience all night long. Won't that make tomorrow's venture fun for you both? A nice night of distress before more exercise.' She chuckled and stepped towards Trisha.

The pony-girl panicked and started bucking, fighting

the tether at her collar and kicking wildly to keep the woman away from her, obviously terrified of the clamps in her hands and the burden to which they were connected.

'Bad pony!' She backed off, and pulling a small tawse from the box thrashed the leather strap against Trisha's cavorting legs. The steady smack of leather rang through the stable accompanied by Trisha's stifled moans of distress as she was thrashed for her defiance. The woman chastised her with vicious strokes to her thighs, stinging the untouched regions again and again until Trisha was rendered a whimpering wreck hanging nearly limp from her collar.

'Are we done?' the woman demanded coldly, and skimmed the weapon across Trisha's rosy flesh once more. The beaten pony-girl gurgled apathetically. 'Good.'

Mina was determined to be utterly compliant, for she had no idea what sort of terrible things this woman might do should she follow Trisha's rebellious example. Already she was destined for a night of suffering, and even though she was looking forward to it in a strange way, she did not want to compound her misery. On the other hand, she was curious to be rendered helpless to this beautiful woman's cruel intentions, whatever they were, so the seductive notion of doing as Trisha had done crept temptingly through Mina's masochistic psyche. The denial of relief in orgasm had left her full of a dangerous hunger, one that was threatening to eclipse her reason and making her seek that which she might not be able to endure. But right now she did not care if she could endure it or not; she wanted to be tied, bound and punished, helpless to the woman's vicious ministrations.

'Now keep still or I'll beat you some more, pony-girl.' The blonde slave moved towards her and shoved Trisha's slack legs open. The clamps swung in like steel hawks and snapped to a generous portion of flesh, taking her labia in their firm jaws and holding tight. The application of the devices made Trisha jerk upright and whimper in distress as the compression to her most tender parts continued unabated as her reins were removed, leaving her free of the wall anchor.

'You can walk to the chamber now, *pony*.' Her tormentor flashed the tawse across Trisha's well-chastised bottom.

Gurgling deep in her throat from the pain of the clamps, she lurched forward, only to have the chain snap taut and tug at the heavy burden trailing behind her. Trembling with the effort she managed to drag the heavy orb after her, the metal globe moving slowly as she towed it with her sex, the squeeze of the clamps increased by the pull on the chain. Whimpering in torment, she gradually made her way to the door, each step a hell of suffering monitored by the jubilant blonde slave.

'Watch this well, pony, because you're next,' the woman warned Mina. 'Come on you,' she barked at Trisha, 'I haven't got all night.'

The scraping of the metal ball faded along with the sound of uneven hoof beats as Trisha forced herself out into the corridor and to some unknown arena of chastisement. The time during which Mina awaited the return of the woman was long and full of angst as she wondered what was going to be done to her. And what psychological effect would the discipline have on her afterwards? Would the woman push her beyond her ability to find pleasure in the pain? Yet whatever was done to her, Mina was confident she would find the strength to relish the ordeal, no matter how humiliating or intensely difficult it proved to be.

Finally, the sound of high heels approached the doorway and the woman reappeared, her eyes glinting sadistically. 'Mm, that was fun,' she purred, stepping forward with the chain and ball that had been affixed to Trisha's labia. 'And what's best is that I get to do it all over again now.'

Mina kept still and allowed her legs to be parted, refusing to give the woman cause to inflict additional harm. She stiffened and moaned as the first clamp took hold of her nether lips, and gave a whinny of agony as the second grabbed her tender flesh, wringing the sensation from it as it imparted a deep, arctic throbbing that surged up through her loins.

'There, now, come along, pony-girl, and let's see how you respond to the treatment I gave your partner.' The woman removed Mina's reins and slapped her rump with the tawse. Mina staggered forward, and gave a yelp as the slack vanished from the chain and the weight suddenly hauled at the clamps clinging to her vulva.

'That's it, pony, get moving.' She subjected Mina to a hot flash of encouragement across her rear with the tawse. With quaking steps Mina moved towards the door, the weight dragging across the floor pulling at her sex lips and making her shudder with the stress of towing it behind her. The tawse snapped across her bottom yet again, and again, in whimsical strokes that kept her moving at a steady pace.

Gasping and wheezing with the effort, Mina chewed on her bit as her eyes filled with tears, and flowed down her cheeks into her mouth. Trudging drearily onwards, her sex aflame with biting sensations, Mina was abruptly halted by the woman's voice behind her.

'Hey pony, back here!'

Mina turned to see the woman standing a short distance down the corridor next to one of the doors she had passed. Scowling with irritation she turned around carefully and started back the way she had come, resentfully trekking across ground she had already covered to satisfy the spitefulness of what was in all reality just another slave.

'There.' She smiled, and opening the door let Mina trudge blindly into darkness. Once the burden of the ball was in the room, the woman closed the door behind her and flicked on the sombre lights, revealing the chamber in all its nebulous glory.

The exact dimensions of the room were lost in the darkness. Only a single spotlight shone from above, firing a stark beam down onto the site of their duel torment, leaving the rest of the chamber draped in shadows. A stone slab evocative of a sarcophagus rose from the centre of the space, a smooth marble table with a hollow indentation, and lying within this shaped trough was Trisha. The sides of the interior groove bore a layer of black latex, the inflatable sheath pumped full of air so it pressed to her body from the sides and against her back from below, holding her body in a pressurised embrace. The top of the table was a glass panel, allowing Mina to see Trisha's body crushed against it, her breasts flattened. It was as though her friend was sealed inside a skin-tight coffin with a glass lid against which she was hopelessly pressed.

The glass tabletop bore several apertures, none of which served any function other than causing further distress to the entombed pony-girl. Abrasive rope wound around her corseted waist and rose between her legs, the chafing length spilling through one hole to rest coiled on the outside of the table unattached to anything.

Two more holes were drilled through the glass at the level of her breasts, letting her nipples peek through, each sensitive teat captured by a clamp from which hung a slack line of cord with identical clamps on the other end, awaiting application somewhere – and Mina knew where.

The last hole in the table was the largest, leaving Trisha's nose and chin exposed, her mouth stretched open, her bit removed so a squat candle might be thrust into her maw. Two small strips of tape ran over her cheeks to hold it in place, the wick as yet unlit.

With Trisha in bondage, her eyes wide with dismay, Mina noticed the other portions of the table that would obviously incorporate her own physique, which would make her and her fellow pony-girl wreak havoc on each other through no fault of their own. Finally, running around Trisha's head were leather trammels, the stern restraints open and waiting.

'Come on, you,' the woman barked, using the tawse to drive Mina over into the stern light. The clamps were set free and Mina jerked with the sudden detonation as her nerves screeched their protest at having been abused so by the voyage.

Dragged up onto the table, her knees were placed by the uppermost corners and the restraints positioned there were set to her upper calves. Her shins were run parallel down the sides and caught in the fetters, leaving her legs spread wide as she knelt above Trisha's face and the candle, the waxen sceptre aiming frighteningly towards her loins.

Unable to resist, Mina had her collar snagged by the remainder of the crotch rope. Gaining insight she burbled and struggled, trying to free herself as the woman started to forcefully haul at the hemp line. Mina whimpered as she was bent backwards, her spine and neck stretching against corset and collar as the back of her skull was towed down towards Trisha's garrotted vulva. Twisted into an agonising pose, the rope was tied off, leaving Mina and Trisha in a dark predicament.

The spare clamps reached up and around to snap themselves to Mina's nipples where the cord was tightened to a thrumming tension, connecting them both by this mordant towline.

'Goodnight, girls, sleep tight,' laughed the woman,

lighting a match and applying it to the wick. Mina felt the heat swell against her pudenda and inner thighs and she shuddered with calamity, releasing startled and terrified squeals against her bit as she heard the woman walking away. The door slammed shut and the light that dazzled them vanished, leaving them with only the golden aura of the candle as illumination.

The horror of the position became immediately apparent and they knew it would only get worse and worse.

If Mina tried to ease the agonising twist on her back as she was forcibly bent over, she would cause the rope to chew and chafe against Trisha's tender belly. Similarly, any shift of her torso would drag the clamps against both their breasts, escalating the effects with even the slightest twitch of her body, for already even a deep breath lifted her ribs to a degree that applied a marked increase in their travail.

Trisha not only had to endure the compression and complete crushing of her form as well as whatever Mina's plight added to her woe, but also, the candle that would have her jaws pounding with duress was filling with wax and slowly withering in height. Any struggle brought by herself or Mina's fight against her bondage would shake the candle and have it spill its scorching fluids onto her tender lips. And all the while the burning wick was abusing Mina's loins, punishing them with a steady heat that constantly tempted her into trying to evade it, the shift of her body prompting new levels of physical dismay in both of them.

The hours drooled by with lethal sloth, making them wail and quiver, wracked with anguish as they surrendered fully to their ordeal. Mina groaned and moaned as her back continued to bloat with a pulsating strain, her body bellowing for her to straighten as all feeling was driven from her nipples leaving behind only the dull cold throb of the clamps that sent cramping chills throughout her upper body.

The rawness of her hindquarters as they were buffeted by heat became more maddening with each second, the infuriating attack of the torrefying waves hideous in their relentless assault of her.

Seemingly for the balance of the night they were left to the horrible punishment, all time dissolving as the only things they became truly aware of were the various punishing additions to their cruelty-wracked bodies.

When Mina heard the door open, they both instantly ceased the dark grumbling moans that continually poured from their parched throats and listened intently for clues as to who it was. Then the light burst on, blinding them both with its potency.

The sound of heels approached and Mina felt a hand trail along her excruciatingly arched front. 'Having fun, my dears?' asked the woman, returning to the scene of her crime after numerous hours of this abuse had elapsed. 'Have you both learnt your lesson?' she continued, coaxing wailing affirmations from Trisha and sobbing agreement from Mina.

'Good. But you'll have to earn your freedom, and it'll all be up to Mina here,' she added, stepping beside Mina's tear-streaked and flushed face, studying her distress at close range, her eyes having accustomed to the intense glare of the spotlight.

'Are you up to that, Mina? Would you earn a reprieve for you both by showing obedience that this little filly couldn't?' she asked, taking hold of the crotch rope and yanking at it, riding it stridently against Trisha. The girl below her spasmed and squealed in almost infantile tones, Mina's struggles having left her womb raw and tender, the rough jolt of the woven length now bringing unprecedented suffering.

'Or would you rather leave her to suffer, I wonder?

Pay her back, because after all, you are only here because she fucked up.' She was gloating over their ordeal, teasing them with the offer of release, making the position suddenly much worse as the end was placed in sight but not delivered.

'Would you like to earn freedom, Mina?' she again questioned, watching with satisfaction as she nodded as best she could against the efforts of collar and contorted backbreaking bondage. 'Good girl.'

Walking aside, she blew out the candle with a single puff and pulled it from Trisha's mouth, letting the girl finally find relief from its trespass. But it was not for long, for a large dildo was taken up and forced back in its place, making Trisha gurgle and retch as it was shoved rudely in.

'Now, you bite to this and don't spit it out or you'll be spending the rest of the night here,' warned the woman, and moved to release Mina's clamps.

The moment they were set loose, Mina flung herself against the rope responsible for holding her down as her teats screeched their hatred of the crushing jaws of the clamps. Jolting in fits, she endured the steady process of recovery from the abuse, her breasts pulsating with waves of aching pain. Once she had settled, the woman started to unfasten the crotch rope from Mina's collar. Mina tried to straighten up but could not, her long confinement having crippled her responses. With a shove the woman assisted her, doubling Mina up with a croak of mayhem, the flares down her spine and through her stomach a sudden and fierce sensation. Shaking in recovery, she felt her shins being set free and she was brought down off the table to stand on wobbly legs, her senses reeling from her punishment.

'Now, I want you to ride that dildo for me until I say stop,' ordered the woman, standing to one side with her arms folded, her eyes lowered as she looked up and down Mina's body. 'Can you do that?'

Mina nodded her assent as she turned and looked at Trisha, her mouth yawning wide to hold the plastic rod, her cheeks and lips streaked with dry wax.

'Well, get on then,' snapped the woman with irate tones.

With a spry flurry of movement, Mina climbed back up onto the table and lowered herself over the shaft. The rounded head brushed her loins, revealing a thin sheen of lubricant upon it that eased entry. Tensing against her uniform, she groaned with wanton lust as she felt the large shaft fill her, riding deep and making her quake with elation. The long period of her pains and her secret masochistic relish of her ordeal had left her yearning for some pleasure, and now that she was able to help herself, she was exceedingly amicable to it.

Lifting herself up, she brought herself to the tip and then slid back down, shuddering with glee at the wonderful feeling. The woman moved in and tied the crotch rope about Mina's waist, making the strand grind against Trisha with every piston jump of her partner's torso on the toy.

'Quicker, bitch!' growled the woman, making Mina accelerate her motions, riding up and down against the rod sheathed in her comrade's maw. Thrusting her belly against the air, jerking upon the shaft, she rode it with haste, the plastic javelin darting in and out of her womb. Mina wondered as to Trisha's thoughts, what she must be thinking as her belly was rubbed by the harsh rope, her eyes filled with the image of Mina's hindquarters dancing upon the rod emerging from her mouth.

Gasping with joy, Mina felt herself dribbling moisture down the pole, the lines trickling down to Trisha's supporting mouth. Heedless of Trisha's ordeal, seeking only to sate herself and free them both, Mina continued, feeling a climax starting to gather.

'That's it, girl, come on, I want to see you climax,'

hissed the woman, her voice corrupted by voyeuristic lust, her breath swift from licentious craving inspired by watching Mina's salacious form riding a rod sheathed in another pony's maw.

Mina cried out onto the air, letting loose her answer to orgasm as she bounded and jerked upon the length, her body quaking, rising to fight the rope about her waist, her body shivering and doubling up as she continued to try and extract all the bliss she could before she could take no more.

Slowing she settled onto the phallus, lowering until her rear was resting on the glass, the point of the rod pressing to her depths, her sex just touching the lips of Trisha.

'Any reason you're stopping?' demanded the woman, revealing that this deed was no act of generosity, but a further punishment she would have to endure. 'I don't recall telling you to quit. Ride that pole or you're both for it!'

Gritting her teeth Mina recommenced her motions, shaking as her constant shuffle upon the upright phallus bore heat to her innards, making the membranes ache and then start to burn as time continued. Once more she managed to climax, but after that her sex was reviling the simulated coitus too much to permit any pleasure. Stiff and tensed against her bonds, Mina screwed her eyes shut as she sought to endure the distress of her own self-inflicted abuse, bouncing on the rod as the woman watched.

'Okay, that will do,' the blonde eventually stated, making Mina sigh with relief as she extracted herself from the accursed length and stepped back to the floor, her pudenda sore, the flesh vexed by the unnaturally prolonged ride. 'Get off.'

They were both released from their bondage and escorted back to their stable, the clamps mercifully forsaken for the return trip. Clipped back onto their anchoring reins and wall fittings, the woman laughed scornfully and shut the door, leaving them to huddle together and soothe each other's sense of resentment and loathing of the spiteful slave.

Chapter Ten

With the usual repetition, the nurse attended them in the morning, entering their stall and leaving the two ponies clean and fresh.

Their owners stepped out into the doorway, ready for the day's activities. Tethys had adorned herself with a set of leather shorts, the polished hide armed with a dual fastened zip that plunged through the crotch all the way around to the back. Wearing the same tall riding boots, the footwear had again been tongue polished earlier, the residue of the slave responsible for the task still marked upon the dark jet surfaces. A studded leather choker encircled her throat, and a strapless bra gathered her breasts and forged a plunging cleavage with made-to-measure cups. Short gloves covered her hands, the fingerless affairs allowing her black nails to emerge, her palms closed around a riding crop.

Oceanus was clad in a similar style, with the same riding boots, shorts, and gloves worn for the trip. His bare chest remained unadorned, his skin starting to gather a little colour from the sun, after having been denied it for a lengthy time because of their undersea environment. Twirling his own crop he approached the two slaves and unfastened them from their anchors, capturing both their reins and leading them out, their bodies brushing against one another as they tottered forward on their hooves.

Taken across the corridor to another of the featureless doors that hid all manner of locations from view, Tethys opened the portal for them, allowing them to be escorted into a small garage. Here a pair of phaeton-style carriages awaited, aimed towards the ascending metal shutters on the other side.

Both phaetons were slender, the open four-wheeled contraptions formed from varnished wood and gleaming steel. The carriages themselves allowed two red velvet seats to face each other with a pair of small doors stretched between them on either side. The doors were marked with the trident symbol of Poseidon, decreeing their heraldry with pride. On the front two corners, beside a driver's seat, were glass lanterns, the antique style updated with an electric bulb rather than an oil wick.

Two steel arms reached forward from the sides, the arching limbs diverting aside and connecting to create a bar where eyelets were welded into place in readiness for the entrance of a pony. Several dense leather restraints were set upon the steel, the buckled harnesses open and waiting.

A young girl, her head sealed in a leather hood, was furled at the side of the carriage in a tight ball, her face to the floor, her thigh-booted legs curled tightly to her. Her arms were locked together beneath her in a single triangular sleeve of leather that anchored itself with hoops about her shoulders, the twin circles linked by another strap across her shoulder-blades to prevent her from acquiring any hope of sloughing off the restraint.

A stringent corset of black hide compressed her form, the presented back fitted with a plate of boning that made the surface more flat and stable to be trodden upon. The living step also wore her chastity belt and a steel collar, the band about her throat connecting via a silver chain to the rear of the coach, declaring that she was a fixture of the carriage, a piece of furniture who served whomever made use of the vehicle.

Another slave stood to the side, presented at rigid attention and bearing a wicker hamper. The woman was an archetypal maid, but one crafted from fetishistic allure rather than practical household servitude. A short dress of black latex ran down her body, gathering her sedate curves and extending down her arms, the tight sleeves sealing her hands within added gloves. The high neck rolled over her collar, where a slit at the front allowed her D-ring to emerge. Her long bleached-white hair was tied back into a firm plait, with a small cap of rigid latex fixed firmly into it. A white apron, the rubber fitted with a lace frill around the front was part of the dress, the large white bow at the back a fanciful addition. Bleak burnished leggings fell into ankle boots, the laced footwear perching her on tall heels.

Her slender features were servile, her eyes lowered as she awaited her orders, trained in submission to attend the whim of her dominant charges. She was a striking vision to behold, for since her arrival Mina had seen very little of the comprehensive rubber encasement with which she had become so enamoured. The image of the maid, locked within her skin-tight cell of a uniform, roused the slumbering hunger for such attire, reminding Mina of how much she relished the feel of it encompassing and compressing her body like some insidious living entity.

Oceanus showed them both to the front of the vehicle and led them under the metal arms. Tethys joined him in securing the trained girls to their posts, the restraints being quickly buckled and secured to their humble forms. Mina deserted herself to the feeling of being bound, to the steady gathering of weight upon her as the various bonds were tightened to squeeze to her form. Clenching herself against the crotch strap, she held to the trespassers in fits, giving a little struggle so that she might encourage a touch of discipline while she was being trapped for service.

'Stay still, Mina,' growled Tethys, the demand causing her to dwindle her efforts but not stop them. 'I said stay still, pony!' she barked, and brought the crop onto her rear, connecting both cheeks with the strut, making her stiffen and give a sob of reply before sinking more amiably into the arms of the coach. 'That's better,' commented the woman, adding the finishing touches.

Their hands had been removed from their corsets and re-secured to the arm before them, spread apart a little so that their limbs provided some assistance in holding the main bar. A larger strap had reached around their waist, hugging them to the bar, the band resting comfortably upon their backs, making decelerating an easier feat as the main centre of pressure upon them would come from it. Acceleration, however, required them to shove with their hands or use their stomachs against the thick front bar.

Their reins were threaded over them and taken to the driver's seat, the small perch already armed with a slot for a long lunge whip to ensure the two women were kept under control.

'We are done, slave,' decreed Oceanus, tugging on the straps to ensure all was secure before walking to the side of the vehicle. The maid moved forward and opened the door for them to enter, bowing as she did so. Oceanus stepped onto the humble footstool, his weight making the girl sigh with pleasure, her desire to be used running as an extreme thirst that took any opportunity to ease itself.

Tethys followed, and as the two Nobles settled into the comfort of the interior, the maid closed the door, bowed again and retrieved the hamper. Slotting it onto a small ledge at the back of the vehicle she ran two straps over it to ensure the ride did not dislodge it, and returned to the driver's position.

With the soft murmuring creak of stretching latex the girl slid onto the perch and accepted both sets of reins in one hand while taking the whip in her other. The footstool arose and walked to the back of the phaeton, standing patiently, peering through the two small eye-slits that offered her a meagre view of her depraved world of hedonistic excess.

A touch to a remote control caused the motors of the door to chug into stuttering life, the whine of strain preceding a deafening clatter of metal as it was hoisted up onto the roller above. The segmented steel bands rose, permitting light to pour through the growing aperture, letting their eyes accustom to it before they were dazzled by the brilliance of the day.

There was a soft whistle of displaced air and Mina yelled onto her bit as the tip of the whip flicked forth and snapped against her rear. The intense jolt made her throw herself to the bar, thrusting with her arms as their reins were flung, the leather leashes jerking against their bits, making them dig at the corners of their mouths. Digging their hooves against the solid floor, they started to haul the vehicle forward, the process swiftly becoming easier as they continued their efforts. The whip attacked again, alternating between Trisha and Mina, applied without cause just to have them bolster their efforts.

Towing the vehicle out of the building, they found themselves on the paved area behind the stable, the small courtyard accessed by several other doors, proving that other modes of transport were positioned within the various garages.

The whip ordered them straight forward onto a slender road, the paving stones set close together to ensure a near smooth surface that their hooves clattered on as they were brought to a steady trot. The warm sunlight bathed their forms, banishing the slight chill of the interior, the exertion of their bodies helping heat them. The ease of their gentle run was a pleasant change from the full sprint that had been demanded before, and the burden of the carriage soon vanished as they merely kept adding to its momentum. Rapidly timing their strides to fall in unison, the uncomfortable jiggle against the bar began to fade as they grew used to working together and in anticipating the actions of each other.

The road drew them into the woods, the trees parting to let the path wind casually into their depths. Running upon the stone paving, Mina watched the lush scenery pass them by as she savoured the feel of being in her current diminished caste.

The sound of birds and buzzing insects arose to join the soft creak and squeal of the vehicle behind them, the soft purring murmur of their leather uniforms and the steady unified clop of their hooves.

The whip occasionally streaked forth, more to remind them of their station than to actually discipline, both of them starting to relish the sudden addition of intense fulgent sensation to their wiggling buttocks.

The branches that reached out overhead often broke to let streams of light descend upon them, their jog through the small clearings like a strobe light as they danced from shadows to glorious cascades. The smell of the forest was strong after the recent rains, the lingering dampness making the air succulent and moist, heady with the scent of flowers and life. Mina was elated by the voyage, feeling refreshed, satisfied, at peace with herself and her world. Only in the heady afterglow of a session with her owners or a similar agency had she felt so content.

The dense wall of trees began to thin, offering clearings and then small fields where the road rolled across some low hills, faint mimics of the mountain peak, each covered in an emerald blanket of grass.

A pull to their reins dragged their heads to the left, affixing their blinkered gaze to a side path. The paving continued for a short way as they dragged the vehicle in the new direction, leaving the main route behind. A mound of stones appeared beside the road along with various building tools wrapped in canvas to protect them from the elements. The unfinished task of building this section of road suddenly brought them onto the dirt track that had existed prior to the construction. The compacted soil was a little softer than usual because of lingering moisture, but it was still an easy terrain to negotiate, easier even than the trail they had been forced to charge madly down. Cresting a hill they saw the ocean spread out before them.

A drag to their reins pulled the bits deeper into their mouths, tugging their heads back. Mina moaned softly with glee at being so forcefully controlled, her fingers straining against their tight mittens as she savoured the moment. The strap against her corset pushed into her as the weight of the carriage shoved against them both, their hooves fighting the impetus and bringing the vehicle to a slow halt.

Standing on the makeshift road, they panted and caught their breath, the sudden end of their exercise leaving them deprived. While they recovered from the long trot, they looked across the stretched realm of leaves before them, the green sea moving suddenly onto a strip of yellow before surrendering to the vast stretches of ocean. After the barrier of reefs and sandbanks that surrounded the island and created churning areas of turbulent current and white surf, the other islands were visible. The crooked spires jutted angrily from the ocean, some of them little more than malformed rocks or boulders, while others had smoothed areas of jungle clinging to them, or were wreathed by a halo of golden sand.

A pull at the corner of her mouth turned her head left again, turning them from the sight and to the hill once more. The whip snaked out, raking its woven tongue upon their rears, the scorching kisses demanding their compliance. Straining against their harnesses they pulled the vehicle aside, drawing it onto the grass and along the hill. The grass gave a little underfoot, the soft carpet smooth and slightly slippery to their hooves, making their tread more careful and precise.

The reins again pulled back, drawing their heads against the rear of their collars. Their ponytails flapped against their spines and shoulders, wafted by the slight breeze that spilled over the hill. The wind rustled the sheet of grass, the slender emerald fingers beckoning them forth in undulating ripples of motion. The suspension of the vehicle shifted restlessly, making the arms that held the ponies move, revealing to the blinkered steeds that the driver was slipping from her perch.

The sound of the door opening was joined by sounds of movement as the passengers disembarked, employing the woman that had jogged behind them for the whole journey.

Their owners approached and appeared before the two steeds, both of their eyes now hidden behind mirrored sunglasses as they began to unfasten them from their posts.

Once set free of the carriage, their reins were removed and the maid furnished them with leashes, the short chains allowing the two nobles to keep control over their ponies. Removed from the arms of the contraption, their wrists were once more moored to their sides, and they were led to where the maid was busily preparing the picnic. A blanket had been laid down and the woman was carefully unpacking the food and drink from the hamper and arranging it in readiness.

'Lay here, Trisha,' ordered Oceanus, pulling down on the lead to have the girl stretch procumbent along one edge of the blanket. Using her as a long pillow, the two sultry nobles relaxed onto her body, their fingers idly tracing her leather-bound flesh as they observed the scenery.

A pull to her leash had Mina kneeling beside Tethys, her eyes lowered with respect, and also so that she might study the body of the woman, scrutinise the leather and the alluring flesh of her owner as she twirled a crop and held her leash.

'I told you this would be the best place for a picnic,' commented Oceanus, laying back, his elbows against Trisha's corset, propping himself up on her as she lay docile beneath them, her face resting on the weave. Her eyes were closed and her breathing steady, her equable outlook on being used like this soothing her to an extent where she was drifting into sleep, making up for the previous night's deprivation.

'Definitely the best,' whispered Tethys, setting her crop aside and leaning over to kiss him.

'Slave, some drinks if you please,' Oceanus stated absently, reclining onto Trisha as he observed the view.

The maid produced glasses, filled them with red wine and handed them to the two nobles before returning to the task of preparing the food.

'And two bowls of water for our ponies here,' added Tethys.

A pair of small ceramic bowls were filled with cool water and set before them both. Mina leant down against the confines of her corset, her bound arms unable to support her as she put her lips to the cool liquid and began to drink as easily as she could. Trisha's task was a little harder because of her prone position, but the thirst they had acquired from the run had her make the required effort and drain most of the bowl.

Once the Nobles had taken what they wished of the picnic, they ordered the maid to pack away the plates and cutlery that had been used, which she did with her customary exuberance, enjoying her vocation immensely. Then Mina was suddenly turned from her vacant watching of the sea when her leash was pulled, forcing her to shuffle closer to the couple as they embraced and tenderly kissed one another. Tethys straightened up and pulled down, bringing Mina over her lap, her rear raised across the thighs of the woman, exposed and vulnerable to attention.

'Such vivid marks,' commented Tethys, running her nails gently against the pelt of Mina's contused rear, the lines from the lunge whip pronounced and distinct against the older marks of discipline. 'They must be quite tender,' she added, pinching one of the effulgent lines, the increase in pressure on Mina's sore rear making her wriggle slightly. 'Mmmm, that's what I like to see,' she commented, rubbing Mina's rear as it performed its enticing dance.

A leather-clad palm slapped Mina's rump, the shock letting a slight pip of distress emerge from her lips. She stiffened for a moment and then settled, accepting another spank across her buttocks as the woman pressed the small of her back, holding her down to be ready for more. The palm dropped again and Mina moaned, elated that she was being chastised, the delicate pain arousing her immensely. Tethys continued, increasing the heat in Mina's rear, the elderly bruises and fresh weals an incendiary force that helped magnify the temperature. She squirmed upon the woman's lap, her cheek pressed to the blanket as Oceanus stroked the soft pelt of re-growing hair upon her head, the spiky tufts rustling under his soothing caress. Fingers ferreted under the front of her crotch strap and pulled, riding the shafts against her, causing her head to rise from its reclined position and release a licentious purr.

'Ohhh, such a hungry little beast, isn't she, beloved?' commented Tethys.

'Indeed, it seems our little Mina is ruled by animal passions, all caught up in being a beast,' chuckled Oceanus, enclosing a fist to the base of her ponytail and pulling back, lifting her visage so he might kiss her lips, parted by the bit. 'Maybe we should consider giving her some relief?' he offered.

'Perhaps, but are we really decadent enough to consider bestiality? I mean, this is a pony we're talking about. Are we that disgustingly sick?' She laughed, adding another trio of hearty smacks to Mina's rear as they teased her with the prospect of release from her frustrations. 'Mmm, I think so,' pronounced Tethys, slapping Mina's rear once more, bringing tears to her eyes as she strained her arms against the leather sleeves.

The buckles at the back of her crotch strap were opened, followed by the front so that the trespassing shafts could be removed from her.

'Okay, girl, get that rosy bottom up,' ordered Tethys, hooking a finger into Mina's rear and dragging upwards, the sudden intrusion by a saliva-moistened digit causing her to gasp with shock and delight.

Raising herself onto her knees, Mina kept her face to the floor as Oceanus stepped behind her, opening his shorts and taking hold of her hips. Tethys gathered in the chain leash, keeping her fist tightly to the strand of metal, ensuring Mina was well aware of its presence, emphasising her submission. The head of Oceanus's engorged length brushed against her aching loins, its passage bringing her to a quaking fit of expectation.

'Steady, girl, steady,' he smirked, teasing her, brushing her inner thighs, running the length through the valley of presented moist vulva, gathering the slickness along his length as she ached to feel him run the hot spear into her. She wished she could somehow manipulate her own sex, have it suck to his shaft and drag him in and give her that which she so fervently craved.

Tethys's other hand reached under her and snagged a nipple, squeezing the erect teat in a firm pinch. A drawn moan poured from Mina's throat as she felt the compression begin its customary menu of effects upon her, the deep throb starting to well within them, increasing as the woman slowly turned her hold, rotating the nugget with casual indifference to Mina's gurgling moans.

'I think she's about ready, my love,' smiled Tethys, pulling slightly against the nylon-sheathed flesh, and no sooner had the words been voiced than Mina threw her head up and unleashed a howl of bestial rapture as Oceanus drove into her, sheathing himself to her very limits.

Unable and unwilling to form words, Mina groaned in rhapsody as he held to her corseted hips, feeling the compacted nature of her waist as he thrust lethargically into her. Oceanus was taking his time, relishing the feel of her as she gripped and squeezed to his shaft, her legs trembling with riots of delight.

'That's it, dearest, make this pony whinny for us some more,' uttered Tethys, with a lust-stained growl, tugging gently at the captive nipple.

Accepting the advice, Oceanus removed himself from her hot belly and instead pressed himself to her rear, the lubrication of her sex allowing him to part her anus and delve down into the furthest regions of her rear passage. Mina yowled with ecstasy, her head dropping back to the blanket as she sobbed and mewled in pitiful tones, overwhelmed by the feelings. She was lost to the intensity of him driving into her. His fingers sank into her buttocks, prying them apart, holding her open for him, her body unable to deny his wishes as he continued to intrude with regular precision.

Removing himself from her rear once more, Oceanus again plummeted back into her womb, lifting her from her knees, the battering ram of sensation that fired into her belly almost more than she could stand. His pelvis bounced against her proffered rear with each drive, Oceanus using her in full as her arms pulled vainly against their intractable bonds, her fingers trapped, her arms flapping uselessly as each breath fought the grip of the corset. Her maw ground upon the solid bit that marked her as their animal, lines of saliva running out to seep into the blanket as tears ran down her cheeks and joined them. Sobbing with pleasure, the dazzling flares of climax romping through her as she quivered upon his manhood.

Still unsated Oceanus continued, making Mina squeal as she was pushed further into ecstasy, her thoughts being scrambled by it until she felt him swell within her and then break into the chaotic fits of final release. She felt a distinct influx within her that spread and dissipated as more was added with his final quivering drives, stealing all the pleasure he could before slowing to a halt. Propped against her hips he paused a moment, capturing his breath, his hands clenching to her, relishing the feel of her nubile flesh still impaled upon him. Drawing free, Mina shuddered and croaked with the return of potent sensation, her body sagging as though his length were a vampiric force that had siphoned away her very essence.

Settling back onto the thighs of Tethys, Mina closed her eyes, breathing softly, her body flickering with an occasional spark of animation.

'There, good girl,' said Tethys, stroking her stubble, the backs of her nails running along the dark fuzz as Mina lay inert upon her.

She felt her hindquarters being manipulated and she groaned as the dildos were threaded back into her wetness, the buckles of the crotch strap being tightened.

'Are we all packed?' asked Tethys, as her husband massaged the leather bond, rocking the intruding weapons within their fleshy scabbards.

'Yes, mistress,' answered the maid, her voice soft but strained from having witnessed such an erotic exchange while remaining starved of her own relief by the belt and the smothering folds of her latex attire.

'Shall we be off, my sweet?' asked Tethys, turning to her husband as he sprawled on the blanket, stretching into the sun like a contented predator mulling over the full belly wrought by its latest kill.

'Whenever you're ready,' he answered with little attention, his mind wandering through its stupor.

'Re-harness our mounts, slave,' commanded Tethys, reaching over and stroking the braided tendrils of her spouse as he lay with eyes closed, his hands behind his head, resting on them as he breathed softly.

'Yes, mistress,' certified the woman, taking up both sets of leads, pulling the two ponies from their positions and drawing them back to the vehicle. She worked with indifference, and fastening them back into place returned for the hamper, which she again placed on the rear of the phaeton.

Opening the door for the couple, the human footrest scampered into position and Tethys and Oceanus climbed back into the plush interior, making the conveyance rock with the new burdens.

The maid retook her seat and furnished herself with the whip and the reins of her steeds before whipping them back into activity. Mina was still in the heady afterglow of their coitus, and each sting of the whip was a further excitement to her sense of jubilation.

The carriage turned around and they drew it back along the dirt trail, pounding their hooves steadily to the earthen floor before riding back onto the paved road.

Once more upon the main route, Mina spied another vehicle heading their way, travelling closer with each galloping step of its paired mounts.

'Whoa!' demanded the maid as the passenger of the other vehicle waved to them, beckoning them to stop. The reins drew back more forcefully than ever before, making Mina sigh with licentious longing as her head was craned back, the bit digging in as the whip gave her a stinging bite of encouragement. Their hooves skidded a little on the stone as they fought the velocity of the carriage, stopping the vehicle.

'Who is it?' asked Oceanus.

'I believe it is Lord Poseidon himself, master,' answered the maid, familiar with the subtle nuances that would betray the identity of the imperious ruler of the island.

'I wonder what he wants,' pondered Tethys.

The fragile looking gig bore a soft seat, almost like a padded armchair, in which reclined the form of Poseidon. The man was clad in leather trousers and tall boots with spurs shaped like rows of tiny tridents. A close-fitting vest bore the same emblem of his heraldry, and studded bracers covered his forearms, his bared hands clutching the reins and a lunge whip.

The gig was led by two centaurs, the two arms of the gig extending forward and parting into a pair of forks that ran each side of the paired beasts, holding to them with leather straps.

'Good afternoon, Tethys, Oceanus,' began the Noble, drawing his steeds to a halt before Mina and Trisha, letting them study up close the intricacies of the centaurs. The women were panting from their run, their eyes full of tears from Poseidon's liberal use of the whip to make them sprint.

'Good afternoon, Poseidon. What's up? Why the rush?'

'I'm just taking these two out for a spin, get them more used to their lot,' he answered lightly, giving a slight pull to the convergence of reins in his hand. The centaurs mewled as the delicate tips of their breasts were pulled.

'New recruits?' asked Oceanus.

'No, they're experienced ponies, but its their first

132

week as centaurs,' he replied.

'Exquisite,' murmured Tethys, with a libidinous tone as she beheld the anxiety of the doomed slaves. 'They look wonderful, all distressed and confused.'

'They'll come to love it soon enough, they all do with the right encouragement,' stated Poseidon.

'You're such a wicked slave owner, Poseidon,' remarked Oceanus, chuckling.

'It's for their own good, really,' added the ruler of the island with a grin. 'They're both very submissive, I'm just throwing them in the deep end, that's all.'

Mina watched tears roll down the cheeks of the women, both of them clearly knowing it would be true, that they would indeed come to enjoy their lot, but only after hardship and grief, dreading the time of adjustment.

'Mmmm, a wise decision,' commented Tethys.

'So how is the little filly I rescued for you?' he asked, indicating Mina as she stood to attention, suddenly turning her eyes to him as she realised she'd been noticed. 'That's her, isn't it?'

'She's been fine, exceeding every expectation… as usual,' answered Tethys.

'I saw her the other day, running wild and free with her partner there,' said Poseidon with an ominous purr in his voice, his eyes rolling over Mina's form as he revealed that he had spied her on their recreational excursion. 'And quite a sight it was…'

'Why the sudden interest, Poseidon?' quizzed Tethys, seeing where he was going with his line of conversation, that he wasn't just exercising some novice steeds, but after something concerning Mina.

'I've a favour to ask… a somewhat big one,' he began, his words considered, placed delicately, tact being of prime importance in his mind.

'We are in debt to you already for rescuing her, what do you wish of us?' replied Oceanus, careful not to rashly promise anything.

'As you know, I'm trying to organise my Pegasus project for the party. Hephaestus has forged the outfit, and it works fine, but I'm having extreme problems finding someone who can fill it,' he explained, his tones even, hiding his exasperation.

'No one?' said Oceanus. 'I thought you had been preparing possible candidates for months.'

'Indeed, but they're not shaping up, they just can't handle the demands of the costume. If half of what they whisper about Mina is true, she could well prove to be the salvation of my dignity.'

'How so?'

'Word has spread about the unveiling,' he revealed. 'Admittedly some of this is due to me circulating hesitant rumours to build interest, and its going to backfire terribly if I don't come through with it.'

'I see,' said Tethys.

'I don't follow, you never made any definite proclamations,' interjected Oceanus, puzzled by Poseidon's concerns.

'People will be flocking here to see this event, and if he doesn't provide it his standing could be gravely affected,' explained Tethys. 'I mean, all those weeks of decompression to come to a party just to see this Pegasus, and it's not here? No one will give credence to Poseidon's accomplishments again for years.'

'Precisely, so I'm in considerable jeopardy and I'd love to try Mina for the Pegasus project, if I may,' stated Poseidon. 'I'll return her straight after, I swear.'

'Hmmm, what do you think, dearest?' asked Oceanus.

'We'll consider it on the way home and let you know there, if that's okay,' replied Tethys.

'That'd be fine, I wouldn't want to harass you into a decision before you'd thought it through,' replied Poseidon, offering them every courtesy and refusing to tug at the favour they owed him, even though lending them Mina would not only erase it, but place the Titan deeply in their debt.

'In that case, we'll see you back at the stable courtyard,' announced Tethys. 'Driver,' she added, causing the maid to snap the reins and apply her whip to Mina and Trisha, hauling aside to turn them onto the side of the road and around Poseidon's vehicle. A series of sharp applications of the scourge brought them to a trot, where the clatter of their hooves hid the softly muttered conversation as her owners deliberated Mina's fate.

Could she handle the rigours of the proposal? It was a tantalising notion, that someone had basically laid down a gauntlet, challenging her to be able to master the straits of the costume. She could prove herself better than any other slave and earn the right to announce such to all as she soared forth over a party that would comprise the assembled powers of the global conspiracy of perversity that was Cabal.

Chapter Eleven

'We agree,' said Oceanus, handing Mina's reins to Poseidon.

'Only until the party is over, then we will of course want her back,' added Tethys, ensuring that there was no misunderstanding between them.

'Of course, of course, thank you, I will let you know how her progress goes,' beamed the man, pulling on the reins and bringing Mina in his wake. Blinkered as she was, she was unable to even look to her owners or Trisha as she was led down the grassy path between stable and main building. Her angst was a small distraction, for she knew she would be handed back after the party, so she was not going to be lost from her owners forever, just a short break to try something new and spectacular. Plus, it would make them even more envied once people realised that it was their slave who had provided Poseidon with the raw material necessary for his prototype's test flight.

The man led her to the large set of double doors providing entry into the main complex. The interior was climate controlled, the sudden change bringing riots of goose flesh across her form, causing Mina to quiver as the air-conditioned breeze stripped the tropical heat and the fires of her run from her body.

She found herself in a large entrance hall, the architecture formed of an older style, capturing the opulent extravagance of old English mansions. The white stone walls were inlaid with emerging pillars, the baroque floral designs that were carved into them marked with intertwined naked forms, following Poseidon's interest in iniquitous vice.

A set of wooden double doors stood on either side, with another directly before her. Two majestic staircases rolled up the sides of the hall and curled round on a steady curve to create a balcony, the stone banister smooth and supported by squat columns shaped like curled naked females, their faces blank as though hidden by hoods.

A corridor ran beyond the wall atop the balcony, a row of four vaulted openings allowing passage through, each one incorporating Poseidon's symbol in the carved stone crest above them.

From the lip of the balcony hung draped banners that repeated the motif, gathering the impression that this could be the home of some military leader who brandished the symbol of his might everywhere he could, instead of portraits or works of art.

Her hooves clattered upon the marble flagstones and then were silenced as they moved onto the elaborately patterned rug covering much of the floor. Escorted beneath the right stairwell, a plain metal door was presented to her, the surface like a faded mirror, reflecting a hazy image of her in the pony costume to which she had become so used. The image of her in black leather and white skin, bound and controlled, seemed almost detached from her true self, the outlandish nature of her appearance catching her by surprise. It was still a shock because she so rarely saw it; she had enough trouble seeing what was around her, let alone her own reflection.

Placing his hand to the side of the portal, their was a click and a light poured through the masked surface of the wall, running a vertical beam down his hand, assessing the ridges and whorls of his prints. With a series of muted clicks the door slid back, revealing an elevator, the interior a solid construction of polished steel akin to the front door. Drawn in, the door closed behind them and they began a steady descent into the bowels of the island, leaving Mina to staring blankly into the distorted image of herself in the interior door.

There were no buttons, no controls, no indications as to floor; this conveyance went to one place and one place alone – Poseidon's secret den.

They slowed to a halt and the door slid back, revealing a small hall, the walls, floor and ceiling covered in polished black marble slabs of shattered paving, the jigsaw-patterned decor roughly placed together with white mortar to hold them in place and contrast them.

In the corners of the chamber, upon small pedestals, were bound women. Each was shaven bald and tied with the use of thick latex straps into a tight ball, huddling them upon a black marble pillar. Slender pipes wound into their mouth and chastity belts, furnishing them with food and waste management, removing the need to ever remove them from their isolated doom. Faced down, their backs were adorned with numerous candles, the waxen stems of black drooling their midnight tears across the forms of the living candelabras, offering the image that the women themselves were melting. The cumulative glow of their candles bathed the corners in a warm amber hue that spread reluctantly upon the mirror-like panels of obsidian coating the rest of the room.

A pair of doors was located in each of the other walls; the mahogany doors without handle or lock. A pull to her reins led her out of the elevator and across the room to one of the doors on the left. The wooden sheet slithered aside at Poseidon's approach, exposing a sizeable rectangular chamber decorated and lit in the same manner as the previous room. In the middle was a magnificent statue of black marble. The rearing form of Pegasus threw out its wings, dominating the room, an awesome and striking sight, the sculptor having captured perfectly the awe and majesty of such a wondrous beast.

Escorted past Poseidon's obsessive goal, a door beyond moved aside and revealed the workshop where he was trying to bring his dream into fabulous reality. The chamber was bedecked in walls of technological equipment, much of which still remained on, exposing itself and its neighbours in the soft coloured glow of its private lights. As well as the array of computers and design equipment required to run through schematics and produce workable models and blueprints, there were tools for heavy-duty mechanical construction. In addition there were also the tiny assortments of apparatus needed for micro circuitry and cybernetics, the elaborate collections neatly placed along various workbenches amidst half-finished parts or pieces undergoing checks and scrutiny. It was beyond state-of-the-art, and was hoarding advances to itself that Mina had been waiting to receive before her assignment to the Charybdis project and her betrayal by Jupiter.

A dark shape lurked in the middle of the room, covered by ample shadow, the light from the other room and the machines that had crafted it doing little to expose their progeny. Flicking a switch, Poseidon revealed his masterpiece.

The uniform was presented on a female mannequin. The artificial woman was bent over, her arms turned into a set of forelegs by constructed sleeves that formed into hooves. The white latex suit that encompassed it covered the dummy entirely, even turning the face into the extending snout of a pony, the stylised image an ivory form with silver glass eyes.

At the body a pair of wings emerged, the articulated appendages spread wide, the skeleton of steel within allowing them to be retracted or spread at the command

139

of the wearer or another agency.

'This is the Pegasus suit you are going to be tried for, slave,' attested Poseidon with a smile, looking only to his inanimate offspring. 'Come, let us get you out of that uniform,' he snapped, flinging himself from his mesmerised wide-eyed look across the ivory form of the mythical hybrid.

A yank to her reins turned her from the image and towards another door, whirring gently aside to expose a smaller chamber beyond. The room bore a low bed, the soft mattress without sheets or pillows and of strange dimensions. Lit by several overhead bulbs set in the ceiling the chamber had no other features save a metal hatch in the wall behind the bed, and a treadmill set in the floor to one side. The long and wide corrugated rubber roll extended from the wall for three yards by three yards, with a metal hatch to one side, the locked panel hiding the controls as several riveted rings hung against the wall directly before the broad treadmill.

Two maids were already present, the women clad in lingerie. Both were shaved bald, even their eyebrows removed to give them an eerie appearance. A white satin basque hugged their bodies, taking hold of fine denier albino stockings that plummeted down their shapely legs into court shoes with a silver buckled band about the ankle. Their dagger-shaped fingernails were painted white, and a slender thong of snowy satin embraced their loins.

'Strip her of this uniform, slaves,' ordered Poseidon.

The women worked quickly and deftly, and in moments Mina was utterly naked, the pony attire that had encased her for so long a forsaken opaque skin on the floor. The maids withdrew to either side of the door, standing like sentinels as Poseidon wandered about her, assessing and scrutinising.

'I am impressed,' he commented. 'Normally a

prolonged spell as an eel would reduce a girl to a feeble wreck. You must have worked marvels during your decompression to recapture such a physique.'

'I only seek to please those who own me, master; what use would I be as a weakened wretch?' she replied humbly, having trouble with the words after her long silence, the removal of the bit and her uniform breaking her state of being no more than a mute beast.

'That was considerate of you, though I more suspect you did it out of fright of the unknown—' he began, cutting of his words as he saw Mina stiffen a little with injured pride at having her courage questioned. 'My apologies, I phrased that poorly. You had no clue as to who had captured and taken you from the ocean. You were just seeking to be prepared.'

'Did I do wrong, master?' she replied, watching his boots pass by her again, the man circling her still as they talked.

'Definitely not, such a feature will serve me admirably. If you want to be able to handle the Pegasus uniform, you will have to show the same sense of diligent dedication. I have a whole stable of psychologically and physically shattered slaves. They will recover in time, but I need someone far hardier than a normal woman, I need a veritable living machine to be my Pegasus, someone who can override her instincts, push herself to the limits of mind and body and then exceed them. Is this you, slave? Or have I made a miscalculation?'

'No, master, I can do this for you, if you wish it,' she answered.

'Oh, I most certainly wish it, slave,' he said, placing his hands on her shoulders, his palms running on the smooth flesh, his fingers tracing up and down her upper arms as she stood tensed before him. She could feel his eyes on her back, looking across her rear, her legs, her curves. 'But you have to be sure, slave. This regime will be even harder than before because of the limits of time. If you are not up to it, you could well be broken by it. If you have any doubt, any second thoughts, even the most minor questioning of your ability, then feel free to decline with no reprisal. I would rather have you refuse than waste my time and disappoint me, and then end up aggrieving your owners by being returned to them a fractured mess.'

Mina turned around and faced the Noble, meeting him directly eye to eye in an act of sudden boldness. With absolute sincerity and no sense of exaggeration or false conviction she addressed her new owner. 'I *will* succeed, master.'

Poseidon merely looked at her for a moment, their eyes locked, unblinking as he watched to see if her façade of confidence would show weakness or crack. Mina's countenance remained like wrought iron, bringing a blossoming smile to the lips of the Titan.

'Excellent, you have given me new hope, slave,' he crooned, and moved closer, raising a hand and closing it about the nape of her neck. Drawing her in he met her lips and demanded a kiss. Her hands arose of their own volition and ran across his athletic form, caressing his skin, stroking and pawing as his free hand took up her breasts. Teasing each in turn his dextrous touch brought life to them, making the teats rise and her body shiver with elation.

She ran her lips across his chest, her hands closing to his trousers, blindly picking the fastenings and pulling them down, exposing a rapidly swelling member to her attentions. Settling onto her knees, Mina swallowed his length with reckless abandon, her hunger for gratification boiling within her. Closing her lips to him, her tongue flitted and danced on his tip, making him swell in her mouth, growing to his full size before her head began to dance back and forth, thrusting deep so that she felt him brushing the back of her throat. Her hands found new diversion in the soft caress of his testes and inner thighs, accentuating the sensual feast.

Her mouth felt him growing more significantly as he stiffened with imminent orgasm, whereupon the man pulled free, bringing her up to her feet. His length brushed against her thighs as he ran his hands over her breasts, tracing his fingers in whirls and spirals upon her.

A sudden turn span her about by the shoulders and he pushed her towards the bed. Mina rolled with the direction and flopped onto the soft mattress as the Noble removed his boots, bracers and trousers in full.

Naked, he climbed onto the bed and pushed her onto her back, acting forcefully. He drew her legs apart and grabbed her hands, lacing his fingers into hers and pinning them down beside her head. With sparkling eyes he watched her, guiding himself by feeling alone into her moist sex. With a pelvic jolt he filled her, opening her suddenly and entering deeply, causing Mina to arch her back, her mouth stretching wide with a silent gasp of rapture.

Holding her down, he kept his body above her by his grip, supporting himself on his arms as he thrust into her with slow relish. Mina locked her legs about him, the feeling of skin on skin adding to her delight. It felt wonderful just be thrown down, held and ravished, no bondage, just control of her physique by another and her own willing submission.

Again the Titan dragged himself free, moving back and flipping her over onto her front. Mina offered some faint struggles of resistance as he took firm hold of wrists once more, and left herself vulnerable to the relish of having him use his strength to defeat the token offering of rebellion. Slamming her hands forward, stretching them high over her head, he placed the wrists over each other and used one hand to press down on both and capture them. The free hand took hold of his penis and guided it back into her, her parted legs shaking as he sheathed himself back into place, riding her, his hips slapping to her pert and welt-marked rear, reviving the bruises in soft murmurs of contused protest.

His hand rolled up her side, his nails presented to the skin to leave rosy scratches, prompting her to vent some soft squeaks at the grazing touch. The hand took hold of her mane of hair, enclosing a tight fist to it and pulling, her roots protesting vehemently as her head was craned back to its limits, lifting her breasts from the mattress, revealing her gasping face. Heady kisses adored her neck, the mixture of tender pecks and the stern haul to her scalp an intoxicating mixture of vivid sensations.

Continuing to ride into her, the hand fled her hair and cupped her chin before her features fell back to the mattress. He let fingers rise and enter her mouth, offering her them to suckle on, and Mina complied with fervour as Poseidon continued to ride her.

With such provocation Mina was jerking beneath him in climax in moments, her squawks of rapture spilling around his intruding fingers as he tightened his hold, keeping her captive as she cried out and broke into paroxysms. And when she felt him swelling with the approach of orgasm once more, she gained a repeat of the peaks of bliss, riding through her tumultuous pleasure before having it accentuated when his length spat warmth into her depths.

The holds upon her sagged slightly, and with a roll he collapsed at her side, the flight of his length folding Mina instantly into a spasming ball where she held to herself, fighting to endure the flares of sensation his departure had filled her with.

'Bring me a collar and leash,' ordered Poseidon from his sprawled position. Mina looked across to the door to see if it were her being ordered, or as was more likely, the maids. One of them opened the door, letting new sounds of activity emerge from the workshop, and as she was still in the process of leaving, Poseidon amended his words. 'And one of my robes.'

Together they lay in recuperation while the maid gained what she had been ordered to acquire, returning with a silken gown embroidered with flowing dark patterns of the sea and the trident in burning emerald across the back. The collar was a leather-studded affair, like one would place about the throat of a dangerous hound. The chain leash was already in place and the whole ensemble was handed to Poseidon as he arose with a disgruntled growl of effort. Climbing from the bed he extended his arms so that the maid might slide the gown onto him and then tie the belt into place.

'Come here, slave,' he commanded, and Mina rose as well, stepping before him, her gaze lowered as he buckled the collar about her neck and ran the chain through his hand until he had hold of the leather hoop at the other end.

'Come, let us see what's happening, slave,' he purred, walking towards the door, the maids following well behind as Mina was led from the room. She already suspected that this would be her quarters, the bed being of a right height and size to allow a pony-formed female to recline in meagre comfort when she was not being run on the treadmill.

Two older men in white coats were looking over the Pegasus uniform. Wearing gloves, masks, hoods and protective glasses they were obviously being careful to ensure nothing contaminated the mechanism. The wings were currently open and exposed, the white rubber skin peeled back as though being dissected, revealing the delicate interior. Drawn closer she looked across the array, her eyes assessing and identifying the components within from personal knowledge and intense study of the subject.

'Evening, Poseidon, who's the new girl?' asked one of the men.

'She's the new hopeful; I think we may have found our pilot for the party,' he replied, scrutinising what they were currently working on. 'Still trying to improve the deployment mechanism?'

'Yes, it's not easy, but we'll get there. What we really need is a pilot who can handle this. You think she can?'

'If anyone can, I believe this girl will be able to.'

'She'll need amazing reflexes if we can't improve the control ratio,' he added, lifting a new section of rubber hide to expose more of the wing anatomy.

Mina looked upon the interior, rising to tiptoe for a better view. Frowning, she regarded the older parts being deployed, ones she was well aware could be updated. Secret advances were being tested in the field of fibre bundles that she knew from personal experience worked well enough to rely upon for this type of duty. Such creations were not unlike artificially grown muscles, save they were many times stronger than their organic counterparts. Tiny impulse generators would make the responsive bundles contract, acting like a cybernetic nervous system, creating wings that could work better than versions nine times their size if these engineers stuck to the clumsy and current means to control them. Poseidon had to have access to the relevant technology, his devotion to finding a pilot slave diverting him from upgrading the design from its initial specifications. She didn't want to embarrass or seem as though she were boasting, but she could seriously assist the project by applying her own considerable knowledge.

'May I speak, master?' she asked softly, all eyes turning slowly to her with befuddlement, wondering what she could possibly be about to say. Mina noticed worry in Poseidon's eyes, clearly afraid she might withdraw her consent to be the test pilot for his prototype.

'What is it, slave?' he asked with trepidation.

'Well, master, the wing mechanism you're using is employing old cybernetic struts and outdated micro-hydraulics. They're about a year or two out of date by now. I think you'll find electrically motivated fibre bundles would refine your weight and drag coefficient and improve aerial dexterity as well as speed of response...'

After a moment's stunned pause, Poseidon smiled and turned to the blank-faced engineers. 'Is this true?'

The men shrugged and reluctantly gave some soft bobs of their heads. 'It might work, but they're still experimental at best,' stated one, trying to exonerate their efforts, their pride wounded by the expertise a mere slave girl had shown.

'But the main reason is time; we just haven't enough to overhaul the entire design and replace everything except the basic skeleton,' retorted the other, with more than a trace of indignation.

Poseidon looked at them with a dubious frown, and then turning back to Mina, he raised his eyebrows, offering her the chance to rebuke. She stepped forward and indicated the relevant areas as she spoke, the strangeness of a naked slave on a leash explaining details that were beyond cutting edge cybernetic technology to the scientists being one that did not escape any in the room.

'Keep the original pulse generators; the fibre bundles use the same frequency parameters. Sharpen the output and response vectors and you can run the bundles in place of the hydraulics. It should be a fairly simple series of replacements providing you anchor the fibres directly to the superstructure rather than the hydraulic bases.' She noticed another lapse in their design.

'And look at this, you've used titanium pivots in the

main articulated joints. These should be diamond-bored plasteel. Try any of the main centres of advanced metallurgical research in Alaska, they should be able to have the parts moulded the quickest, and while you're at it, see about these fibre-optic control veins.'

'Now we know those can't be improved… slave girl,' bitterly retorted one of the engineers.

'Yes, but they're carrying the entire data load. Use older strands; they'll break it into smaller portions. Overall they'll be quicker on reactions and use less room and be less heavy. The ones you've got would be ideal for something much larger, but they're designed to carry heavy traffic. You need lines that are small and deft, working on a single response procedure, direct routes rather than larger, more meandering paths.'

'Anything else, or would you like to take over for us?' growled one of them, before being hushed by his more sedate comrade, this one less easily inflamed by the questioning of their work.

'How the hell do you know this?' he enquired, seeking to confirm her sources before taking her word as genuine.

'I worked for Turan Incorporated until a short time ago,' she replied calmly.

'A *secretary*,' accused the other man, folding his arms, his eyes glaring at her with contempt. 'She saw it on memos or something.'

Mina didn't care, she was above trying to boast, she knew what she knew, and she knew she was right. She wasn't trying to impress them; she just wanted the suit to work properly, as best as modern technology could offer.

'Slave, tell them what you did,' said Poseidon with a drawn smile, revealing that he had all the information about her nefarious existence prior to Charybdis.

'I was their operative, master,' she said without

148

inflection, addressing her current owner rather than those who were questioning her abilities.

'What do you mean, "their operative"?' ranted the agitated engineer, throwing his arms up in frustration before the other calmed him, placing a hand to his shoulder and regarding his comrade eye to eye with sudden gravity.

'No, Jackson, she was *the* operative, as in *one*, as in...'

The eyes of the man suddenly widening with realisation as he followed the chain of words to what his partner was getting at. He suddenly became nervous, his eyes flitting to Mina, more than fear in them.

'Oh, I see,' he burbled, and quickly shifted away to lose himself amidst the hardware. 'Well, that would, er, explain it. I'll, erm, get to making the orders.'

'A pleasure to meet you, miss,' said the other with better-hidden anxiety, and after a curt bow he swiftly followed his companion.

They knew what she was, and knew what she did. She was the person people such as these dreaded. As employees who worked in the shadowy world of private and ultra-secret development, their discoveries moved power across the globe like the tides of an ocean. They created and manufactured discoveries no government would see for years. Scientists such as these were entities Mina had snuffed out on many occasions, snubbing their advances with murder to allow her paymasters the chance to beat the sponsoring rivals to the goal. A delay of mere days could offer billions in potential profits.

The men before Mina would have lived like she had – in hidden corners and pampered luxury. But also they would dwell in constant threat of someone like her coming to their lab or home one night, sabotaging, booby trapping, hobbling their efforts and perhaps liquidating those responsible for them.

Turan Inc was a global power, and as such it confirmed that Mina was one of the elite in her class, a ruthless professional right arm that extended outside the law to smash whatever Turan wanted out of its way.

Poseidon smiled and shook his head, leading her across the room and to the opposite door. Led through the separate room, she was presented to a slightly convex hatch.

'Don't worry, they're the best in their field,' said Poseidon, with an amused smile. 'They've just been kept behind on the latest advances by their work here. I wouldn't judge them too harshly.'

'I meant no offence, master, I just thought—'

'Don't worry about it, you did the right thing,' said Poseidon, removing her collar and lead. 'If you're suggestions work out it will make the Pegasus project more effective. Now, to the matter of your training. First, I'll be testing your reflexes and stamina. If you pass these tests, you'll be fitted with the basic uniform that you will then wear until you have earned your wings, so to speak.'

Opening the hatch and revealing the interior of a smooth white sphere, the large orb easily accommodated Mina, leaving her standing at its base, looking up at the ceiling and bland dimensions of the interior. The hatch closed and locked and she was left naked and alone within the test chamber. She could guess its purpose; the ball would spin and rotate, try and confound her ability to adjust to its ever-altering directions.

With a mechanised murmur the ball began to roll on the spot, bringing Mina to a slow jog along its base, her bare feet slapping softly upon the interior plastic surface.

With a smooth and swift deviation it rolled around until she was running in the opposite direction, moving quicker, making her accelerate to a sprint. Keeping focused to the task, she regulated her respiration and kept her mind and awareness razor-edged and ready to assimilate any problem the sphere threw at her.

For seemingly hours she ran around and around, the sphere drastically changing direction at random intervals. Sometimes it jerked to a halt and reversed, carrying her up one side. If she were not quick enough she would be toppled and rolled on the floor, but Mina had the celerity and agility that kept her upright. The programme continued to get more and more harsh, the ball hurtling around, changing speed, direction, trying with ever-increasing stress to defeat her.

It was a pleasing workout, the feeling of pushing her tolerances never ceasing to stoke Mina's sense of pride in her own body. Dancing along the floor of the ball, her heart raging in her chest, alive with tingling heat from the exertion, she was possessed by euphoria as she battled the machine, pitting herself against it.

At last the sphere ceased movement, and with an agile twist she landed in a tensed squat, her balance tilting left and right, her senses confused by the rigours of the event.

'Well done, slave, you did exceptionally well,' stated a synthesised voice, Poseidon's words corrupted by the hidden microphone he was using to address his imprisoned test subject.

'Thank you, master,' she panted, keeping her position and striving to once more fixate herself on what direction was what just in case he continued the test.

The hatch opened and Poseidon appeared, beckoning her out, her collar and leash in his hands. Once she emerged she accepted the symbol of her servitude, feeling wonderfully secure for the simple addition as she was led back out of the room.

Escorted through the chambers, she was brought to a fitting room. A black metal sawhorse resided in the middle, and a series of small black wood chests were placed to one side along with a plain chair. The corners flickered with the lights created by the candle-adorned female prisoners, the women hidden from their own source of illumination, their hunched forms squashed into the compacted and terrible fate of eternal captivity and use as no more than furniture.

Three glass doors were equally spaced on the left wall, each entering a white-tiled shower cubicle. The two maids from before were already present, standing on either side of the sawhorse, awaiting Mina with a grim intensity. Their lush forms still resided in the seductive lingerie and Mina's eyes found keen arousal in studying them, her heart aching to run hands across the smooth materials, to touch and embrace the beautiful women, her exercise having roused her thirst for carnal experience once more.

Poseidon caught the fervour of her stare and smiled to himself, removing her leash and collar and indicating to the middle shower room.

'Remove your clothes and clean and prepare this slave for her uniform,' he ordered. 'And while you're at it, see to relieving yourselves, and her. I want your full attention on the fitting.'

The women looked to each other with jubilation, ecstatic that they would finally be able to end their frustration. Poseidon walked over and grabbed the chair, drawing it up and settling into it before the transparent pane that would allow him to view their acts. The women moved closer and began stripping each other rather than doing it themselves, taking pleasure in running their hands over the form of the other, fanning the flames of their swollen libidos.

Mina watched the erotic display of their teasing strip with glaring eyes, her mouth watering, her mind yearning to taste and feel them.

Once their bare bodies were exposed they sauntered over to Mina, their motions fluid and graceful, showing their curves off to their waiting and expectant subject. Taking her by the wrists they led her into the small chamber and turned on the warm flow. Twin jets from either side launched a soothing deluge of water across the trio, making Mina gasp with joy as she felt her perspiration being washed from her, the flows of crystal warmth causing her to shudder and run her hands across her slick skin. As she traced her breasts she felt other hands merge onto her, the women using cakes of soap. The suds flowed down with the passage of water, the bars slithering upon her flesh, her head draping back, her ponytail hanging as a limp tentacle down her spine as she moaned softly at the excellent sensations.

Hands parted her thighs and started to run up and down the inside, the soft touch causing Mina to sway with giddiness. In answer to her decadent stupor, the other woman embraced her from behind, her sultry breasts brushing Mina's back, the nipples distinct against her skin. The assets slipped against her, the lubricating waters making them slither against one another as the woman's arms rolled around her, caressing and supporting her, holding her up as the other female continued her task.

Lips brushed her neck, running down the wet flesh before a tongue started to lick at the water. The woman suckled at her earlobes, taking them in and gently nibbling upon the pliant morsels as hands rose and lifted her breasts, the thumbs tracing small spirals on the tips of Mina's nipples.

Letting her head laze against that of the woman behind her, Mina left herself vulnerable to their every whim, the two maids filling their senses with the feel and taste of their subject.

As a pair of hands worked her inner thighs and rolled

around to attend her rear in alternating sessions of cleansing and massaging, she felt a mouth kiss her sex. Rising onto tiptoe and shuddering as the warmth of the shower saturated her, the fingers dug in and pulled down upon her buttocks, keeping her in place as a tongue rolled like a plough through her vulva. Taking a long slow lick through the parted lips, the organ skipped upon her clitoris and departed, ricocheting from her. The single tickle almost dissolved Mina into their arms, the hands on her rear and her breasts keeping her stable as the woman paused for a moment, looking up across Mina's heaving chest and smiling with glee before burying herself back between Mina's quaking legs.

The frisky tongue worked with a marvellously deft effort, pouring its widest part against the sensual nugget, the waters that flowed down their bodies running a compressive caress over them all, emphasising and magnifying every touch.

Mina's mouth spread wide, allowing tickling jets to pound her mouth, filling it with a pool of warmth that she let dribble from the corners as kisses once more took to covering her throat.

Treating her to such a luscious event for a short while, the women released her, manipulating her pliant form with quick movements. She was pressed face first into a corner, her cheeks against the wall, her gaze fixed on the shadows she cast into the tiles. Palms slapped her rear, holding the cheeks and pulling apart while pushing forward, holding her in the corner as a mouth dove through the parted flesh and poured a tongue into her anus. Mina sobbed with delight against the tiles as she rode the organ, the slithering length driving deep, thrashing against the muscular ring, penetrating, the sensation indescribable and intense.

As the woman licked her, the other female rolled onto her back and positioned herself between the parted legs of her partner, pouring her own efforts into detailed cunnilingus. Straddling the face of the supine woman, feasting on the feeling of such oral gratification, the woman's tongue became all the more energetic and capable, gallivanting against Mina's rear. One hand relinquished the task of holding Mina open and rose between her legs, the fingers starting to thread into her sex, using the waters to ride in before changing their mind. Instead, they began to beat small circles against Mina's clitoris.

The woman grabbed her buttocks once more, using the soft mounds as handholds by which to demand that Mina pivot. Turning her around so that she was staring directly into Mina's loins, the woman lodged her hands over Mina's hips and pulled down, bringing Mina to her knees, their eyes meeting as waters poured down their features and dripped from nose and chin.

Moving closer their breasts touched, nipples grazing, the gentle meeting making both parties shudder with ecstasy. The taste of water slipping into their mouths as they kissed frenetically only added to the exchange, the wet kisses being wild and full of furious passion. Mina took the opportunity to help herself to a serving of the fellow slave's breasts, her hands savouring the feel of another woman as they caressed, slick against the warm rain that pelted them.

The other female shifted beside them, her hands sliding between their closely pressed bodies, reaching between their legs and rising against both pudenda. The embrace and kiss of the women increased, the pair of them able to exchange their passions as they wished while being serviced by another. Moving from Mina to the other and back again, the woman drew out the exchange, the flight of her deft fingers allowing each to gain a moment's calm before being worked back towards climax.

Acting together without even exchanging a single word,

the woman before her pushed Mina aside, while the other pulled her in. She was drawn down, the woman pressing her back into the corner by the door, parting her legs wide and hauling Mina's willing features between them. Mina buried herself in the smooth flesh, letting her tongue assault the woman's pudenda. The taste of her was strong, even when diluted by the waters still raining down on them. Mina relished the meal, kissing and suckling, rolling her tongue into the woman with zealous dissipation.

The other woman grabbed Mina's hindquarters, lifting her rear and sliding a leg between Mina's own limbs. The woman's knee found a place against Mina's belly, the joint rising between the acutely spread limbs and using the wet floor to slide gently back and forth while simultaneously using the toes to wiggle against the puckered anus of the woman Mina was servicing. Hands again fell upon her rear, pulling the buttocks apart as streams of water bounced upon them, a tongue finding its way through the cleft and again tasting her.

Holding the hips of the woman before her, Mina quivered and continued to adore her sex, the female slave running her hands across Mina's sodden stubble, assessing it before stealing a razor from the shelf. As Mina darted her tongue against the slave girl she drew the three-bladed implement across her scalp, leaving behind naught but smooth skin.

Even her ponytail was attacked, the razor running against the roots, severing the strands, leaving an uneven series of tufts that were then cut away with steady and careful strokes. As this deed was performed, she felt another razor working on her as well, the other woman using her position to blindly run the identical implement along Mina's legs.

The feel of the knee riding against her, the tongue within her and the roll of razors and warm waters across her form as she feasted on another woman left Mina in a languid haze, her thoughts numb, filled with nothing save hedonistic indulgence and glee.

The female jerked and groaned, setting her razor aside as she finished her task and started to give in to the flashes of pleasure Mina's tongue conjured again and again. Her hands clapped to the back of Mina's head, forcing her deeper, smothering her as her thighs clenched to the sides of her face, holding her tightly. The control that was levied on Mina made her wilt with rhapsody, magnifying her efforts, her tongue becoming a baton that conducted an epic suite of ecstasy in the slave.

The hands on her head lifted once the woman had taken her fill of the attention and could withstand no more. Raising Mina's face, she offered it to her lips, congratulating Mina with kisses, tasting the flavour of her own pudenda.

Her comrade removed her face from Mina's bottom and started to finish her job in full, working her instrument across Mina's sex, sweeping the blades through the cleft, taking her nakedness a step further, and once the task she was obligated to finish was done with, the woman turned her attentions back to sating a more primal need.

A bright clap shattered the gasping quiet of the shower as the woman dropped a palm onto Mina's rear, the sound emphasised by the sheen of water coating the skin. The spanks came at random periods, the slave sending shocks of feeling into Mina's bottom, increasing her pleasure as the fingers continued to beat small circles against her clitoris, working her towards release. Mina's fingers clenched in fits as she was soundly spanked. The girl beneath her continued to diligently attend her fellow slave, the woman unleashing rasping gasps as her spanks were used to free her pent up sadism.

Mina started to tense and her moans and gasps started to gather speed, accelerating to a throaty groan until she finally erupted into paroxysms. Clasping tightly to the woman beneath her for support against the exquisite sensations, Mina rode through the climax, a finger continuing to work and conjure more and more against her belly. With her cheek pressed against the woman she wailed into the air, fighting the urge to fling herself away, unable to withstand such reckless straits of rapture.

Choking back their screams, the exchange slowed and finally came to an end, the parties involved each sinking down to lounge against each other or the walls, gathering their breath as they let the pounding rains wash away the sweat of their exchange.

After recuperating some hint of energy, they arose and turned off the shower. Running hands down their limbs, they wiped away the excess moisture and took hold of Mina's wrists, before leading her out of the room. Curling tendrils of steam flowed from their hot bodies as they walked across the floor, leaving behind wet footprints and spattered droplets.

Poseidon was still on his chair, his face full of happiness at having watched such a teasing dance of lesbian passion. Without addressing them he turned about and continued to study them as the women produced towels from within a box. Running them over Mina's form they soaked up the moisture, her complete lack of any hair making the process swift.

Once they had attended her, they left her to dry each other, and once this was done, they began to slip back into the ivory clutches of their lingerie.

'You may proceed with putting your playmate in her uniform, slaves,' confirmed Poseidon as they looked to him for new orders now that they were again fully dressed. Together they returned to Mina, her belly aflutter with excitement at being placed within the confines of rubber captivity one more. She had greatly missed the clinch of latex upon her, the squeezing embrace of the impermeable shell as it clung to her as an auxiliary skin, smothering, controlling, serving her up to the whim of others, rendering her little more than a helpless possession.

A rubber cat-suit was removed from the insides of a trunk by one of the women as the other used an open dish and a cloth to wipe talcum powder across her form, smoothing a pale layer of dust upon her skin to ease entry into the garment.

The women worked together, opening the back of the latex garment and helping draw it onto Mina's body. The firm clinch started to swallow her form, clutching to her, compressing her, making her sigh with bliss as she was devoured alive by the vestments. How long would it be before her bare skin once more tasted air and light? It was an intriguing uncertainty.

'This is your basic skin, slave, the rest will follow shortly,' stated Poseidon, monitoring the work of his two slaves as they cocooned Mina, turning her from a naked sex slave into a rubber smothered pony-girl.

The sleeves rolled down to her hands, leaving them in fingerless gloves. The maids gathered clippers as soon as her digits were in pace, trimming them back and running a nail file against them to smooth the tips.

The zip was drawn up her back, enclosing the grip of the cat-suit more forcefully to her, squeezing her torso and pressing her breasts. Her feet were in moulded socks, the neck of the garment rising to her jaw, the zip terminating at the base of her skull.

Looking down she found that slits existed between her legs, while small apertures at her breasts let her nipples and aureole peak through. Plastic fastenings were attached in circles around her upper thighs and arms, the open fixtures revealing their purpose when she saw hoofed stockings and gloves being taken from another box.

The women drew her to the sawhorse, laying her along the padded top, her arms and legs hanging down the sides. The stockings were drawn up her legs, forcing her feet into the moulded stiletto hooves. The hem was peeled back and a layer of rubber glue drawn in a circle around the lower reaches before the latex was lifted back into position. The clips upon the rim of the stockings were snapped into the waiting clasps, holding them in place as the glue set and created a water and airtight seal.

The gloves were overtly long, the sheathes being glued and clipped to her arms, leaving her hands in an interior pocket, sealed tight within a moulded grip at the end of the sleeve. The garment continued down, the extra portion weighted and ending in another hoof, rendering her arms the same length as her legs, turning her more effectively into a genuine quadruped. With four hooves now resting on the stone flagstones of the floor, the garments for her head were gathered and laid beneath her.

'I'm sure you remember this manner of gag, slave, so you know what to do,' attested Poseidon as one of the deep throat-penetrating tubes was taken up and offered to her mouth. With complete compliance, seduced by her latex bonds, Mina let the woman feed it into her. The other held her down as she jerked and choked, her body reacting instinctively as it was violated. The slick device slithered down her oesophagus and the gag plate entered her mouth, opening up and capturing her teeth, setting her jaws wide and preventing her from spitting out the device. With her tongue trapped speech was crippled, and she wheezed softly through her nostrils while watching the rest of her transformation occur.

The sculpted solid mask of latex that was lifted up was of a size to fully encompass her entire head and neck. The long snout of a pony was marked with two reflective mirrors at the eyes, small perky ears, and a cascading white mane that absolutely contrasted the deep abiding black of the rest of her new skin.

The women carefully placed her head into the mask, where a sudden click sounded, revealing that the gag had been grabbed by inner mountings. Stretching the elasticised neck down over her throat so that it ran over her cat-suit, the two were glued together to ensure she was properly sealed within it.

The interior suddenly welled with life, the insides of the mask billowing out to squeeze her head, pressing from every direction to mould itself perfectly and tightly to her skull, making it impossible for any of her efforts to even budge her new artificial countenance.

Breathing through the internal vents that accessed the nostrils of the mask, Mina peered through the shaded eyepieces, watching the women as they brushed their hands through her mane to clear it aside and then brought forth a leather bridle. Unlike any other, this one was completely normal, her new face accepting the standard riding tack. The bit slid into her mouth, able to steer her just as easily by holding the front of her mask, and the leather harness was tightened to her head.

Reins were clipped into place and used to bring her off the sawhorse, leading her slowly forward so that she could experiment with her initial steps while still having the sawhorse to support her should she fumble the attempts.

Lifting her forelegs she set them forward, the hooves clopping to the floor as her rear legs timed themselves to keep up and maintain her balance. Her infant steps were unsteady and weak, but it felt glorious to be diminished so absolutely. She now resembled nothing more than a four-legged animal, a beast owned and controlled by others, without will or speech of her own.

Clearing the sawhorse she wobbled forward and was drawn to the side, where a new garment was taken up. The halter-necked leotard could be broken into two halves, the garment forged from a much more solid fabric, almost like rigid plastic. Two circular sockets existed at the crotch of the shell, ready to accommodate plugs or some other manner of intrusion into her body.

Setting her legs and arms through the apertures, the two slaves lifted them onto her body and pressed them together, the two sides meeting with a chorus of clicks. The leotard now squeezed her body, resting firmly against the strict hold of the cat-suit. Its sculpted collar acted like a posture band, lifting her chin and serving it upon a solid tongue, keeping her face upright.

Two translucent shafts of plastic were taken up, the separate rods formed as a hollow tube coated in a layer of the ridged jelly substance that Mina found so delightful. The rounded heads of the phalluses bore a cluster of holes that accessed the interior shaft and which would allow her to be pumped up or drained as the designs of her owner wished.

The apertures of the carapace on her torso and the slits in her cat-suit allowed them to slither into her, making Mina shudder and sway. The women quickly held her to ensure she did not collapse, her equilibrium still trying to acclimatise to the new form in which she had been moulded.

The two lengths locked to the fixtures so that she was completely sealed away from the outside world, all her bodily functions being handled by internal hoses.

A plume of snow-white hair was grabbed and clipped to the leotard at her tailbone, gifting her with a tail to match her mane.

'Very pleasing, slave,' commented Poseidon as he rose from his chair and walked over to where Mina stood, watching him through the reflective eyepieces. Hidden from view, she flexed herself against the confines of her new uniform, the strain of it already starting to rise, feeding her masochistic cravings, her loins squeezing to the soft outer layer of the plugging shafts.

Extending his hand, Poseidon was furnished with a small remote control that he took and examined before addressing Mina. 'The uniform you wear has several other functions. For example, should you try and rear up, the sensors in the body shell will scold you for trying to break your designated caste. Such discipline can also be meted out at the touch of button, like so…'

As soon as his finger depressed a tab on the device, Mina screamed into the gag as her clitoris and nipples were savaged by voltage bites that made the skin erupt with scintillating pulses. The momentary jolt had her chewing on the gag, sobbing against her mask, pulling at her uniform, trying to get free of the attackers that were now her most intimate and immobile companions.

'Not pleasant, but it's a vital part of the uniform. It'll help push you as far as you can go. We have scant time before the party, and I'll have to drive you mercilessly to get you ready for it. You assented to this training regime, so you had better get used to the fact that you are totally under my control. If you do not perform as I require, you'll be chastised until you do, it's that simple. I will not tolerate failure in you, because I know what you are capable of. Any failure on your part will clearly be the work of laziness and rebellion and as such will not be tolerated.

'So, let's get you to your station and begin your training, we have much work to do before you're ready,' he revealed, moving away and using the reins to draw Mina along, her four hooves struggling to find order against their stringent bonds.

Walking awkwardly, but gathering new knowledge on what she could and could not do with each hesitant step,

Mina was taken back into the bedroom where her naked form had been ravished by Poseidon – the very same female form that now lay an infinity of space away from the outside world.

Drawn onto the treadmill, her reins were attached to the wall rings, leaving her nose almost touching them, preventing her from getting off the apparatus.

The hatch was opened, exposing controls and several sockets. Poseidon took one of them and pulled it out, a long metallic segmented hose spilling behind it. The hose was fed over her bit and clipped to an internal fixture to provide her with food while she toiled.

Flicking a switch within the hatch, a more covert panel flicked open in the floor at the end of the treadmill. A telescopic pole started to rise with gradual speed, locking itself at the same height as Mina's rubber encased rump.

From the tip Poseidon took more of the hoses, the coils spilling from the summit to pass between her legs and lock to the base of her dildos, ready to regulate her insides with their mechanised influence. 'There, you're ready for your lessons now, pony-girl,' he testified, flicking another switch, slapping her bottom and then marching from the room.

Once the door had closed and locked itself Mina was left in silent contemplation, wondering what was going to befall her. Calming her thoughts and relaxing into the arms of her uniform, she looked blankly at the wall, waiting for her training to begin.

The belt beneath her started to move, rolling slowly at first, bringing her to a slow walk where she could practice using her complement of legs. Adapting as quickly as she could, she soon grew more confident in flipping a hoof forward, the sprung joint at her hands letting the rest of the metal-shod hoof thump against the corrugated rubber. The treadmill started to increase its speed, moving her from a slow walk to a swifter pace.

Her reins pulled back as she tried to accelerate, having difficulty changing her rate. When they tugged at the wall rings her loins were nipped with angry sparks of voltage, chewing on her most tender membranes to have her croak against the gag and bolster her efforts. As soon as she was meeting the speed of the treadmill and thus had taken the pressure from the wall anchors, the attacks of encouragement stopped.

Continuing the walk, she started to grow more fluid in her movements, the constant use making them second nature as the hours trailed lethargically by. Occasionally she let herself dawdle a little, fall back and gain a few kisses of discipline before restoring herself to the required position on the belt.

The hunched position started to become tedious and she tried to straighten a little to ease some of the stress, only to find that the sensors were intolerant of the slightest change in her stance during this period of devolution. The shocks emerged again, but this time others were added to her breasts, the nipples that rested against the stern shell being savaged by swirling flashes of discomfort that quickly forced her back onto all four feet.

Over the course of several hours she was relentlessly pushed towards a steady gallop, her hooves pounding the mat beneath as it span past. Once again she was subjected to the ordeal of fighting to have her physique meet the demands required of her, applying her resilience to the task to ensure she succeeded.

The rubber prison became a horrendously sweltering bane to her flesh, the rubber squirming against her motions, filled with ample sweat. Her body ached and burned, her pulse stamping through her head as she kept to the rigorous gallop, her occasional failures earning her bouts of discipline.

It was not long before she started to pray for an end,

so she might rest, her weariness growing more potent, making her stumble on occasion, the electrical castigation quickly galvanising her back into a full run as she vehemently cursed it. There was nothing she could do. She could not take any more, but if she tried to stop she would be disciplined so severely that no matter how enervated, how emotionally and physically shattered she was, the uniform would have her back at the required speed in no time. The longer she ran, the more her head swam with giddiness and the more difficult it was to keep to the parameters proscribed for her training.

The periods of voltage assault grew longer, the agonising teeth that gnawed at her becoming more venomous, increasing their vicious settings until she gave up and found the effort to restore herself to a run. The fiendish machine was never going to let her rest, it would keep going, keep increasing the agony it could impart until it found the setting to make her comply.

Mina could see now how other girls had been reduced to shattered insane shells by this horror, for already she was in turmoil, resenting her treatment, hating it, yet unable to do a single thing to affect it. She had foolishly agreed to this fate, and Poseidon would work her until she dropped, succeeded, or went insane. She couldn't take this, she would lose her mind or suffer a coronary. How could they do this to her, to a woman who only wanted to please them?

Mina had no idea how long she remained on the running machine, her first awareness that her lot had changed coming when the door opened and Poseidon entered. The man moved beside her, standing just by the rolling rubber mat as it forced her onwards, making her sprint, her limbs bounding against it as her sight wavered and rocked, her mind full of woe.

'You've been running well, Mina,' he stated, and flicked a switch in the control panel. 'Few ponies have lasted this long on such a setting.'

Mina sighed with utter relief as the machine swiftly slowed and came to a stop, letting her sag. Her legs folded beneath her until she was hanging by the cables and tethers that remained sternly fixed to her body, holding her a few feet up, her limbs loose under her hanging torso.

'You must be exhausted,' he offered as Mina closed her eyes, sobbing to herself within her private cell, unable to fathom how she could hope to make it through this evil tutoring. 'Let's get you cleaned up and to bed.'

Chapter Twelve

Mina stood upon one of the small hills, her hooves sinking a little way into the soil with each step, burdened by the added weight of her new attire. The shell that encompassed her torso had been swapped for another white version, this one bearing the fixtures that would allow the wings to be attached. The carapace was far more solid, constructed from a plasteel alloy, an amalgamation of plastic and metal that combined exceptional light weight with incredible strength, a strength emphasised by the erasure of the brittle nature of a metal, giving the material a far higher tolerance for stress. Plasteel was being kept quiet for now, hidden while it was fully developed and the manufacture of it prepared, the factories readied, the uses worked out, even basic plans for marketing arranged. Thus while it ran through government approval, the entire machine behind it could confidently be set in motion, completely certain that it would pass. This would allow the corporations to flood the world with their product and beat all competition by years, creating a cartel impermeable to outsiders.

With soft clicks of acceptance her fittings grabbed the wings, the white upgraded versions furled neatly at her sides. Her body stretched against its new albino uniform, and her fingers clutched at the internal sleeves of her gloves, scratching a hoof against the turf as she awaited the order to begin.

A tingle of static charge brushed across her scalp, the neuronic sensors charging themselves. They were placed to the most deep setting possible, where only a concentrated devoted force of the will would register against them, the flashes of impulse through her synapses having to be singular enough of purpose to deploy the new appendages to her body. It was a wise precaution to stop any wayward thoughts interfering with the flight, but also it meant it required a person of unparalleled willpower to operate it safely and competently.

'You may begin, slave,' commanded Poseidon, stepping back with her unleashed reins as the engineers followed. The carriage that had brought them was parked a short way away, the team of six ponies blinkered in full so that they could not see the test flight.

Fixing her eyes forward through the lenses, Mina banished all superfluous thought from her mind, casting away all doubt and speculation, and then flung a single yelled command through her mind, visualising the response to assist her.

The wings flung wide, the artificial muscles making them operate in smooth organic sweeps rather than clumsy mechanised jerks. Pounding her hooves against the grass she bolted forward, her mane and tail flapping in the wind as she accelerated to a mad charge.

With a hiss of exertion she kicked into the ground as she cleared the crest of the hill, closing her eyes and filling her mind with the orders needed to control her winged harness. Her legs curled up against her body, meeting the small clamps upon her underside that snapped to awaiting hoof rings, letting her relinquish control of her limbs so she could concentrate more fully on her flight.

Upon a smooth dip she began to glide downwards, sweeping towards the tree line and certain doom. With a soft grin she pictured the mortified faces of Poseidon and the engineers before she altered the angle of the wings. With a sudden flash of ascent she spiralled upwards, using the ornithopter capabilities of the wings to assist her climb, taking her costume well beyond the realms of a mere glider.

Gathering height, she beat her wings against the air, the strong thrashing sweeps hauling her up in steady jolts. The land began to drop away, the edges of the island becoming visible as she gained more and more altitude. Against her gag she laughed and giggled with glee, enthralled with the magnificent sight of the world below her, her rubber-clad form gleaming in the bared rays of the sun. The sense of elation was immeasurable, the feeling of being able to fly, to soar and swoop, to escape the world while still being imprisoned in her skin-tight personal cell.

With intense concentration she kept going, working in small swirls, her wings beating with precise rhythm as she crawled upwards towards the same height as the mountain itself. Once she cleared its summit she soared forward, extending her wings to their fullest, cruising on the breeze like an eagle, surveying the world in these idle moments, the wings needing no more commands.

She looked across the sea in all directions, spying the sporadic collections of rock jutting from it, the myriad islands stretching in all directions until open ocean extended to the horizon, save to the north she could see the loitering line that was the mainland – distant China, the normal world. To see even this vague glimpse of it escalated her sense of jubilation, for all she could picture was the choking cities, the teeming, closely packed population, the oppression of existence itself. And here she was, riding the air as a rubber-clad beast of mythology, dragged from legend and forged through discipline, erotic bondage and her slavery on a tropical paradise. If she could have defeated the gag she would have howled her delight across the heavens, sent its echo through the universe to announce her pleasure.

With a chuckling growl she banked and dove towards

the mountain, her wandering having buffeted her with a few choice thermals that had taken her even higher than the lofty peak. She rolled around the craggy surface, hugging the stone, watching the uneven spire flash beneath her belly as she whirled around it, descending like a helter-skelter.

Peeling away as she neared the lower reaches, she sped over the main building, the area deserted. The guests were attending a display Poseidon had arranged in the sub levels of the building, and the ponies had been set in their stables for the day. No one would see her first flight; she would remain a secret until her grand unveiling.

Swooping around she arched her wings up at the front and then flashed them around, braking suddenly. With a stern thought she set the clamps free and as though dropping an undercarriage, her hooves clopped upon the roof of the mansion. Furling her wings to her sides, she pranced along it and then threw herself from the side. Practiced at command, and without fear or doubt, her wings flashed open before she hit the ground and turned her dive into a sharp ascent. The sudden reversal of direction jolted her body against the uniform and her hooves tore four shallow trenches in the ground before she hurtled upward.

Beating her wings she arced around and began a level run towards the stables. Dropping her hooves upon the lip of the roof, she kept her wings out and half ran, half glided along the building, galloping along the entire length, drumming her hoof beats upon the roof. With jovial mirth she imagined the startled expressions of the other ponies as they heard a pony-girl running above, their confusion as to how she got there and who she was making them struggle and whinny against their bondage.

Leaping from the end of the wooden runway she locked her legs into position and sped her ascent, climbing rapidly, clearing the trees and then ascending higher. Once she had left the ground far below she broke aside and plummeted at a steep angle, streaking down towards the beach.

Scudding along the sand, her turbulence whipped up particles in her wake before she skimmed onto the water. The tips of her hooves caught the peaks of waves as she cruised just above the sea, circling slowly around the bound women, whose eyes widened in shock as she darted past their restricted visual arc.

The image of Icarus struck her mind as she looked across the rolling ocean flashing beneath her and launched upwards with purpose. Capturing thermals and assisted by choice winds, Mina used her wings to carry her ever up, continuing without pause, keeping her mind dedicated to the task, the interior of the uniform growing hot with her mental exertion and the heat of the toiling components in the wings.

A few streaked clouds drew her attention and she passed through them, the wispy lines placing a sheen of moisture to her form as she moved through them and back into unblemished sky.

The lethal ascent of Icarus made her laugh with satisfaction. She was another product of mythology and she was triumphing over him with her flight, but then again, she was a far more advanced aviatrix.

Levelling out her flight, she was startled to see that the island was little more than a vague blotch of green and brown below her. Only the churned white waters that surrounded it marked it from the others, preventing her from becoming lost.

A soft series of beeps entered her ears, testifying that her energy reserves were getting low. Glancing to the horizon she was similarly amazed to see that the sun was creeping down towards the distant skyline, the day drawing to a close. It felt like she had only been up for seconds, and yet it also seemed as though she had always been there. The sheer ecstasy of her flight had stolen the day from her and now she was running low on fuel, her artificial wings succumbing to fatigue from the strains she had placed upon them.

Pausing for one last moment to admire the unequalled view, she looked to the world and then dipped into a nosedive, her snout streaking against the air as she drew her wings in to accelerate her plummet. She knew the capacities of the uniform and let her mind marvel at the image of the island as it grew with increasing haste. The tiny pinprick specks upon a few green bumps became the vague image of Poseidon and the engineers, watching her with binoculars.

Letting her wings emerge slowly, she changed her trajectory and then turned suddenly. The velocity of her screaming descent wrenched her body as the wings fought her impetus, destroying it abruptly. With a nimble flip she swooped up before them, breaking from her dive and folding her wings as she simultaneously released her clamps and dropped onto all fours before them.

Panting softly, Mina shuffled on the spot as the men approached. Poseidon clipped her reins into position and patted her head, running his hand down her mane as the engineers removed her wings and loaded them back onto the carriage.

'That was quite a flight,' he said with a mellow voice, running his hands across her form. 'We were very impressed. You seem to have mastered the uniform with ease. Every other aviatrix had trouble with just gliding and maintaining flight without all the stunts and other feats you were performing. I guess the new wings help, but I think it's more down to you, my sweet Pegasus.'

Mina gave a pleased whinny, delighted to be treated to his touch, for even though she could barely feel it through her uniform it was emphasising her derogated position in life. He was treating her as a genuine beast, a possession, and that satisfaction was a wonderful sense of comfort and security.

'We'll get you back to your training stable, and I think some reward is justified,' he promised, making her eager for release, her flight having fanned her arousal to a peak that rivalled her earlier famine.

Chapter Thirteen

Hitched to the back of the carriage, Mina was drawn to the stables, walking behind the conveyance, stripped of her wings.

As grooms handled the vehicle and its human beasts, Mina was shown back to her training and living module. The engineers vanished to check over the wings, to see if any damage had been caused by the flight and to replenish their batteries.

Poseidon took her to the wall and drew her onto the treadmill once more, signifying that she was to begin yet more training. Sighing with despair, she readied for the humdrum run that would no doubt restore her to the usual rota of exhaustion and sexual starvation until the time of the party.

But instead she felt movement at her rear as Poseidon began to remove the dildos. Unfastening the clips he hauled them free, making Mina shudder, now addicted to their presence and resentful of their flight.

'My sweet Pegasus, I never imagined you would be so magnificent,' he purred, running his hands over her buttocks, his touch seeping through the rubber layer that cocooned her. Cupping the rounded flesh he squeezed and fondled, stoking his prurient lust with the sight of Mina, bound and degraded before him, turned into a beast that he owned and adored.

Mina stiffened and croaked with joy as she felt his penis rub against her sex, slipping through the opening in the carapace and sliding through the slit in her sealed suit. Opened to the outside world for the first time in an unknown duration, she shivered as she felt him replacing the jelly phallus with a far more pleasing variety. The sensation of having him slide into her was almost overwhelming, accepting him with jubilation, letting him glide deep as she quivered and mewled softly.

His hands tightened against her constrained hips, using them as handholds by which he allowed himself to drive into her, working slowly so as to enjoy every moment of this ravishment of his creation. Mina jerked with a flare of climax, the pleasure continuing before another struck, the feel of a real length working her insides making them answer with intense responses.

'That's it, slave, enjoy the feeling while you can, you'll be plugged until after the show once I've finished with you,' he groaned softly, easing back and forth. Mina's mouth chewed violently against the gag as she sought to endure the ongoing eruptions of ecstasy, her sanity bubbling against a trial as fierce as the most pernicious flogging. 'How does it feel to be dragged from your humanity and made a beast to my will?' he mused as he continued to ride against Mina's tensed legs. 'I wonder how long you can keep your thoughts before they start to fade, lost to your bestial caste. Isn't that a pleasing concept, slave? To lose yourself totally, to actually be erased as Mina and simply become a Pegasus?'

The words were like pillow talk to her, erotic statements that fuelled her licentiousness. To some such words would be a torture to the ears and mind, slashing at them like razors of condemnation to be reviled and despised. But to Mina they were a gateway to heaven, a promise she yearned to embrace. Mina ached to be ruled by the crop and by bondage, led by reins, without a care in the world save when she would be permitted respite from her frustration. Even then it would be an all too fleeting relief, negated as the intense pleasure she exacted from her lot re-forged the bane of denial for her.

Poseidon drew free of her and sheathed himself in her rear, a hand digging through the aperture at her pudenda, opening the slit of latex and tickling her clitoris. Occasional pinches made her squeak and wiggle from the distress, but the delight of his length as it glided into her anus, riding against a sphincter that tightened to it to increase the sensations was an admirable reward.

Groaning lasciviously, Mina swayed her head from side to side, the last of her punishment devices sending grinding spikes of duress into her swollen nipples. Afflicting herself to augment her pleasure, she felt Poseidon withdraw from his brief diversion and once more return to her hot and ravenous sex, riding back into the moist depths as his hands worked her rear. Occasionally he slithered a thumb or two into her anus, opening the orifice as he continued to help himself to his slave's body, stretching it to fill the muscular ring with hot rhapsody.

'Are you ready to be filled up, slave?' he said on a panted purl, his rhythm starting to increase slightly as the seduction of orgasm sped his efforts. Mina bobbed her head as best she could against the damning collar, tears spilling from her eyes and seeping under the hood as she wept with strain. When she felt his length spill warm liquid into her belly, Mina jerked with response, the feeling of him feeding her one that almost brought her to a faint. The Noble continued with a few more random thrusts, growling softly to himself as he continued to shunt himself into her, ensuring every nugget of bliss was taken before he chose to withdraw.

Mina had trouble remaining upright as she closed her eyes, mulling over the ghost sensations and the presence of his seed within her belly.

'You, restore her,' he ordered, clicking his fingers in directions to bring the observing grooms to life. 'And you, attend me.'

177

Mina jolted against her uniform as the plugs were threaded back into her and locked into position, restoring her detachment from the real world, if this place of debauchery and perversity could ever bear such a title.

The other groom dropped to her knees and swallowed Poseidon's rampant shaft, cleaning him with her tongue and her lips.

With the dildos back in place, Mina was once again prepared for slumber, ready to rest and begin a new day of training.

Chapter Fourteen

For several more days she received her concentrated regime of training, her fitness at a new peak, her ability to exist within the Pegasus uniform one that was now second nature. She could scarcely recall what it was like to be a biped, the memories hazy, the continuing imposition of the uniform seeming to erase the past, leave her surrendered to the moment and the expectations of what was to come.

It became harder and harder to think clearly. The lack of speech was leaving her on a steady descent into a more devolved state. She could conjure old memories of pleasure, her ever-present urges being fuelled with teasing reminders of what she had undergone in the past. But it was becoming more difficult to add speech and verbal exchange to them, her mind being gradually washed clean of language. Unless indulged, it seemed that her imprisonment would rob her of conversation, further dragging her down, removing another portion of her humanity as she was turned from woman into pony.

The distinct process did not frighten her, rather, Mina welcomed it, untroubled by the erasure and almost eager to see how much farther she would descend, wondering how much of a trained and obedient animal they could make her. The ordeal impressed on her how Poseidon bore similarity to his divine namesake, for was he not crafting a Pegasus? He had taken the raw materials of a woman, and was expertly and with ruthless efficiency remaking her in the image and demeanour he wished, reconfiguring psyche and physique to his specifications.

Without any real contrast or change time followed her

own private devolution, becoming nothing more than the periods of exercise, the moments of preparing for slumber, and the frustrated torture as she tried to ignore her thirst for sensual pleasure and find recourse in the dreams that only fuelled it.

Slowly though, the day of her grand unveiling drew closer until finally her daily rota of arousing tedium broke from its pre-set and eternal cycle.

Chapter Fifteen

Mina's hooves echoed though the tunnel as they clopped onto the stone floor. The passage was roughly hewn, carved carelessly though the island towards the mountain. The jagged subterranean artery wound onwards, leading her through the bowels of the island, a line of insulated wire swinging between distant wall lamps, filling the hall with shadow and tentative light.

The two grooms led her, the women marching steadily along, holding her reins together, her wings folded at her sides, ready to be thrown open and permit flight. Poseidon was with his guests, the party well underway and having been so for most of the day.

A lift that was little more than a metal cage supported by an automated winch appeared before them, the bare elevator accepting her body as the grooms led her in and slammed the gate shut behind them. With a whirring grumble the lift jerked and began a rough ascent, occasionally scraping against the walls as they rose through the closefitting vent.

The lift issued a deep clunk as it reached its peak and the gate was thrown back with a squeal to allow her grooms to back her out and off the steel grate floor. Reversing her in the more spacious dimensions of the tunnel, Mina turned around to find herself facing a short passage, the end of which was a set of plain steel doors mounted and held forward by articulated metal arms.

Brought before it, one of the grooms slapped a button on the wall to have the corridor resound with deep rumbles of hydraulic strain and the doors slowly peeled back, swinging inward to pain Mina's eyes with the glare

181

of the late evening sun.

The sight of the ocean below them, spreading out across the world, pockmarked with islands as the waters slammed against the rock took her breath away. The sun was in the final stages of its defeat, slinking towards the horizon and hurling its dwindling rays out across the waters, seemingly in a bid to hold on for just a little while longer. During her resumed training, her mind had glazed over the sights of her initial flight. She had assumed she'd exaggerated them, that nothing could have been as wondrous as what she remembered. Now she realised that her recall was actually insufficient to recapture the splendour of the firsthand view offered by this vantage point.

'You may go now, Pegasus,' said one of the grooms, Mina barely aware of them as she stared awestruck at the sight before her. 'Poseidon commanded us to pass on a reminder – you are to take your post and await the call to descend. Ensure that you make yourself known to the guests.'

Suddenly realising that she had just been given permission to fly, she galloped forward and hurled herself out with a mighty kick of her rear legs. The air embraced her, her hooves leaving the safety of solid ground. With a squeal of unbridled joy the wind rushed around her, streaking upon her plummeting form.

A collected thought had the wings flash open and she turned from her dive into a swooping ascent. Streaking up past the closing doors of the secret mountain post, she banked and veered backwards, performing a few loops as she locked her hooves to her chest to lower drag.

Beating the white gleaming wings against the air, she forced herself upward until she was reaching the very peak of the mountain. With a final lunge she set loose her hooves and had them stamp onto the rounded pinnacle. Furling her wings she lowered into a small crouch, curled up on top of a mountain, watching the world from this unrivalled spire.

The island far below was bristling with activity. A number of boats were anchored out to sea, each member of the small fleet identical to the vessel that had orchestrated her deliverance from the depths. Poseidon had gathered his guests, and now they were abroad on the grass about the main building. The field was alive with sites where engines of restraint offered elaborate bondage displays and carnal sideshows to amuse the epicurean nobles of Cabal.

Mina watched them milling around far below, the high altitude winds running their hands over her smoothed hide, trying to dislodge her but lacking the brawn to accomplish the task. Smiling against her gag, she clung to her perch and like an eagle watching its quarry, continued to sit on her bland nest and observe the goings-on.

Three soft beeps entered her ears, the remote signal commanding her to begin her descent and unveil herself to the crowds. All her limbs kicked out as one and curled back to her torso, clamping into place as she cast out her white wings to capture the air. The wind rushed over her snout, pulling at it, dragging at the tiny disruptions to aerodynamics across her form.

On a smooth gliding arc she streaked down the mountain, flowing outwards towards the open area of the grounds. Dozens of startled expressions flashed beneath her eyes as the carpet of Nobles sped beneath her, her new body skimming just over their heads before rising at the other side of the field.

Releasing her legs she banked and hovered, her articulated wings pounded the air, making her bob but remain largely stationary above the treetops, and her hidden eyes turned to regard the entire ensemble.

The sea of latex and leather, vinyl, lace, fishnet and steel was locked to her visage. Every maid was stalled in her work by staring at Mina. Some glasses and plates fell to the grass as limbs went limp from astonishment, and suddenly applause was pouring through the air as spontaneous respect was paid to Mina and her creator.

She hovered for a moment, her heart leaping with joy as the entire throng became livid with rapture, their eyes not even blinking lest they miss a split second of the show.

Tilting her wings she recaptured her legs and swooped back across the crowd, launching up into the sky, firing herself into a rigid ascent, gathering height and leaving the people far below. Every portion of her body was tingling with excitement, in feeling so adored, so brazenly acknowledged. She had done what no other had come close to doing – mastered the transition from woman, to slave, to pony, to Pegasus. She had exceeded all others; she had finally achieved the perfection that had eluded her in her previous life.

Throwing herself up, she performed a reversed loop that turned into a dive before rolling effortlessly into a figure of eight manoeuvre. The feel of her wings was wonderful as they obeyed her commands, her body defying gravity, mocking it with her stolen ability to achieve flight. Spiralling around the clearing she cruised gently on the soft thermals, winding slowly down, descending as a tease, making the people wait for her, their eyes aching to see her in more detail. But now *she* was the one in control. She could make them hang on her arrival, their mouths watering with lecherous hunger pangs.

As her hooves brushed the leaves of the treetops she veered drastically away, shooting across the foliage before arching upwards. Spilling around, she began a swift run back towards the clearing, dipping towards it.

Formed into a dart of white she flung herself into their midst, speeding over their heads and then jerking her wings up, braking sternly at the middle of the area, instantaneously countering her momentum. Eyes flashed onward, lured into following her speeding path, tricked by her aerial agility. Her mid-air stop left her hanging for a second and then she dropped to the ground, her wings folding in immediately, her legs dropping down to stamp into the soil.

Standing tense and panting before Poseidon, she stepped forward and nuzzled into his side, the Noble rubbing her head as she listened to the awed applause spilling from all directions, the crowd wild from the show.

Poseidon took the praise with humble gratitude, nodding his head calmly as they continued for a few minutes and pressed closer, everyone eager to see up close the creature that had astounded them so.

Taking a bridle from a maid, he threaded the straps onto her artificial face and tightened it into place. The blinkers were snapped down, obscuring her eyes, preventing her from seeing anything as she heard his voice address her softly.

'You did very well, Pegasus,' he soothed, as he closed a fist to the base of the reins, making his hold distinct, easing her anxiety and welling sense of bizarre claustrophobia. 'Now keep calm, people will want to touch you. I'll look after you, I'll hold your reins throughout.'

Here she was, sealed skin-tight within a pony outfit, her body encased in figure-squeezing rubber, every function under complete control, and yet it was the thought of dense crowds pressing in on her that spiked her sense of unease. Bondage she could handle, smothered in an orgy of flesh during obliquity was a pleasure, but somehow the thought of large numbers of people, pressing in on her from all directions, leaving her no way out, made her heart start to race and a chilled sweat form on her skin. She was on the verge of losing control, of breaking into a panic, kicking and swatting at them until she could throw open her wings and take back to the air. The only thing that stopped her and soothed her distress was Poseidon's calming hold on her reins. He would not let anything bad happen to her, he was looking after her personally and would allow no guest to take liberties with his prized pet. Her respiration started to ease, and she closed her eyes against the darkness and surrendered her body to the inquisitive hands that descended in droves.

Fingers stroked her body, caressed and squeezed, traced her rubber skin, marvelling at the woman trapped within the astounding uniform. Mina told herself that they were adoring her, that she should feel the same amount of relish in being worshipped by those who ordinarily would use her as a slave in any way they wished. These people never really noticed their servile caste, they used them as though they were furnishings. The women that eagerly scampered forward to do whatever their owners wished were objects, with only a few rare exceptions standing out to receive actual acknowledgement and special attention. Now Mina had captivated their interest, and all were zealous to feel and explore the creation that had dazzled the assembled force of dominants and sadists.

Questions flowed freely with the praise, offers were made, but Poseidon never accepted, keeping to his deal with her real owners, and eventually the groping dwindled, the crowds parting as Poseidon whispered into her ear once more, his hands freeing the bridle.

'Good girl, now fly for us again, and return when I call for you,' he ordered, the straps to her equine countenance vanishing, the blinkers coming away to open her view once more. The paltry light was a little

186

dazzling to her eyes, the flaming torches that had been stationed throughout the clearing creating a flickering amber halo that served to force back the night.

As Poseidon retreated she flung open her wings, gathering her mental dexterity and applying a singular consciousness to the task of take off. She had yet to try vertical ascent straight from the ground and wasn't sure if it was even possible. But casting away the doubts lest they interfere with her attempt, Mina lowered into a tight crouch and fired her limbs like pistons. Closing her eyes tightly, her mind roared for maximum effort, the wings obeying every command with broad sweeps. With relentless effort she started to gain height, lifting herself in jolts until she was high enough to exploit her capacity as a glider.

Dropping forward she swooped down and then curled back up, sweeping into the sky, using her wings to give added velocity. Arcing up into the night, her form was vaguely brushed by the lights of the party, the orange and yellow hue staining her pure white form until she escaped it.

Whirling and weaving through the heavens, Mina's form was now completely revealed by the light of stars and the exposed spherical face of the full moon, which rendered her an incandescent silver form dancing through the sky as though she owned it.

Three soft pips of sound entered her ears, calling for her return to earth. At first she thought she was low on fuel, but the trio testified that she was merely being commanded to return. Mina ignored it; her addiction to flight would not tolerate a premature end, she wanted to fly until she was on the verge of plummeting from the skies. In some ways that was the end she would have sought, a martyr's dive from the heavens, to perish as an extravagant spectacle rather than ever lay a hoof on the earth again. It was a fanciful notion and little more than that, but one that helped convince her to disobey and remain aloft.

Her plugs started to come to life as they obeyed the remote order of her owner, Poseidon seeking to bring her down with them. But she was well out of range, and as she climbed even higher than before the momentary spark of infant influence from them vanished. Mina wailed with glee at having found freedom in the sky; she was beyond influence now, no one could touch her. The entire sky was her playground, a sanctuary where the influence of those who sought to control her was removed, sloughed off with each flap of her wings.

It took her a few moments to notice the rhythmic stammer of her earplugs as they betrayed dwindling power reserves. Cursing her reliance on technology, Mina began a solemn descent, aware that she had only a few more minutes of energy left. If she got the chance she would recommend that the wings be fitted with automatic locks for the main struts to conserve energy when she was gliding. Implementing these anchors would allow the wings to remain out and not use any energy to have the fibre bundles hold them in position. As a glider she could live in the sky, exploiting thermals and winds to stay aloft. She could perch on the mountain when she needed sleep, and if she could have them add a few solar cells to her body, she could even replenish her power during the day.

But there was always the looming and undeniable necessity of sustenance. With her gagged mouth she was reliant on others to keep her alive. She had the means to spend the rest of her life in the sky, but unless she could find a way to become self-sufficient for food, she would be doomed to dependence on others for survival. Perhaps she could convince Poseidon to place a food dispenser of some kind atop the mountain, to reconfigure her suit to give her more freedom, make her a permanent creature of flight that would haunt the skies of his island for the rest of her days.

All previous allegiance was gone, she had never before experienced anything that came close to this love of flight. Her time in the seas had helped craft it by laying a foundation in the sense of gliding, of being untroubled by gravity and land. But in the depths there was a sense of oppression, of the sea pinning her down, crushing her and smothering her. Only in the air was she undeniably free.

She could not return to land now; she had tasted untainted bliss. How could she be expected to endure captivity upon solid ground after such giddy thrills as a Pegasus? She was the first, the one who had made it possible. She wanted to stay in this caste, have others created to fly with her, to be the head of an airborne herd of Pegasi.

The clearing before the mansion beckoned, an area in the crowd already open to accept her, their parted ranks like a makeshift runway. With wings wide she swooped in, her legs dropping free and delivering her into a sudden run. Slowing down, her gallop swiftly dropped into a trot and then a walk, her wings folding into her sides with an absent command, the skills of flight now second nature.

Looking around, she suddenly felt panic as she noticed that the guests carried a variety of implements of corporal punishment. She looked to the end of her runway and saw Poseidon beside a set of stocks. Far from ordinary, the wooden pillory had two sets of slats at the base to snare her hooves, with an upright sculpted panel to grab and hold her head in place, consciously leaving her helpless rear exposed to the assault of the guests.

Filled with rebellion Mina turned and cast open her wings, breaking into a gallop as the wind gathered beneath the bared membranes. Her hooves left the grass, there was a shimmer of movement before her eyes and she felt something drop about her neck. The lasso of rope snapped taut as its wielder dug their feet in, the hoop snapping against her collar, the dense material preventing strangulation but proving a most effective anchor. Wailing in horror as she was captured, Mina beat her wings with as much force as she could, the draining power making them more difficult to operate. She screamed to get free, the process of being apprehended after her flight a traumatic and intense one.

She was succeeding in dragging those holding to the rope when another landed, slipping down over her head as others bounced against her sides and legs, seeking to snare her but being shed before they could tighten. Another lasso did lock to her left foreleg, adding to the variety of bonds helping defeat her, bringing her forcibly back to the soil.

Mina collapsed onto the ground, driving the wind from her lungs. Before she could fight back hands were upon her once more, pinning her down, and she could do nothing as she was quickly laced into a web of rope. Sobbing, she was lifted up and drawn towards the stocks, the wooden jaws opening to accept her as she struggled, defeated by the humans, for she herself was no longer a member of such a breed. She had become a Pegasus, and it riled her that they had defeated her. She was surely doomed now. They would hold her, whip her, make her pay for her defiance until she was once more tamed and their slave, the light of her revolt extinguished.

With damning snaps the timbers were closed, the stern hands of the guests steering her into the grooves and trapping her extremities. Despite fighting as best she could, her head was placed in the main slot and captured, leaving her pulling at the stalwart restraints.

Hands brushed the roots of her wings and she wailed in abject dismay as she felt them being removed.

Throwing herself against the pillory with berserker fury she sought escape, the feel of being clipped and turned back into an ordinary creature of the land bloating her mind with the purest rancour and utter resentment. Nothing that had ever been done to her before had ever been this cruel.

Her fight started to subside until she was hanging lose against the stocks, lost in a morose torpor of defeat. They could do what they wanted with her now, she didn't care. They had taken away her wings, anything else would be a minor infliction compared to this most grievous of mutilations to her. The wings may have been mechanical appendages, but they were more a part of her than any other portion of anatomy. For all the effects they had on her, they might as well have taken her heart, for she could have survived more easily without that than her wings, and the loss of her Pegasus status had effectively performed that mortal dissection anyway, leaving her hollow inside.

The first blow sank into her rear, the cane sending a jolt of fulgent terror through the costume, sinking its burning weal into her flesh, making her gurgle and squeal, spasming wildly against the pillory. A different weapon struck her, and then another, the guests taking turns to apply a stroke or two of reparation for her refusal to return when ordered. It was now a ceremonial event, a party to tame the Pegasus, giving it a strange sense of closure.

Her bottom and thighs were alive with pain, each new lash feeding the swell of agony they were applying to her. But despite the unimaginable duress of the ordeal, it soothed Mina to be punished so, to make her feel more like martyr, a captured wretch struggling against the will of her captors, misused and maltreated by her hated oppressors. Her mind was rocking to and fro on the hurricane of pain, her sight wavering, the endorphins pumping through her veins gathering the residue of her excitement from her flight and driving her to higher plateaus where the pain started to merge with pleasure. Despite her misery she was lost in a trance of euphoria, an almost spiritual event as she was thrown beyond all tolerances, her mind feeling as though it were drifting from her body, seeping away in a bid to escape, or set lose by the intensity of the harrowing trial. Grizzling in apathy between the moments where her soul-torn screams battled the ability of the gag, she looked through her tears to see Charybdis standing before her.

The owner of the underwater domain that had started her on this road of voluptuous craving stood defiant and proud, refusing to join in the circus of punishment. Instead he stood still, arms folded across his chest as he watched Mina's hidden eyes, staring directly into the mirrored eyepieces as though he could somehow pierce them. At his side was the rubber-clad zombie that seemed to always be with him, never leaving his side, lost in her rubber doom, bound and contorted, utterly commanded by her skin-tight prison.

The man did not move, merely continued to study her as she was hauled through the full consequences of her act of disobedience. Unable to break free of his stare, Mina was entranced by him, her own eyes locked to his, captured as effectively as her body. The scourging of her rear and thighs continued on and on, the escalating level of mayhem she was being submerged in welling around her, drowning her senses in a banquet of algolagnic horror. Unable to detect anything save her dismay and Charybdis's eternal scrutiny, Mina started to lose her hold on consciousness, the highs and lows of the day and the severity with which the group were hounding her delivering her into a faint. Darkness encroached suddenly. Without warning the world suddenly started turning as though being spun left and right, making her think briefly that she was flying again until she vanished into oblivion, her overloaded senses shutting down, unable to brook any more input.

Chapter Sixteen

Mina was catapulted from her torpor with a sudden jerk, flinging herself against the stocks only to find they were gone. Her hazy vision condensed into more definable confines, restoring her vision as her mind tore off the haze that muffled it.

Her rear still ached terribly, the whipping she had received leaving it pulsating with an unbearable life of its own. She had no idea how long she had been out, but it had been long enough for some drastic changes to be perpetrated on her appearance.

Her arms were locked behind her in a single triangular sleeve of latex, the dense fabric hugging them together. Her hands were sealed within the tight bag that served as the culmination of the restrictive garment, and two dense straps flung over her shoulders to hold it in place. Another ran across her collarbone to connect the two hoops and prevent any hope of shedding the distressing sleeve.

The metal hoop at her fingertips had been snared by a slender line of chain, the silver links running up to the ceiling, lifting her arms, forcibly bending her over a metal bar. The steel trapeze was supported by chain, the dense strut digging into her stomach as she was folded over it, her legs splayed wide, a set of latex fetters holding her ankles and spitting forth chain to distant rings in the floor. The bonds kept her legs split and stopped her from falling over the trapeze while serving her lewdly to whatever other forms of punishment were destined for her. Held against it, unable to move or escape, she surveyed her surroundings with a cool detachment, the saturnine temperament conjured in the aftermath of terrible loss and anguish.

Her mouth was free, her lips untroubled by any form of intruder for the first time in as long as she could remember. It felt strange to be free of her pony uniform, it had been a companion for so long that she felt almost dependent on its impositions on her, her body relying on them after such long and arduous friendship.

The room obviously pandered to what she had correctly assumed was to be more education as to the folly of disobedience. The black tiled walls were adorned with numerous hooks, each holding a vast variety of weapons, while shelves held toys and other implements of darker intent. A few trunks ran the base of the walls, leaving gaps on either side of her where an alcove reached back to access a featureless door. Immediately before Mina was a single metal door that was set in the wall, the material obviously far more dense than the others, revealing that this was probably the entrance.

In the corner behind her was a room within the room, the tiny box chamber a confining cell of steel with a restricted door. The portal had a slim hatch at the base to introduce food and another hatch higher up to allow a view on the prisoner within. Was this to be her new home, a cell to be confined in when not being tormented for her crimes?

A strong light above poured a stark white beam down, spotlighting her, leaving her in a dazzling column of light while the rest of the room accepted only the most minor illumination.

Mina lowered her head, letting it hang limp as she wept freely, lamenting the loss of her wings and her pony status. Tears rolled down her cheek and fell to the floor, splashing on the tiles as she mourned softly to herself.

For seemingly hours she hung on the trapeze, the

discomfort growing steadily. She occasionally tried to find an easier position, but that only served to heighten the distress, quickly making her resume the normal docile pose that the bondage had so meticulously enforced upon her.

There was a click and a hiss of strain as the door peeled back into the wall, revealing that it was a dense vault-like slab operated by heavy hydraulics. From the darkness beyond came movement and two people emerged into the hesitant light outside of the main beam that exposed Mina. The first was Poseidon, the man dressed in leather trousers, with tall boots and a loose waistcoat of the same polished hide. His look was grave.

Behind him was a young woman, her youthfulness making her appear almost as a mere girl. She had a playful innocent expression, her painted ruby smirk matching deep hazel eyes that sparkled in the glow, rimmed with subtle shades to highlight them. But there was nothing young or spry in the darkness behind them, in the malevolence that skulked behind her eyes, making her exude a cultivated and barely suppressed malice.

A cascade of shimmering tan hair fell about her shoulders, the strands highlighted in places to bring them to an almost golden shade, the parted veil revealing her peaked eyebrows. Her body was slender, her chest and arms completely bare. Her breasts were round and attentive, lifting her nipples upon buoyant flesh. Her subtle curves were smothered from the hips down by latex trousers, the polished skin fastened with laces at the back, leaving the front smooth and unblemished. She walked barefoot, her toes and fingers long and filed to points before being painted the same sanguinary hue as her lips.

The door whirred shut behind them, and as the woman stood still and to attention before it, Poseidon walked towards Mina.

'That was very foolish of you, slave,' he stated firmly. 'Disobedience will not be tolerated here.'

'Please, master, let me go back, I'll be good, I swear, I just got carried away,' she wept, desperate to feel the close embrace of the uniform, to have her wings again.

'It's too late for that, slave,' he replied callously.

'Master, *please*, don't do this to me, I beg you,' she whimpered, her voice burbling the heartfelt words. 'I can't take it. I can't lose my wings. I'll do anything for you, I'll undergo any torture, just let me return afterwards. I don't want to live without them.'

'What you want is of no consequence to me, slave,' he commented, walking back and forth before her, gesturing absently with his hand, his eyes raised as he pronounced sentence over her. 'You transgressed and you will be punished as an example to all the other slaves I shall transform into Pegasi.

'You, however, will not be amongst them again... ever!' he snapped, turning to Mina to see her reaction, his spiteful malice suddenly snapping her from despair, turning it instantly into choler.

'Bastard!' she roared, fighting the bondage, desperate to break free. 'I'll kill you! Let me go back or you'll not live to see another Pegasus spread her wings!' Diplomacy and begging had gained nothing; threats were her last recourse.

'Oh, such a little harridan, aren't we, slave?' he stated lightly, standing before her, taunting her with how ineffectual she was. 'I can see I'll have to upgrade the punishment devices on my other Pegasi if they all get as moody as you after a flight.'

'I escaped before, I'll do it again,' she vowed.

'I doubt that, slave. I'm going to ensure your security. You'll not slip the rule of your owners again.'

'Let me go!' she howled, interrupting him before he could continue, her limbs aching from battling the bonds.

'Let me out!'

'Tut, tut, little slave,' he chuckled, making Mina sag, sobbing afresh. 'You should know by now that fighting is useless. You'll never fly again, I can promise you that.'

'Please, master,' she mewled, her heart tearing from being denied a chance to ever experience the giddy thrills of being airborne again. 'Please don't. Not this, anything but this.'

'Ah, the whimpers of regret. Your tears amuse me, slave, but they are not a currency I am inclined to accept. You see, I have made the necessary arrangements, and there is to be no changing them now.' He stepped back, waved to the girl, and she sashayed forward, slinking with grace as she moved beside him.

'This is Rache,' he announced, stepping behind her and taking hold of her shoulders, showing her off to Mina's appalled eyes. 'I use her for special circumstances, employing her skill while she waits patiently for this day. She is deaf and mute, so feel free to scream all you want; you'll not affect her in the slightest. She will be responsible for exacting my chastisement on you.

'You will be held here, and will not leave. Here, Rache will be your absolute ruler, and will ensure you suffer. She is an excellent sadist, and will slowly escalate your trials over the years to ensure you never get used to them. There are a few monitoring devices, so I may comfort myself some nights with your screams of anguish or sobs of despair. Or I may even terrify disobedience out of other slaves with images of your tortures. You've proven your physical superiority, your endurance and stamina, and they'll now serve me well as you become the most terribly abused slave on this island, one who I can be sure will live out a long and nightmare life of degradation, agony, and despair.'

Letting go of the girl he wandered behind Mina and laid his hands to her bottom, making her struggle against the touch, loathsome of the man who now intended to rob her of the object of her obsession.

'But first, before I leave you to Rache's not so tender mercies forever, I think I'll make use of this hole one last time,' he announced.

'No!' she roared, writhing against the latex that served her up to her captor. 'Fuck you, Poseidon! Don't touch me, you bastard!' She heard a zip lower and yelled curses until Poseidon addressed his malevolent gaoler.

'Rache, if you would silence her?' he said lightly, rubbing his length against Mina's rear, her buttocks clenched frantically, trying to stop him from entering her, her every fibre resentful of his rule. If he would not give her what she wished, he would get nothing from her.

Reading his lips, the girl stepped forward and turned on her bare-soled feet. Mina gazed into the rubber-clad rear of her, the material stretched taut across her seductive buttocks. The scent of it caught her nose, catching the reins of her fetishism.

The sight suddenly moved down and then rose towards her, pressing the cleft of her rear against Mina's face and then using it as a means to crane her head back. Mina wailed against the smothering sheet as she stared wild-eyed along the naked spine of the female. Her neck throbbed as the woman pushed herself firmly against Mina's face, totally stopping up her mouth and nose, leaving her unable to escape or respire.

Leant over, holding to her knees, the girl merely stood still as Mina tried to snort fresh breath through the wall of latex across her face, unable to make anything save resonant moans against the living gag.

'There, much better,' mused Poseidon, digging his fingers into her buttocks, pulling them apart so he might plunge into her anus. Mina wailed as she was penetrated, employing her muscles to try and spit him out, her hatred finding a delicate satisfaction in being so forcefully taken, melting her resentment a little.

'Ah, I'll miss using this passage, slave, but I'll sleep better knowing you are here, in torment. And as to the point of your escape, I almost forgot to mention before you so rudely interrupted me. Rache here was raised for just such a purpose as this. She has been conditioned only to find her pleasure in another's pain and humiliation. She has been trained to wish only for this moment, where she would be locked away with a slave, to use and abuse her for the rest of your lives, spend them together so she might exact every single crumb of anguish from your shrieking body.' He ground his hips against her rump with each drive of his shaft into her, the vivid weals exploding with new torment, making her croak and let valuable air slip free through the cleft of the female's rear.

'All she sees you as is a means to gain her own enjoyment. Mercy? Compassion? Regret? Guilt? These were never even introduced to her during her isolated upbringing. You see, when her disabilities were discovered her uncaring parents deserted her, bringing her to our attention as a candidate for just such a job as this. I think she turned out just fine, don't you?' he crooned, stabbing into Mina as she groaned in apathy, unable to fathom how such a terrible fate was going to befall her. She had to escape it. She just had to.

'But you will,' he went on, running his hands over her rear, punishing the contusions and taking one last feel of her before he gave her up. 'You two will have all the time in the world to get acquainted. You see, once that door closes, it locks itself and can only be opened from the outside, and only I know the code. The two of you will live in here for the rest of your lives, together in

200

sadistic bliss. Isn't that romantic, slave?'

Her face started to burn, her mouth straining against the leggings with rising panic, her eyes bulging as she tried to throw her head aside and find air. But she was trapped in the valley of the girl's bottom, the buttocks on each side of her face like dams that refused to let her slip free.

The feel of Poseidon ramming himself casually into her was mortifying, the pleasure a meagre one as she battled to try and find air. The girl shuffled forward a little, letting Mina find a scant vent for her nostrils. She wheezed in deep gulps of air as she sobbed and whimpered, and once she was deemed sufficiently recuperated, the girl pushed back onto her.

'Everything you'll need to survive is in here, and as long as Rache lives, I'll keep supplying food and air to this chamber and those rooms attached to it. Mmmm, doesn't that ass taste good, slave? I know yours does,' he giggled, his length swelling within her, the image of Mina being pressed into Rache's buttocks fanning his ecstasy, and then he was filling her rear with his seed and scalding her with his mocking laughter.

Dragging free, she whined with disgust as he deserted her, his length drawing at her burning rear before vacating it in full. 'There, that'll be a fine enough memory – I'll leave you now to Rache, slave,' he chuckled, feeding himself back into his trousers before leaving her to her entrapment.

'Oh,' he said, pausing and turning his gaze over his shoulder as he stood in the doorway. 'Seeing as these are the last words you'll ever here again, I might as well make them count.'

Poseidon turned and walked back and regarded her as she was submerged against the latex rear, her eyes fixed to him, full of tears, unable to answer anything he might say, guaranteeing him the last word.

'You've failed, Mina. Have a fun life.'

The door hissed shut and locked itself, throwing heavy and damning bolts of condemnation. The girl waited for a moment and then stepped forward, letting Mina's head drop forward as she gasped for air, feeding her ravenous lungs.

'Poseidon, you bastard,' Mina said sorrowfully, tears trickling down her face.

The girl crouched before Mina, looking at her with bland intensity, no trace of emotion apparent in her eyes. Mina felt new levels of sorrow well within her. This girl had been raised for this, there was to be no reasoning with her, no exchange, no love, nothing save eternal suffering. She was in hell, a slice of Gehenna carved off and served just to her.

'Please, if you understand me, you don't have to do this, I—!'

A stinging slap to her cheek span her head aside and left her looking at the wall. She paused for a moment and then looked back to the girl, her expression and demeanour unchanged. New tears welled in Mina's eyes as she regarded the impassive torturer.

'You have to listen to me, you—!'

Her words were cut off as another slap span out and caught the other cheek, filling the flesh with heat and jerking her gaze aside with its severe impetus. The girl was silently educating Mina in the ways of silence. She could not hear her words, so Mina guessed that was maybe a source of resentment, that she had been abandoned because of her imperfections and now reviled them in others. Now she had the chance to exact all her bitterness and rage on Mina, and the mere thought had a deep pit opening in Mina's stomach as she contemplated briefly all the horrors such a beast might be capable of.

Returning her eyes to the girl, Mina lowered her gaze in humility, her will to fight back gone. She couldn't win here, she was beaten, they had taken away that which was most precious to her, and left her to this miserable end.

Without word the female rose with the subtle creak of latex. Wandering to the wall, she removed two clover clamps, each one spilling a long line of slender black cord from their end.

Mina whimpered softly as she walked back and knelt below her suspended form, taking the clamps in her hands and squeezing. The jaws craned open, revealing their padded interiors. With deliberate sloth she started to lift them towards Mina's hovering breasts. Hanging upside down, the assets were easy prey, and even though Mina desperately shuffled them from side to side, paining her belly all the more from struggling against the trapeze, the mordant contraptions snapped to her nipples without delay.

Mina groaned and gritted her teeth as the compression started to take hold, wringing all feeling from the points of her breasts, save the standard throb that started to grow worse as Rache paid out the cord.

Grabbing her left big toe, she threaded the cord around it and yanked tight. The clamp hauled suddenly at Mina's left breast, pulling fiercely at the nipple, stretching it out and making it erupt with havoc. Mina threw her head up, a grimace ruling her features, her eyes screwed shut as she stifled her howl.

Snorting for breath, she felt the girl lift her toe up. She tried to resist, but bound so effectively there was nothing she could do as the tormentor simply grabbed her foot in both hands and wrenched up, ensuring that her extremity was raised as much as it would go. Tying off the cord, Rache left Mina hopelessly wracked by anguish. Her foot was painfully contorted against the demands of the fetters, and her raised toe was linked to her stretched nipple. Any attempt to lower her foot from this position would inflict more havoc to her breast, and in seconds she felt the muscles and tendons of the appendage start to pulsate with strain as she tried desperately to maintain the required pose. She could not keep her foot up forever, but the consequences would have her striving to.

The fight to resist the raising of the other foot was sterner when Rache grabbed it in her red-nailed hands. Mina hissed and channelled the pain into her strength, using it to help her resist. Suddenly she let loose a squeal as Rache merely grabbed the dangling cord and tugged it, afflicting her breast, trying to coerce Mina into obeying. She refused, holding to her stubbornness, the girl unable to defeat Mina's fight to keep her foot down and free of the cord.

Without any change in her temperament, Rache stood up and walked calmly to the wall where she selected a rattan cane. Locking her fist to the crooked handle, she took hold of the other end and flexed the weapon as she walked past Mina's face. Mina looked at the stern device with a sense of calamity, knowing how brutal the effects of such a weapon would prove, even without the compiled layers of bruises from her previous intense session. But she could not give in – she just could not.

The girl stepped behind her and thrashed the cane down, the slender sceptre of bamboo releasing a damning hum upon the air before a sound thwack echoed through the room. Mina tensed, every muscle suddenly flying to attention in answer of the impact, the virulence pouring through her buttocks, feeding on every other welt that had been laid on her the previous night. The strike made her foot kick down, suddenly wrenching at her nipple, making her scream rise to new levels of clarity and pitch before she jerked her foot back up, shaking as her nipple and rear pulsated abominably.

The cane descended thrice more, Rache employing

swift and terribly hard strokes to break Mina's resistance. As soon as the fourth had landed the girl poked the tip of the weapon into Mina's rear, the issue of Poseidon lubricating its entry. With a startled croak she felt it push in a short distance, and remain lodged there.

As Mina tried to fathom the mental machinations that conjured such whimsical deeds, her foot was grabbed. Before she could reapply herself it was yanked up most painfully and the cord pulled extra tight to have her wailing, all sense of dignity forsaken. She pleaded and begged the girl, promising anything if she would just take the horrible devices off her, but the girl merely looked at her blankly, observing only her suffering. With a satisfied smile she plucked the cords, making the taut strands vibrate like guitar strings as the cane fell from Mina's rear and clattered on the floor behind her.

Mina bellowed her vituperative exclamations, spitting insults and hatred at the girl for her actions. It was taking effort to hide her masochism, to hide away the fact that there was a secret portion of herself that loved this mistreatment, that was enthralled with the idea of lifetime captivity and servitude to a pitiless sadistic force. But she was more enamoured with being a Pegasus and she could not afford to lose herself to the pleasure she was covertly finding amidst her agony. If she relented, if she let herself be swallowed by her vices, she would give up and perhaps never exploit a valuable chance to escape. Hope was still in her heart that she might gain reprieve, but the more the enigmatic girl paraded her salacious body and cruel intentions before Mina, the more she was finding it hard to resist her.

Rache watched her spill her false venom for a moment and then lifted a finger to her own lips in imitation of a 'ssssh' gesture.

Stepping to the wall, she furnished herself with a roll of bright red duct tape. With a tug she pulled out a foot long ribbon, which she bit into and tore off. Attaching this to the side of Mina's ribcage, she let it dangle as she added two others in readiness for use. She then laid the roll down between Mina's raised shoulders, using her as a makeshift table while she worked. Opening the laces at the back of her trousers, she hooked her thumbs into the waistband and wriggled her hips, peeling down the tight black skin to reveal her naked, hairless loins. Mina fought the rising urges of lust and turned them into a renewed struggle against her bonds, her efforts paining her breasts all the more effectively as the clamps tightened with every motion.

Reaching behind her, she ferreted in her buttocks and drew at something. A rustle of moisture and motion reached Mina's ears as she strained to keep her attention on the torturer.

With a twinge and a gasp Rache removed the jelly butt plug from her bottom, bringing it around before her. The implement was a large pink ball, the semi-translucent orb held by a brief stalk on a small oval base. The flat base revealed why Mina had failed to notice it when buried in Rache's rear, but not what she was intending to do with it. Was Mina going to be plugged with something that had been in her oppressor?

As the girl stepped forward with the plug in one hand, Mina's expression changed to one of dismay. 'No, surely you're kidding,' she gasped, only to have the girl act with a burst of celerity. Her free hand clapped to Mina's cheeks, squeezing, the pointed nails exuding spires of discomfort as her jaws were kept forcibly parted. 'No, please!' she wailed, her words distorted as she wriggled and bucked, the words being cut off as the warm sphere was forced into her mouth, acting in mockery of a ball gag. The humiliation tore at Mina, making her excited and full of hatred simultaneously. The girl held it in place as Mina gurgled and choked, fighting to get it out as a strip of tape was pulled from her skin. The extremely sticky ribbon tugged at her skin as it was torn free and smoothed over the base of the plug and onto her cheeks. Mina mewled in pitiful tones as the plug was taped into position in her mouth, the other two strips running as a cross over the base, leaving her unable to get the accursed thing free.

Humbled by the deed she felt her submission rise, her capacity to loathe the girl melting as she proved again just how ruthless she was going to be. Mina could not help but think how marvellous a dominatrix she was. Any other female would fail to satisfy Mina's hunger for such depravity, but this girl was raised to it, knew nothing else, she would never stop, never relent, she would make Mina suffer forever. She tried to tell herself that it was the pain deluding her, but deep down she knew she needed this, and if she could not be a Pegasus, she would happily loiter here. But for now she had hope, and until that was extinguished she was unable to fully lose herself to her role as a hapless slave to debauched appetites.

With the taste of the tormentor ruling her palate, Mina watched as the girl lifted her trousers and refastened them, stretching herself back into the tight fitting sheaths of latex. With her single garment back upon her, she walked to the wall and removed a long dressage whip. Clutching the lengthy weapon she settled down before the main door, sitting back and laying against the heavy vault that sealed them in together.

Using it with lethargic touches, she reached out and absently played the cords on Mina's body, twanging them, using the long strut to reach across and pull at them, increasing their woe in brief sessions. Her features never changed as she worked, her innate need to cause distress being fed by Mina's suffering. On occasion the whip flashed aside, giving a light flick to a trapped breast, making Mina scream as she was tormented by the venomous girl, who simply continued to sprawl as though watching television, tormenting her interactive viewing programme whenever the mood took her.

For hours Mina was left in such a state, her mind burning with the need to get out, her body awash with mayhem. Every part of her hurt, and nothing emerged to counter it, her suffering complete and worsened by the knowledge that this was merely her initiation.

A final swat had Mina squawking onto the gag, chewing on the soft instrument as Rache arose and replaced the whip before starting to unfasten her additions to Mina's form. Her toes were released, and the clamps removed simultaneously to prompt Mina into a wailing fit where she jiggled and wept freely, the sudden intense flash of returning sensation to her crushed nerves bringing about a vibrant jolt of pain.

The fetters were unfastened and a tiny chain locked them together, hobbling her as the chain holding her numbed arms aloft was taken away. Mina whimpered as they were brought down, the muscles held too long to this pose to accept any other.

Brought from the trapeze she collapsed on the floor, crying out as her stomach was freed, the residual pains coursing through her like lightning, crippling her for long minutes as she slowly recovered from her prolonged bondage at the hands of the harridan.

The tape was torn from her face and her slack lips let the gag dribble out and roll onto the floor as Rache stood over her, towering like some despicable deity of torture, brooding over her victim. Looking up across the jet mirrors of her elegant legs, Mina panned her stare up across her bared breasts to eyes of uncaring acrimony. The image burned into her mind, dissolving her loathing, making her melt before this goddess that ruled her so efficiently, a creature bred to make Mina pay.

Looking back down she shuffled her head over and placed her trembling lips to the girl's feet, taking lingering licks of the toes, running her tongue upon them and between them, her breathing irregular, broken by lust, her loins damp with hunger.

Rache did not interrupt Mina's worship of her, and once one foot had been licked, she placed it on the back of Mina's head, her balance excellent, allowing her to place weight on the toes and force Mina's face deeper against the other foot. The expression of dominance made Mina wilt further, her tongue between the girl's painted toes.

The foot came down and pushed into Mina's shoulder, rolling her over onto her back. Lying on her rubber-entombed arms, she looked up from her humble pose and saw the girl lean down and run a finger though Mina's vulva. Mina jerked and croaked, the mere touch almost having brought her to climax from her ultra aroused state. The girl straightened up and rubbed her fingers together, assessing the moisture she had discovered.

Stepping over Mina's form, she recovered one of the clamps and returned. Winding the end of the cord about her palm, she lowered the implement between Mina's legs. 'Oh no!' Mina wailed, trying to rise. 'Not there, please, mistress!' A naked foot pressed just below her breasts, the weight shoving Mina back to the floor. There was a soft snap and she flew into paroxysms as the awful tool gnawed at her wanton clitoris, the engorged morsel an all too easy target. Rache rode Mina's suffering for a moment until it started to subside, whereupon she started to give small tugs to the cord, the yard of excess forcing shudders of new mayhem into Mina's pudenda.

'Stop, I'm getting up!' she cried, fighting to rise, her body exhausted, and surprisingly Rache did not hamper her, allowing Mina to stand, wheezing and panting with effort.

Turning towards the door on the right, she then gave pulls to make Mina whine and scamper behind her, the impossibly short steps making her slow, a limitation that resulted in constant pulls to the cord.

The door whirred open and Mina wandered haphazardly behind Rache. The corridor beyond bore six more doorways on either side, each of them accessing a dark chamber wherein she saw a catalogue of devices she would no doubt come to enjoy and dread. She could vaguely detect stocks of various configurations, gallows, pits, cages, poles and beams, hanging chains and all manner of strange eldritch forms that she could not even hope to identify.

The image of these numerous sources of sadomasochistic pleasure curled in Mina's heart, making her regard the girl responsible for cruelly towing her with a lewd prurience. Mina's eyes met the image of her rear, riding against the latex, the smooth rounded peaks black and catching the refractions of light across their tight panes, the grip of it down her legs as her elegant back swayed with her steps, her long hair swishing from side to side as they went through the doorway at the very end of the corridor.

Flicking the overhead light on, the spotlight beam dropped down to reveal a bland room. It looked almost like a site of execution – the dominating chair of steel riveted in place at the heart of the dazzling beam, its surfaces sparkling with wicked glee. The polished steel structure seemed to glow as she stared across its rigid dimensions, the chair made to contain even the most berserk struggles to break free.

The metal seat bore slight grooves so that a female bottom might settle in, her thighs being parted wide to run down the two flat panels descending on the front legs. The tall back of the chair was just short of being as wide as her torso, withering in further at the shoulder area so that it could remain smaller than the dimensions of the head.

From the back, two metal poles curled around to hold steel plate armrests as long as her forearms, and all across the stern device, dense leather trammels had been riveted into irrevocable place. The various belts hung lazily from the metal chair, awaiting their first victim, the chair clearly being new and unused.

Underneath the four stout legs of the device was a grill, like a drain, and Mina then noticed the subtle hatch in the seat that would allow access to her most intimate and vulnerable areas.

Led by the cruel leash, Mina was delivered to the chair and turned around before being shoved into it. As her buttocks landed on the hard seat she jerked and cried out, her bruised cheeks becoming livid with angst from being so rashly sat upon.

Rache gave spiteful pulls to the clit clamp, crippling any hope of resisting as Mina spasmed, wriggling against the arm sheath. Rache exploited this debilitated state to open her hobble and use clips at the base of the chair to catch her fetters, anchoring Mina temporarily to ease the full process of restraint.

With her legs spread lewdly, the inner tendons strained from such a pose, Mina could only watch impotently as a belt at the back of her head was pulled around and presented to her mouth. At first she resisted, refusing to open for the girl, but a slap to her cheek made her will melt and roused her desire for more. She again declined to obey, gaining another stinging swat from the gorgeous dominatrix. Another slap stung her face and she finally relented so the girl might run the leather ribbon through. The dense hide was inflexible, and even when she crushed her jaws to it, it failed to collapse and allow her to close her mouth. Rache tightened the strip with a stern yank, pulling Mina's skull tightly against the headrest.

Resting in the solid arms of the chair, Mina felt the buckles down the latex sheath being unfastened and the girl started to pick at the laces. The opportunity to try and break out was close. Against all reason, Mina found herself deliberating whether to try or not. Yes, she wanted escape, but also, she had a mistress dedicated to her, who would never stop, never leave her again. She had suffered loss and anguish when separated from her previous owners and beloved castes and fellow slaves, if she would just surrender herself to Rache, give the girl her body and soul, she could find paradise. But every time she pictured life it wasn't in the skies, and that was where her true love lay.

Unable to bend over now, Mina wailed as the clamp was removed, the eruption of stolen feeling making her rear clap against the seat as she jiggled up and down, her loins thrusting into the air as though they could fling free the loathsome sensations.

Again her enfeebled and distracted condition was used to condemn her, and acting with speed and skill Rache slipped the latex sheath free and stretched an arm down. A buckled belt grabbed at the wrist and the leather strap tightened with a brutal yank, pressing the flesh against the steel sides of the backrest.

Mina tore her other arm free to try and unfasten the restraints and get out before she was fully immobilised, but the girl had defeated her already. Rache grabbed Mina's arm and held tightly to it with both of hers. Full of rage Mina burbled against the gag, sending rivulets over the leather barricade as she tugged and thrashed, trying to get it free. But the girl was stronger than she appeared, and Mina was wailing in jeopardy as Rache forced the limb down, bringing it slowly towards the side. A knee pressed into her forearm, paining the flesh and making Mina croak with the discomfort as the restraint was tightened into place.

Rache stepped back to admire her handiwork, her dull stare panning across Mina as she lay bound to the chair, her body straining against the bonds, a slight glaze of sweat being conjured from her skin by the fight to gain her freedom.

The girl began her work with steady precision, taking up the rest of the trammels and setting them firmly to Mina's helpless frame. Added strips ran over her upper arms, over her forearms, and about her throat. A pair of leather ribbons acted like strangling jaws, running closely above and below her breasts, scooping them up between them and squeezing to her ribs, oppressing each breath and making the feminine flesh swell with added feeling. Another captured her waist, hauling in the softer region as another secured her hips, dragging firmly back to pin her hindquarters into position. Straps ran over her inner thighs and above her knees before another was set below the joint.

Every inch of Mina was immobile, and she tensed her muscles, the feel of the straps rising as they dug into her flesh. It felt good to be left so helpless, to be left utterly compliant to another's will. The girl could and would do anything she wished now, and there was nothing Mina could do to stop her.

The girl stepped up and straddled Mina's lap, settling in, making her libido churn with the feel of latex-coated buttocks seating themselves on her, the thighs of this goddess of pain resting on her own petrified ones. The naked breasts of the girl were just short of her own, Mina's eyes wide as they regarded the torso of the exquisite female, studying her, aching to kiss and lick her, to even just touch her would be a blessing. But the girl was spitefully teasing, letting Mina strain and struggle, betray her hunger for Rache and be starved.

The pointed nails of the girl rose and closed on Mina's breasts, running the daggers gently over the skin before inflicting gentle prods about the aureole, introducing flicks of distress. After tapping her nails steadily all about her nipples, she began to point them into the swollen nuggets, jabbing them lightly so as to make the engorged flesh shudder with discomfort.

The girl tormented her thus for a while, leisurely testing the full spectrum of Mina's responses to it before she merely closed her fingers to the assailed morsels and squeezed. Mina's respiration rasped over the gag, her chest fighting the straps with each gasping breath. The effects of the fierce holds were magnified by the straps and by the recent prods, and as the girl began to roll her fingers, Mina was groaning and sobbing for mercy, but Rache merely continued to watch Mina's expression as tears slid down her features. Rache continued the maltreatment until Mina was a sobbing wreck, and then merely released them and stepped from Mina's body.

Sighing with relief, Mina could still feel the residual ache in her breasts, the glorious lingering trace soothing her, the act having rekindled her masochistic need. With endorphins flowing again she was hungry for more discipline, to be made the girl's slave. It was not a futile wish, and though she knew she would regret such thoughts when the worst of her punishments were being applied, she knew she would love them afterwards and want more, and be all the more sated the harsher and more callous they had been.

The girl moved behind the chair and settled down, the soft murmur of stretching rubber making Mina's desire curl within her. What would this girl do when she realised just how aroused Mina was by her? Would her torments be affected when she discovered Mina's insatiable hunger for abuse and humiliation?

The girl strode to the wall and pressed her hand to it as Mina watched through tear-flecked eyes, the beads of moisture hanging on her eyelashes distorting her vision, making every refraction of light wink like an angelic star. A hatch opened up and she reached in, drawing free a magic wand, the black stem of the handle bearing the small strut and bulbous vibrating head of the exquisite sex toy. Mina bit the gag with glee as she beheld the device, for it was a source of pleasure that made any vibrator a pathetic runner-up by comparison. A roll of red tape was also removed and brought over, Rache closing the concealed hatch and leaving Mina wondering what else was hidden in the very structure of the chamber.

A socket hidden on the back of the chair accepted the wand and the girl paid out the cord, bringing it over and between Mina's parted thighs. Dipping it into Mina's sex, she tensed with the feel of it sliding against her, the girl pushing so that her clitoris rested gently upon its soon to be thrumming head. Two strips of tape were used to secure it in place, leaving Mina unable to escape it, not that she would even wish to.

Rache turned it on, using the more lethargic setting, the device breaking into an oscillating rhythm that sent astonishingly intense vibrations through her sex. A rattling exhale poured from Mina's throat, the heady bliss galloping through her, making her wither into the stern arms of bondage, her eyelids fluttering, her jaw dropping open.

The girl watched her reaction for a moment and then stepped forward to turn around and present her latex-sheathed rear to Mina's ravenous gaze. Shuddering on the wand, Mina yearned to touch her, to feel the flesh that owned her, wrapped tightly in the fetishistic shell.

The girl shuffled back, bringing herself a little closer. Mina's hands stretched against the wrist straps, her fingers straining forward, her tips just short of being able to touch, the fabric beckoning, making her livid with need. She would give anything to just run her hand over the rear of her owner, just once, just to hold it and feel Rache's power over her. The quivering head of the wand blithely continued its singular mission, drawing intense pleasure from Mina's womb, making her tremble, every depraved thought and segment of longing bolstered by the bliss, turned from a simple peccadillo into a raging insatiable obsession.

Rache moved back a little more, offering herself to Mina's senses. Her arm was burning from the effort she was placing in trying to brush a finger against the girl, the straps digging painfully in. But she needed this more than anything and was all too willing to endure to acquire it.

Another small move finally let her very tips brush the fabric, the smooth black skin running under her touch, elating her senses. Rache moved closed still, permitting Mina to actually employ her fingers in full and to ease the need to stretch so acutely. Mina's unblinking stare was locked to the sight of the glorious rump before her, tight thighs set apart a little as the girl stood to attention, her hands on her hips in a classic dominating pose, allowing her servile wretch to touch her.

Was it a reward for all her suffering, and that which was to come? If so, it was more than adequate. Mina would undergo ten times what she had already just to earn this pleasure, to be tied tightly down, mounted on a wand and allowed to run her lowly hand upon the hindquarters of her taciturn deity.

Again the girl moved back onto the fawning touch, permitting Mina to run her hand upon the pert buttocks, to trace their contours, her mouth watering with the fantasy of licking it, of being smothered by it as she had been when Poseidon ravished her. At the time she resented it, but now she was here, riding the buzzing head of the wand, she could think of nothing she would rather endure.

Her hand slid between the cleft of Rache's rear, the latex stretched tight upon, swinging from the peaks of her buttocks, slung across the valley as it dipped down between her legs. Running her palm between the girl's thighs she felt the taut flesh, rubbed the latex-bound hide, the back of her hand being tickled by the other inner thigh.

The girl gave a small shudder of response as Mina continued to stroke her, Mina's mind burning with arousal, making the wand's work all the easier as she felt a climax develop in sudden bounding waves. Her hand held tightly to the rounded stem of Rache's inner thigh, clasping the firm physique of her private tyrant as she jerked with orgasm, the sensations overwhelming.

Again she climaxed, this one merged with a growing pain, her sex growing raw, chafed by the continuing attack. The eagerness with which her sex had met the arrival of the wand quickly vanished as it grew intolerant and then hateful of the implement.

Rache moved away, Mina's finger sliding on her latex hide and then falling free as she was deserted. Rache turned about and continued to watch as Mina started to grimace and wriggle, trying to get herself off the baleful tool that was continuing its work, crafting rising discomfort instead of pleasure, as though a setting had been changed to completely alter its purpose. Rache had turned an implement of ultimate pleasure into a weapon of unprecedented frustrating angst.

Mina gurgled and wept, fighting her bonds, writhing upon the humming head, her thighs flickering with bursts of tension as she struggled to find some way in which to alleviate the ongoing havoc. Burbling pleas spilled freely from her, her spread lips leaving them distorted and virtually unintelligible, not that it mattered to the girl in her world of eternal quiet.

Mina looked to her oppressor with pleading, her eyes dripping salty trails down her cheeks, her body fighting the chair with fervour as she suffered for the pleasure of Rache's innate and cultivated sadism.

Suddenly the girl stiffened with a small twinge and reached behind her back, bringing a small dart into view. She looked aghast at the steel projectile and brushed a thumb over the bright blue feathered plume, then her eyes rolled and she collapsed, the dart chiming brightly on the floor as it fell from her grip.

Mina stared with confusion down the corridor to see two shadowy forms approach, one of them moving boldly, the other approaching with less ease. Flickering her stare down to the crumpled form of Rache, she could see the softly regulated breathing of unconsciousness, the girl merely sedated, not slain.

Stretching her physique against the bonds, Mina wondered just what the hell was going on, this event being contrary to everything that had been explained to her about her incarceration.

Chapter Seventeen

Mina looked up and found the regal owner of all she had known and loved. Clad in his ragged robes, he slid the tranquilliser pistol back into the internal folds of his garments, slotting it into a shoulder holster.

The eternal ghost was at his side, her tubes connected to the portable mechanism that sustained her, the wheeled box following her like a metal dog. The zip down her face had been opened, allowing the two flaps to be pulled back, unveiling two plastic eyepieces, the interiors damp with condensation.

'Charybdis?' she quizzed, her words corrupted by the belt as she raised her eyebrows, the astonishment making her forget a moment about the pain between her legs.

Stepping forward he opened the gagging belt and pulled it out of her mouth, letting Mina lick her lips and stammer her words as she continued to ride the throbbing toy.

'Please, master, turn it off,' she sobbed, her head able to droop a little to stare at the accursed thing oscillating against her. 'Please, it's too much pain!'

'Of course, Mina, I don't want any outside forces impeding your judgement,' he announced, and flicked the switch. Mina sagged with a rasp of relief, her loins still scorched from their chafing experience but at least no more distress was being added to her already considerable reserve.

'Judgement, master?' she murmured after a moments consideration, wondering what was going on. No one was supposed to be able to enter here. She was supposed to be here forever, so why had this intrusion taken place?

Had Poseidon sponsored it? Or was he oblivious to the actions of Charybdis?

'I have a very special offer for you, Mina,' he said softly, kneeling down and looking up at her as beads of sweat trickled down her brow. 'But first I have a question... are you ready?' he smiled, his wicked leer hiding some terrible secret that he was relishing unleashing.

'Do you recall a woman in my employ... Melissa was her name?' he began, causing Mina to peer at him curiously. He knew of the prime informant who had allowed her to delve into his affairs. How long had he known this? Had he watched her from afar, traced her progress as Jupiter had? 'You see, someone had been hacking into my little empire, poking around and doing a very good job of concealing their tracks. The best of my elite could not find the source,' he continued, running his hand down her cheek as she sat bound and vulnerable before him.

Why was he talking of a life she had deserted long ago? It was an existence destroyed by her time in the complex, then further erased by being made into an eel before being forced further back into her mind during her stint as a pony, and even more distanced from her thoughts during the time of training and experiences as a Pegasus.

'So I ordered all personnel with the relevant access to be watched, and I found that a spy for Turan had been using one of my people to gain access,' he elaborated. 'The spy was a particularly nasty piece of work. She confused my employee with notions of lesbian love, exploiting her, using poor Melissa like an object. Which is ironic, because that is pretty much what she has become,' he laughed, turning to face the latex form behind him.

'M-Mel... Melissa?' she stammered, recognising the

curves she had run her hands over and kissed, the Asian woman sealed deep within her own latex tomb.

'You got it in one,' he smiled, rising and walking behind the contorted display of wanton latex bondage that had been Mina's lover. Sudden guilt struck her, regret for having delivered the woman to this fate. 'You always were a smart operative, Mina.'

Mina was now besotted with such deeds of extravagant bondage and control, but Melissa was an innocent, someone she had just used and abused to get what she wanted. Now the woman was doomed to an eternity of smothering confinement.

'So, little Melissa takes the fall for industrial espionage and treason – we handle some very sensitive government information. But before the authorities came for her, I called her to my office and extended an offer to this crying emotional wreck. It was a life of imprisonment no matter what she did. Either the state provided it, or I did. I had barely said the words before she agreed. I can't blame her though, can you? After all, imagine this luscious little form locked in some state pen? She wouldn't last long, would she? And it would have been a crime in itself to let her be wasted like that.'

'Why, Charybdis?' Mina asked with meek effort, anger and guilt choking her words. 'Why did you do it to her?'

The man span around and jabbed an accusing finger at her, his teeth bared, his face a mask of fury. 'Because I saved her life after you ruined it!' he spat, then calming his tones as Mina was left reeling from the stark truth, he straightened his sleeves and took a sigh of composure. Stepping behind the girl, he reached around and placed his hands on the smooth flat plain of her stomach, submerged beneath a smothering layer of stretched black.

'I told her she would be my companion, that she would be kept bound in latex, and that she would stay with me

221

forever,' he summarised, rubbing the tight artificial skin, savouring the feel of the nubile woman locked beneath it.

'Why are you telling me this, Charybdis?' she asked, tears spilling down her cheeks. She had never really borne any emotion towards Melissa, because she had none within her. But now that she had been shattered by her delicious slavery, her pent-up psyche was set loose to thrust such long denied traits upon her in abundance, making up for the years they had languished forsaken and lost in the bleakest recesses of her soul. The guilt she felt was overwhelming and had her wishing for her old cold dispassionate edge.

'Because I want another companion, another someone to rescue from one mode of incarceration to install in another, and I think you would be ideal, dear Mina,' he said, causing her to suddenly stop her breath, stare at him for a moment, and then move her glower to the latex spectre haunting his side.

'You want me to… to become like Melissa?'

'Exactly. An indistinguishable twin sister. Except for the height, of course.'

'But I…' she began, trying to form a denial, to refuse out of hand, but the sight of Melissa was captivating, rousing her depraved libido, devoured alive by rubber, a prisoner in her own body, tormented and abused every moment of her life, pleasured, teased and frustrated.

'I want no misconceptions. You will be sealed in the uniform for the rest of your life, like Melissa here. I'll torture you, I'll pleasure you, and you'll come to love them both, just as Melissa now does. She probably bitterly regrets her decision, but you, Mina, you can appreciate it in ways she cannot. I've seen you, I've seen your eyes and I know your soul. You want to be mine, to trek at my side, to be with me every second of every day as a defenceless and utterly vulnerable toy. And all the

222

while you can know that I have a wonderful glow in my heart from seeing you bound thus, a prisoner for the rest of your days, every facet of you controlled and regulated only by me.'

Mina stared long and hard at Melissa, a curving sculpture of burnished jet, her eyes glistening within the confines of the inner hood, full of tears, for though she probably hated Mina for using her, she would not wish her doom on anyone. But Mina was unlike her former lover in that she actually craved it, that such bondage was not going to be imposed, it was going to be adored.

'And if I refuse?' she asked.

Charybdis waved a dismissing hand as though such an eventuality did not trouble him in the slightest. 'If you refuse then I simply leave you to the fate Poseidon prescribed for you. I switch the wand back on, lock the door, and when Rache awakens, everything will be as before.'

Mina looked down at the fallen form of the girl, realising that when she awoke she would be even more spiteful. But that was not a consideration. She had to choose what was best for her and forsake everything else. She knew now there would be no return ever to the caste of Pegasus, but with one change in plan, Charybdis's offer could give her something of equal bliss.

'I'll do it, on one condition, and its not negotiable,' she stated firmly, brooking no defying of her wishes.

'I am listening,' replied Charybdis, intrigued. Folding his ragged arms across his robes he regarded her from beneath an intense and studying brow.

'Starting from this day, and every year thereafter, Melissa and I are released from the uniforms to spend one full night and one full day together in a private room with food, drink, no monitoring and whatever other luxuries are currently on offer,' she stated, staring into his eyes with purpose.

Charybdis looked back into her defiant stare and then let a smile creep through the corners of his mouth. 'Done, sweet Mina, done. I'll have you released and brought back to my domain. Once there, you'll be sent to a room where Melissa will join you. Make the most of it, slave, your uniform awaits after your little lesbian tryst.' He turned, drawing Melissa after him, her head fighting the posture collar to try and keep a startled look to Mina.

Clapping his hands a flurry of activity emerged from deep in the corridor as six women in latex cat-suits emerged. No portion of them was visible, the black garments covering their hands, setting them on stiletto heels, their hoods fitted with acute silver eyepieces and a small respirator nozzle at their noses, their mouths stretched wide by an internal gag. They were tall and strong, their muscles pressing against the latex shell that smothered them, the stern guards like wraiths, their mirrored eyes spotted in the corridor long before they emerged from the darkness.

Two of them carried folds of latex stretched between them like a hammock, the body bag flaccid and empty, clearly Mina's means of transport down to the underwater domain of her one true owner. It felt like she was going home.

Another pair held a weeping girl between them, the slender young woman grizzling in despair. She was obviously aware of her fate, and Mina could guess that she was going to be her replacement, to be locked in with Rache for the rest of her life. What horrors Rache would inflict on her would remain between them and languish in the realms of Mina's darkest fantasies.

The final pair began to unbuckle Mina, removing her from the chair as the rubber sack was opened up. Exploiting her weakness and willingness to obey, Mina was taken down and slotted into the bondage bag. Loose internal slots accepted her arms and legs, and the hood piece was pulled down to let a gag be placed in her mouth, the ball transfixed by a small tube so she could breathe.

The bag was zipped up, leaving her sealed within a loose cocoon of cold black darkness that clung to her body, making her squirm with delectation at the sensation of being so methodically entombed. The sound of inflation began as the women started to force bulbs onto various nozzles and begin the process. The bag started to swell around her, growing slowly, applying a soft squeeze to her form, relentlessly swallowing her up in its folds, making her feel as though she were dissolving, all capacity for movement evaporating with every new squeeze of a latex gloved fist to an inflator.

Mina sighed and groaned as the pressure continued to mount, the latex vice closing on her, hugging her from all directions, seeking to compress her even further. Finally, once she was crushed tight, unable to even curl a finger against the pressurised coffin, the women stopped.

Lost in darkness she was taken up, ready to be spirited away and begin the voyage home. Deep in her tomb Mina wept with joy, elated, eager to begin her sentence once she had stolen a day with her cruelly jilted lover.

Chapter Eighteen

After an eternity contemplating her future and past, Mina felt the nozzles being touched. A hiss of pressure sounded as escaping air rushed from the tight balloon suit, the sack deflating upon her. The zip was opened and Mina was dragged roughly out, her eyes granting her a shimmering white pane for a view, her captivity in absolute darkness leaving the outside world a dazzling source of unbearable brilliance.

She was lifted up, her body drenched in sweat. She saw the vague image of a door being opened by one of the black rubber spectres and as the portal swung wide one of the latex ghosts shoved Mina in the shoulder, sending her staggering forward. Her limbs were stiff and weary from her long sentence in the inflated sack and they folded beneath her. She dropped to the floor, flitting her gaze back to see the heavy door slam shut and be locked from without.

Shielding her eyes as they slowly accustomed to seeing things other than pitch-blackness, Mina examined her new location.

The small room had another door before her without lock or handle. The chamber itself bore a shower cubicle in the corner, with towels and other toiletries set on shelves beside it. There was a toilet, and two dressing tables. The first was a cosmetic table, the dresser having a soft chair before it, with angled mirrors rimmed with lights. Elaborate boxes before the reflective panes bore arrays of make-up and the brushes and sponges required to apply it. Upon the other there had been placed several varieties of lingerie, the seductive garments a delightful consideration from Charybdis. Mina traced her fingers over the silken fabrics and smiled with glee as she looked beneath and saw a menagerie of shoes. Charybdis was intent on letting her preen herself and look as alluring as possible for her lover, a consideration she felt immensely grateful for.

Opening the shower door she turned it on, changed the settings until a hot cascade spat from the nozzle. Stepping into the jets she shuddered with exquisite merriment as she felt the perspiration slide from her. Taking the soap she washed and started to use a razor to shave away all excess hair.

Stepping out of the shower she dried herself, checked that she had shorn every follicle and missed nothing, and turned her attention to her appearance.

Her hair had grown back a little since last she had been tended, and after a quick towel dry and the application of a hair dryer to desiccate the strands, the small spines stood up to attention as a bristling carpet. Mina smiled, the severe look suiting her well as she opened the boxes and began to ferret around for colours that fulfilled her purpose.

Highlighting her eyes with shade, running a pencil over her eyebrows after plucking them to a more slender shape, Mina ran a subtle lipstick across her lips and assessed the finished product.

It had been so long since she'd seen her own image this clearly, and even longer since she'd refined her features thus. She had to admit that she was greatly pleased with the result, and couldn't recall ever looking so attractive. She mused that slavery must agree with her and then turned to the matter of attire.

Sliding her smooth legs into dark fine denier stockings, she straightened the seam down the back and stepped into a thong of midnight satin. Hooking it over her hips she settled the crotch into place, slipping it though her buttocks to press to her rear. She turned and looked at her bottom, the marks of discipline faint and hard to detect, the firm flesh ripe and eager for more.

A strapless bra increased the appeal of her breasts within their shimmering jet cups, and on a whim she added the set of matching opera gloves to the ensemble, the fingers removed so she could file and paint her nails with an ebony sheen.

Sitting back to let the varnish dry she admired the final product, turning on her stockinged feet and assessing her physique. The training of a pony and Pegasus had rebuilt the muscles her eel caste had atrophied, and she was once more a toned and elegant form. Her skin was a wonderful pale colour, the various latex uniforms that had entrapped her like vampires had siphoned out the pink, leaving her an ivory beauty that contrasted the black of her lingerie perfectly. The image of her body tempted Mina to maybe toy with herself, masturbate and exploit the fact of her utter unbound freedom, but she didn't want to take the edge off her hunger, she wanted to save it all for Melissa.

Blowing across the smooth ovals of her nails, she touched them to ensure they were dry and slipped her feet into black stiletto court shoes. Without cause, the door leading out of the room slid aside, exposing a large chamber beyond.

Taking a deep breath, Mina walked through into the bedroom, her heart fluttering with excitement and yearning lust.

The room was furnished solely for what they wished, giving them all Mina had requested. A large four-posted bed sprawled at the heart of the room, the pink satin sheets glistening in the amber haloes of the flickering candles spaced along the walls on opaque steel curls. The dance of the flames sent shuddering shadow across the scene, making it gloomy and mysterious, inviting iniquity.

A table on the left wall was arrayed with selections of food and drink, a minor feast so they might indulge more ordinary appetites. The other wall had a similar table, this one offering far different fare. This table catered to carnal hunger and was armed with a variety of vibrators, toys, lubricants and other sexual devices for their pleasure. Mina smiled at the sight, doubting she would need them, but amused to know they were there just in case.

The opposite wall bore a door through which Melissa had already entered, the slender Asian girl kneeling on the bed, the two of them fed through preparation rooms.

The girl was naked save for a silver thong, her tawny skin smooth and soft of appearance. Her once long hair had been shaven for inclusion in the latex mummifying uniform, and had now grown back down to her ears, an abrupt bob that she had tended as best she could in her own dressing room.

'Hello Melissa,' Mina said softly, wandering slowly towards the bed so as not to frighten her.

'Who are you?' snarled the woman with venom, questioning just who it was who had used her and condemned her to this fate, the revelation that Mina was something else irking her.

'So, you're pissed that I lied to you, that's understandable, but I had no idea I would get you into trouble, you have to believe that,' replied Mina, trying to erase the resentment and fury her imprisonment must have created. Lost in the latex folds, Mina's betrayal and use of her was probably something that had bloated to insane proportions, giving her something to fixate on other than her sensory deprivation and pain.

'I always knew you were using me, Mina, or whoever the hell you are, but I couldn't have imagined how much. Then you left me to… to *this*,' she growled, waving a hand around the room.

'Melissa, I was a spy,' she stated, sitting down on the end of the bed. 'I had no choice but to do my job. But I never meant to hurt you, I looked after you, made sure I covered my tracks so you wouldn't be suspected. My own employer betrayed me, that's what doomed us both. I'm not Cindy, I'm not even Mina any more, I'm a captive here, just like you.'

'Is that supposed to make everything right again?' she hissed, shuffling back across the sheets, retreating from her nemesis, the person she heaped all blame upon for her trials.

Mina sighed and shook her head, looking to the floor. 'Melissa, look, it doesn't really matter what happened. We can banter about who set who up, whose fault it is, who came off worse in this, but the fact is, all I've had recently is torture and punishment, and you've just spent endless months in that latex hell. We're both free for a short time, so do you want to use it, or shall I just call for Charybdis to come and put us in those rubber cells?'

The girl visibly blanched at the thought and gave a slight shudder as she recalled the smothering embrace of the suit.

'Good, I can take that as a no, then?' Mina stated abruptly and climbed up onto the bed, crawling slowly to the cowering girl. Mina had forgotten how gorgeous Melissa was – her curves, her petite form alluring and seductive, her delicate features, her soulful eyes and inviting breasts. It seemed as though a statuesque beauty had been condensed into Melissa's diminutive form, concentrating her beauty, carrying it far above normal. As her gaze wandered across the huddled body of her former lover, Mina felt her insides ignite with need, her arousing journey in the belly of the rubber sack and process of dressing having filled her with a volcanic appetite.

'There was one thing I never lied to you about, Melissa,' she said, closing in on the luscious form.

'And what's that?'

'I do love you, Melissa,' she offered, realising now that she actually did. Before, the very same words had been made up, used to get what she wanted from the girl, but now she meant them, her old dispassion had been removed and when she said the word, it felt right.

'Yeah, of course you do,' the girl retorted sarcastically.

Mina extended a hand and touched Melissa's shoulder, causing her to shy away with a disgruntled shrug.

'Melissa, we don't have much time together, is this how you want to spend it?' Mina stressed with frustration, growing tired of the delay.

Moving in she grabbed hold of the girl, locking one hand about the nape of her neck and pulling her in for a kiss. Their lips pressed together and for a moment Melissa accepted. Then, with a sudden violent pull she sought escape, shaking her head, pushing her hands against Mina's shoulders to get away. 'No, I won't,' she protested, holding Mina off as she continued to try and reel her in.

'Okay, Melissa, I had intended for this to be easier, but you leave me no choice,' Mina said, and shoved instead of pulled, catching Melissa off-guard and casting her to the sheets. Before the girl could react Mina pounced, straddling her torso. Her hands captured Melissa's wrists, pinning her down, her weight keeping the girl under control.

'Get off me, you bitch!' she wailed, struggling against Mina, her head flailing from side to side, her legs kicking and pummelling the mattress as she fought to get out from under the physically superior beauty. 'I *hate* you!'

Mina studied her distress for a moment and then dragged her arms down, running the girl's arms down her sides and then using her stockinged shins to pin them

231

in place.

With her arms freed, Mina reached down and ran the fingers of her left hand into Melissa's hair, feeling it between her fingers before she moved them to the back of her crown and then closed a tight fist to secure a hold. Her right hand moved in and caught Melissa's chin, holding it tight, the two grips upon her head keeping the girl's visage facing up and utterly still.

Mina lowered slowly and placed her lips to Melissa's and kissed her gently, brushing those of the trapped girl. For a moment they remained tensed and rigid, but as Mina let her tongue gently run swirling traces Melissa's resistance started to quickly fade. The tensed jaws of the girl began to grow less firm, and Mina loosened her holds a little to show that she was seeking compliance, not dominance over someone who was going to fight her every step of the way. Her right hand lifted away from Melissa's chin, and the girl stayed where she was. She left her other hand in place, keeping her rule in force, revealing the girl's submissive nature as she relented to Mina's authority because of her displayed power.

Running the back of her nails down the girl's cheek, she shivered and her arms strained against Mina's trapping legs, not to try and escape, but to ensure she was secure. The delicate hands of Melissa curled up and cupped the sides of Mina's rear, stroking the flesh as she lay trapped beneath her.

Melissa's passion exploded like a dormant volcano, her gasping pants being accompanied by frenzied kisses. Mina could feel the hands groping at her, their hunger to trace her contours hampered by the pose. Lifting up a little, she grabbed Melissa's hands and brought them out, keeping no question as to who was in control.

Mina placed the hands to her own hips, letting Melissa feel the thong before raising them, dragging the girl's palms up her curves until she brought them around to her breasts. The girl audibly groaned with libidinous response as she cupped the firmness. The feel of satin and wanton flesh under her hands after the prolonged denial of anything save latex imprisonment had her wilting with sudden and pressing need.

Releasing her holds, Mina let her left hand drop and brush against Melissa's breasts, tickling the nipples with a cursory touch before wandering the hand up and enclosing it to her throat, holding her in place as the girl sighed and her hands began to caress and fawn on her. Trembling fingers slid under the bra cups and felt her nipples, the small swirls Melissa imparted to her teats bringing Mina to attention.

Mina's right hand rolled down her own torso, tickling her skin and sliding under the front of her thong, her finger running through her sex, covering itself in a sheen of moisture. With this physical proof of her arousal, she lifted it free and kept her hand pressed gently to Melissa's throat before holding the finger above the girl's lips.

'Taste,' she ordered delicately, lifting her hand a little so the girl could raise her head. Closing her lips almost to the knuckle, Melissa rolled her head back, running them along the finger as her tongue flashed across the skin, spreading the taste of her lover across her palette. As though affected by a narcotic, her eyes rolled and her body quaked. The hand at her throat shifted round and enclosed the back of her neck, and as Mina fed her back onto the finger, she shifted her body, moving down Melissa's body while bringing the girl upright with her.

Cradling the girl's head, Mina removed the finger and drew down her right bra cup, exposing the turgid nipple. Another soft pull brought Melissa's freed mouth onto the bud, Mina's hand keeping her upright, the other running her nails up and down the smooth back of the girl, leaving soft rosy lines from her light scratches. Melissa's tongue was lunatic upon her breast, sucking and kissing, lapping and flitting as she adored the teat in all its joyous intensity.

Mina's head rolled back with the glorious feel of the attention, holding the girl tighter, pressing her to her breast as the other clawed and ran across the fields of her shoulder blades. The meagre discomfort was a lethal aphrodisiac to the girl, her attentions escalating wildly. Her hands flashed around and held Mina's rear, groping with fervour, filling her prurient senses with the feel of Mina's buttocks. Melissa's fingers traced the satin thong as it plunged between her cheeks and then started to run wildly across her back, her devotion spent on exploring every inch of the female who ruled her.

The supporting hand moved the girl back for a moment, her lips coming away from the moistened nipple. Without word Melissa's hands rose behind Mina and expertly picked the fastenings of her bra, opening it and letting it fall away, revealing her goal in full.

Mina pulled her back in onto the other nipple, filling Melissa's face with her flesh, relishing the feel of the eager tongue as it zealously serviced her. Mina drank her fill of the event, and then decided to change the nature of their exchange a little.

Shoving back, she pushed Melissa onto the sheets and moved off her. She flipped her onto her front and placed a knee into her back. Melissa mewled softly as she was held down, Mina exercising a moment of control. Flinging her hand down, she spanked Mina's thighs, aiming inward, driving them apart and then by soft slaps to the inner regions she made the girl spread herself even wider.

With a spry jump Mina dropped between Melissa's parted thighs, clapping her hands to them, applying her palms to the flesh as searing spanks that echoed through the room. Melissa gave a whimpering lust-filled gurgle and sank into the sheets, lost to the storm of sensation. Mina held her there for a moment and then moved her hands up, pressing down, running the thighs and then the rear of the girl beneath her palms.

A hand ferreted into her underwear, curling around the back of it and then hauling up. The material dug into her crotch and started to exert its demands. Melissa moaned softly and gathered her legs, shifting her knees forward so that her haunches rose up with the hoisting pull to the underwear. Mina smiled and wrenched more distinctly on her hold once Melissa was at the required altitude. The soft fabrics ripped apart with an angry shredding noise, and the garment came away in Mina's hand to be thrown casually aside.

The startled croak of distress from Melissa melted into a prolonged moan as Mina's mouth dropped against her rear and sheathed a hot tongue into the orifice. Thrusting in, Mina rolled it back and forth, driving as deep as she could while Melissa squealed in depraved rhapsody.

Peeling off her gloves she flung them onto the pillows and used her hands to dig into the soft buttocks of the girl and pull the barring mounds open so she could penetrate deeper. Melissa whimpered with ecstasy as she was devoured, her thighs shaking with random fits while she was lost in a storm of utter pleasure. Mina let her hands drop and slide between the parted legs of the diminutive woman, riding her knuckles through her labia, bringing soft squeals from the girl's throat. The knuckles gave way to fingers that began to slither in and penetrate her, while another digit began to stroke and slither against her clitoris. Melissa wailed and sank her fingers into the sheets, dragging at fistfuls of satin as she tried to endure the stern ferocity of the dextrous touches.

More fingers began to come into play, one hand starting to insert more and more of its lengths into Melissa, stretching her, making her sex resound with flashes of sensation as the other hand continued a more devoted toil upon her clitoris.

Mina took her time, ensuring she offered only a minor havoc with the drives of her hand as she slowly fed her finger deeper into Melissa, and then retreated once she met resistance. Occasionally she dropped her face between the quivering legs and feasted on Melissa's rear a little more, darting her tongue into the puckered opening, leaving the girl awash with physical joy.

It was difficult to tell when Melissa was giving vent to orgasm, the acute nature of the input being thrust upon her making the bursts of rapture hide amongst her general writhing and squealing as she revelled in the feel of riding Mina's fingers.

Finally though, as Mina's hand was moving with more speed, Melissa jolted up, her arms ripping grooves in the sheets as she broke into spasms and shrieks. She collapsed onto the bed, spasming, the ghost traces left behind in her nerves like footprints in the snow bringing her to shaking fits, her voice spilling half syllables and sobbing croaks as she rode through the aftermath of the most intense of orgasms.

Mina lounged back and mulled over the feel of the girl, when suddenly Melissa was upon her, her eyes glazed as she grabbed Mina's forsaken opera gloves and used them as impromptu ropes, throwing up Mina's arms and using the fabric to tie her wrists tightly to the bedposts.

Mina wriggled a little, offering token resistance simply to have it crushed. Pulling at the tight bonds she watched the girl move down her body and slip between her legs, digging her nails into Mina's inner thighs so that she was forced to spread them further apart.

The hands of Melissa rolled up and down the stockings, the whispers of the fabric rising around Mina's panting gasps of excitement. The girl grabbed her torn underwear and forced it into Mina's mouth, driving it in as Mina gurgled and whimpered, pretending to be resisting.

Melissa leapt from the bed, ran to the table and grabbed some items that she kept from Mina's gaze before returning. She bounced into position and took hold of Mina's thong at the front. Lifting up, the slender crotch ate between her sodden lips, slipping through as the girl kept her fist to the intersection of satin, watching with glee as Mina was forced to lift her hindquarters. It was a delightfully humbling act, one that aroused her even more.

Melissa teased her with this deed for a while and then took hold of the thong in both hands, ripping it free and then using it as a wet cord to wrap around Mina's face and ensure she could not spit out the underwear already inserted. Mina chewed on the fabric with joy, feeling wonderfully subjugated by the girl.

A finger suddenly smoothed lubricant into her rear, the fingers of the girl working it inside and out before she felt an anal bead brush through her buttocks and press against the sphincter. The ball exerted more and more force until Mina arched up with a croaked moan when it slithered in and started to ride into her, the passage of the cord connecting it to the next one distinct as it rubbed against her. Her innards gulped in the next ball, and the next, Melissa feeding her rear a glut of solid spheres that flowed into her.

With the last one entered she deserted the remaining cord, casting it back and slotting her big toe into the metal ring at the end of the slack. With this hold on the toys, the girl clapped her hands to Mina's thighs and lowered her face into the humid pudenda.

Mina shuddered, her mouth stretching open as her body tingled with warm riots, her belly rolling over with delight as she felt the flat of a tongue troll against her clitoris. The sensation was beyond exquisite, and Mina pulled at her bonds, her muscles flexing as she shook, her legs held tightly down, her rear chewing on the balls as the girl performed a session of cunnilingus that almost had Mina fainting from the exquisite rhapsody it sent charging through her nervous system.

Melissa paused on occasion to rise and attend Mina's nipples, giving her a moment to calm, to let orgasm retreat so she could work her back towards it again once she had finished kissing and sucking at her breasts. Occasionally she threw a soft bite into the assets to have Mina gasp and send soft wails into her intimate gag.

Finally though she could resist no longer and kept her tongue flitting and suckling, devouring Mina's sex until her target began to air ascending groans, the panting howls rising in pitch and volume as a climax started to muster in her belly, growing stronger with every delicate lick of the betrayed Asian girl.

Mina's spine arched, lifting her head up as her cries rose towards their peak, her arms pulling at the bonds. When she finally climaxed she slammed back down, her back squirming, her head burying into the pillows as she yowled with utter bliss. As final release exploded through Mina, Melissa kicked steadily back, rattling the balls from her rear, her anus riding the drastic rise and plummet of the linked spheres, increasing her pleasure to a new and soul-tearing peak.

Mina's scream poured from her throat, the gag unable to even muffle it as she unleashed her howl to the heavens she felt she was already deeply immersed in. The last orb popped free and the tongue buried within her eased its work, letting her settle and relax, flashing with spasmodic jerks as she recovered from the ordeal.

Melissa unfastened the gloves and together they buried

238

themselves in the arms and kisses of the other, ruled by tenderness, gratitude and satisfaction. Collapsing onto the bed they held each other tight, shaking on occasion as tiredness started to swell. But they refused to succumb, holding it off as it continued to gather in strength, trying to have them fall into the soothing depths of recovery.

'Mina, do you know what you've let yourself in for?' asked Melissa.

'I have a fairly good idea,' she whispered in response.

'Why did you pick this fate?' Melissa quizzed. 'I had no choice, but you?'

'You could have gone to jail,' said Mina.

'Maybe I would have preferred that in retrospect,' replied Melissa.

'I doubt it. We both know you would have ended up in a far worse situation in there.'

'You still haven't answered my question,' pressed the girl, causing Mina to pause before answering her.

'You chose the lesser of two evils. I had a choice of being imprisoned and punished for the rest of my life with that torturer, Rache, or serve my imprisonment with Charybdis. At least with one of them I get to spend a day with you, like this,' she stated, hiding the fact that she ached to feel the eternal embrace of the uniform, to be smothered and mummified, served to the utter control of Charybdis. Melissa wouldn't understand, and there was no sense in spoiling the mood of her annual one day of carnal vacation.

Mina closed her eyes and finally relented to her fatigue, drifting into sleep as Melissa stroked her spiky mane of hair.

Chapter Nineteen

'Good morning, slaves,' crooned Charybdis, making them both jump awake from their restful snooze. 'I trust you are ready, it's time you were put in your uniforms until next year.'

They looked up and found their owner in the doorway, the squad of black-clad enforcers at his heels, the rubber clad women ready to capture his slaves should they prove resistant. A wicked twinkle flitted across his eyes as he contemplated seeing the two lovers separated by an eternal wall of latex.

'No, not yet, please!' begged Melissa, as Charybdis nodded to his anonymous entourage.

The watching women advanced quickly, stomping towards Melissa as she cowered and wept, hugging to Mina for protection.

'I love you, Mina,' she wept, kissing her quickly on the lips as rubber-gloved hands grabbed hold of her, hauling her from the bed.

'I love you too,' replied Mina, sitting on the bed as she watched Melissa being dragged away and out of the room, her feet dragging as the women marched swiftly, heedless of whether she co-operated or not.

'You're not resisting?' asked Charybdis, once Melissa had vanished.

'I agreed to this, why deny that?' she replied frankly. 'I want this. What would fighting accomplish?'

'Ah, so you've finally accepted your masochistic submissive streak then?'

Mina said nothing as he smiled at her.

'Ensure she is chaste,' he ordered, and the women

produced a chastity belt of the variety she had first endured. Grabbing her, she was bent over, her haunches raised and they roughly installed the device before they walked from the room.

'We'll be back for you shortly, slave,' Charybdis announced as the door slammed shut in his wake.

Mina spent her time alone feeding her hunger. She ate her fill of the foods on offer, drank what she wished, relaxed into the opulent covers and let her mind drift, enjoying her last portion of freedom.

The door opened and four of the women entered, grabbing and hauling her from the bed by force. She did not resist, merely hung in their hands as she was led to the chamber that would change her life for the rest of the year.

The door whirred aside, revealing a small room. Lit by several strip lights, a table lay to one side, a set of clippers on it and a pile of Melissa's shorn hair next to them. The white walls of steel bore a few rings, one of which accepted the chain leash of Melissa herself, the girl now restored to her blind state, lost in her bondage once more. With her pipes locked to the appropriate wall fittings she tottered back and forth, trying to accustom her body to the rigours of the uniform as the three women who had done this to her stood aside and watched their creation's panic. The umbilicals snapped taut as she wandered too far, the thick hoses more than able to defeat her feeble struggles against them.

Faint whimpers were seeping through the costume as the rubber creaked softly with her despairing fight against it. Mina smiled, eager to follow her, to lose herself in the dark and sweaty oblivion of the uniform.

Charybdis was standing by the wall, and with a wave of his hand he indicated the latex cascade hanging beside him, a portable unit parked at its feet. 'Slave Mina, your uniform awaits you,' he beamed, eager to see her swallowed up. 'Take a good look, for you won't be seeing the outside of it again for another full year.'

Mina stared across the slack folds, her mouth dry as the leash was removed and hands pushed her forward, in a trance, fixated only on the sight. It would be the last thing she saw without the obscuring eyepieces of the hood, and she intended to commit every detail to memory.

Taken to the table she was roughly bent over, her body refusing to resist as they ran the clippers across her scalp, trimming away her hair. The tresses tumbled before her eyes once more, joining Melissa's, the soft groans and squeals of the girl's distress merging into the sound of the device as it toiled.

The chastity belt was opened and drawn from her, the plugs slipping free and letting her tracts finally close. She had assumed that the belt still existed on Melissa, but it seemed that a different example was to be used.

Steel bands were locked above her knees and to her ankles, set against the skin in readiness to grab the chains of the bar that would hobble her every step and prevent her ever sitting down.

The cat-suit was taken up and with a shake to straighten it, the garment showed that the dense material flowed out to a set of gloves, socks, and a basic open-faced hood. The suit opened down the back from the nape of the neck to the base of the spine, the doubled density of the area of rubber about the zip fitted with eyelets for lacing on either side.

The brawny women started to feed the tubular sheaths onto her body, encasing her in a thick layer of impermeable fabric. The cold arms of the suit stretched onto her, the thickness making their elasticity minimal, the fit of the uniform exceptionally tight.

Mina groaned as she felt them settling it into place, tugging along her extremities to drag away every wrinkle, leaving her with a fight to bend her legs because of the density across her joints.

'Exquisite,' commented Charybdis, watching Mina with wide eyes, licking his lips as he lounged against the wall.

Her head was forced up into the hood, where she found two electronic nodules that were set into her ears, cutting off almost all external sound, leaving the voice of her master as the only thing she could hear.

Her breathing started to quicken as her breasts were forced through two tight circles, the women employing a casual indifference to their subject. The holes made them swell from the grip around their base, and as she wriggled against the hoops, the slits across her crotch and rear were straightened into place.

Again she was laid against the table, her body resting on it, her arms pinned forcefully down to ensure she did not forget that resistance was not an option. The thigh boots were drawn up onto her legs, setting her feet atop the high heels. A line of glue was added to seal them perfectly and the buckles locked them to fittings on her suit, condemning her to their eternal companionship.

Hands clamped about her ankles and brought them together as the steel bar was brought forth, the chains chiming softly as they swung and bounced against the metal. The shaft connected to the band of her replacement crotch-piece, welded into place to prevent it moving in the slightest. The half circle of steel had far more obvious armaments upon it than her last such belt. A large, drastically ridged black rubber dildo awaited entry into her sex, the dark material laced with circuitry to stimulate and chastise. Her anus, however, was destined to accept a long pliant tube.

Lubricant trailed a line across her openings as the waistband was installed over the cat-suit, and Mina tensed as she felt them threading the pipe into her, paying it in and letting the work of her internal muscles swallow it up. The little struggles she gave caused the women to lean more weight to her, keeping her under firmer reins, perhaps because of her reputation, or just because they liked to subdue slaves.

The dildo kissed her sex and slithered in, her lips tight upon the trenches and peaks of the articulated intruder. The size of it made her lift her head up and mutter soft cries of discomfort, her channel aching as it was filled. She would of course get used to it, but for now it was a strenuous burden to bear, her legs quivering with tension.

A hearty shove sent the crotch-piece slamming between her legs and to the suit, throwing its teeth into the locks and fixing it to her. The dildo jabbed against her deepest regions, making her cry out from the sudden flash of pain.

'Easy, Mina, you're doing just fine,' commented Charybdis.

Mina went slack against the table, her spasming orifices chewing against the trespassers, her muscles trying to drive them out, only to find them immobile. She would be wearing this for a year.

A line of thin wire was laced through the long slit down her back, drawing it in, and as the women applied their full brawn to the task, Mina hissed and gasped as they crushed her torso against the corset-like body of the cat-suit. Tolerating no slack, they continued the process of tightening again and again as Mina whimpered softly from the compression. Once the two sides met, the wire was riveted to a fixture on the back of her crotch-piece.

A thick leotard was next to be added, the neck being the raised posture collar that would stop her from ever moving her head more than a few millimetres. The hips of the garment descended like shorts, the brief legs ready to meet the hem of the thigh boots. The areas for her breasts had been removed again, leaving Mina wondering when they would be covered and what the sensation would be like. For a moment it looked as though the leotard was for a male, for there was a penis sheath set at the crotch, but then she saw it was placed too low down into the crotch for male anatomy to use.

The top was pulled over her legs, the prepared hole in the crotch squeezing tightly to the hobble bar with the inch long tube of latex. Twisting her arms back, they forced them through the sleeves and dragged it up into place, adding more weight to her body and increasing the clinch to her torso.

The relentless procedure of Mina's transformation continued as they produced the tube of glue, using the substance to run a thick line under the rim of the shorts, creating a hermetic seal. They repeated the act of perpetual closure on the armholes, and then on the upper rim of the collar once they had tightened the band into place. The chains of her bar were set through the layers of rubber and clipped into place, to be swiftly drowned in the resin, as was the small tube gripping the meeting of belt and pole. With airtight seals running around the leotard Mina was rendered utterly watertight save for her breasts and her face, and she knew that this oversight would soon be corrected.

Standing upright, she found that balance was no longer something to be taken for granted. The imposition of the chain kept her legs curtailed and she had to be constantly careful of every movement else she stumble, topple and fall.

The hands of her tailors once more fell upon her, grabbing her arms, helping to steady her a little as they were twisted up her back. Mina grimaced as they were hauled well back, making her thrust her breasts forth against the hoops. Straps were set across her upper arms, the first stage of trapping her limbs and rendering them useless to her complete. When they started to bend her forearms up and around, running them parallel to each other up her spine, Mina struggled and gave whinnying protests of distress, her arms reverberating with pain as they were manhandled.

'Ow!' she mewled. 'Stop, please, I can't keep this position!'

'Nonsense, Mina, once you're locked into position you'll get used to it quite quickly,' he stated, making Mina wince at the thought of just how long that might be.

Her wriggling fingers were gathered together into a small mitten, the bag possessing two internal slots and being laced tight over them, bunching the digits together before a buckled strap at the wrist sealed them away for good. Groaning, Mina lifted herself from her heels and wobbled on her toes, the women forcing the single sleeve down onto her forearms. She kicked her legs vainly against the bars as they supported her, but it was useless, the time to resist long gone. The tight sleeve was settled into place and they started buckling it shut. Tears were forming in Mina's eyes as she endured the increasing stress of the uniform, but it still felt so good, despite the havoc in her flesh. Buckles from the sleeve were dragged around and snapped to fastenings on her front, the hearty yank the women applied squeezing her arms firmly against her back.

Two rubber cups were aimed towards her breasts, the implements being brought forward with menace. Mina gave crippled struggles against the two women holding her. The stern females clapped hands to the back of her neck, forcing her into a stoop. She sobbed immediately as the pole between her legs was made to fight the belt, churning the rods in her, making them try to shift aside yet be denied.

With her breasts hanging, the cups gathered them up and were pushed firmly onto them. She could feel banks

246

of dull rubber spines lining the interior, the short teeth pressing into her flesh. When the base of the cups were pressed to her suit, the interiors pressurised themselves instantly. The scowling hiss of air being thrust out grabbed every inch of her assets, dragging them fiercely against the spines, making them dig in more distinctly. Mina thrashed against those holding her, unable to straighten against their rigorous grips.

'Oh, what *are* these things?' she wailed, her fingers fighting the bag that prevented them even moving, her arms unable to even twitch.

'They serve a variety of purposes, all of which you'll find out soon enough,' said Charybdis.

The sealing glue was traced around the connection and as they lifted her back upright, Mina could see two sockets where her nipples were submerged.

The women equipped themselves with her two hoods, the first being the under-hood that was pulled down over the suit and quickly glued to her posture collar. Her head was now locked within a dome of latex, the only break in the polished sheet being two nostril holes and an aperture for her mouth. Her eyes peered through plastic lenses, the material fogging her vision slightly. The other hood was held back a moment as Charybdis spoke.

'You recall the gag, don't you, Mina?' he jovially quizzed as the implement was brought forth. The plate that would seal her mouth still bore the moulded interior that would slot onto her teeth and spread her jaws painfully wide. Then the contraption spilled onward as a segmented pipe that they would compel her to swallow, but this one also extended up to the nose, the faceplate holding two long tubes that were ready to snake down her nostrils. Having faced something like this before, she nodded and watched as the disturbing thing was brought over.

She was tempted to try and air some last words before

she was rendered silent for a year, but nothing came to mind so she watched the horrid approach of her instrument of silencing and complete control. A firm hand sunk fingers into her cheek, ruthlessly illustrating the rictus they wanted. As she spread her jaws wide, they started to feed it down her throat. Mina retched and convulsed against them, the serpent slithering down into her gullet. As the plate neared her quivering lips the nostril tubes were threaded down, making breathing momentarily difficult.

The facemask was pushed into place and glued airtight into position, Mina's breath now rasping through the two sockets at her nose. Unable to speak, or hear, and barely able to see, Mina watched the last hood approach. The dense discipline sheath was forced down onto her head, the women having to fight the fabric, forcing Mina's jaws painfully into the posture collar as the infernal thing was hauled into position. Mina wailed in dismay at the treatment, her howls dribbling out through the tubes as mere distant groans. All sight was lost, her head compressed within an iron fist, her body crushed, each breath straining against the rubber tomb in which she had condemned herself.

Immediately air was forced through the umbilical demanding a prescribed rate of breath for Mina, her lungs powerless to resist the mechanised force. She almost wilted into her increasingly harrowing bondage, the feeling of separation, of arousal at being so mercilessly parcelled was a giddy high of the darkest variety.

Suddenly a voice poured in through her earplugs, startling her with its clarity after the deathly silence of her hoods.

'I'm going to let your servants play with your controls for a while, as a reward for a job well done,' said Charybdis, using his own private PA system into their hidden servile world.

Mina took a step forward and found that rather than attach her to the portable generator, she was now anchored to the wall as Melissa was. The cables twanged and she was abruptly stopped, wondering what the three women who had attended her would do first. She was a vulnerable target, any number of choices open to them, and it all depended on just how sadistic they were willing to be.

The answer was delivered when the vaginal dildo started to retract and thrust into her, the harsh penetration delightful and searing all at once. Instantly the clitoral nodule kicked into spurious life, humming and pounding her sex, making her gasp and totter unsteadily, her head swimming, her loins aflame.

The sucking at her breasts commenced without warning, the massaging banks of rubber fangs chewing gently on them while a suckling pressurised kiss attended her nipples, dragging them out into the awaiting internal dimple.

Mina swaggered aside and dropped against the wall for support, unable to sink down, the pole forcing itself to the chains whenever she tried. It was almost too much to contain, her grunts and sighs failing to emerge and illustrate her delight.

Galloping towards climax, the devices suddenly changed settings just before she was taken into such a release, the women expert at telling when one of their own gender was in the giddy throes of pre-orgasmic joy.

Voltage nips scorched her rear, running its length as painful bites sank into her buttocks. Thrusting her hips forward to instinctively pull away from the source of pain, Mina was cast back as the clitoral button turned from a friend to a heartless fiend.

The savage snaps had her dancing on her feet, madly

writing, screeching into the gag. The breast cups increased their attention, applying more force to their caresses, kneading her breasts with hateful spite, as well as firing nips of shock into the contained flesh. Her nipples were suckled upon most vehemently, the feeling convincing her that they were going to be torn off by the oscillating grab of the vacuum cups. Other shocks started to gallop across her body, the suit fitted with an arsenal of diabolic engines, all of which thrust their dire effects into Mina.

Jolting and screaming against the gag, she fought the rubber and bonds, battled the hobble bar, but she could do nothing save suffer unspeakably for the delight of those who had placed her in this terrible fate.

Then all the evil machines suddenly ceased their assault, letting her wheeze and catch her breath. She wondered how Melissa was doing. Had her time already within the suit hardened her against it? Could one even get used to such grand duress?

What felt like a cane suddenly ripped across Mina's rear, the influence of the weapon compiled by a series of co-ordinated electrical jolts that tricked her nerves into feeling something they had not. Jerking onto tiptoe, she dropped back, the ethereal stroke incredibly intense. The pain was soothed as the dildo began its slothful play, a slow, dull bliss that helped take the edge away from her panic. She felt so utterly exposed, so unable to even defend herself, the extreme bondage making her moist with new arousal, even as another phantom switch etched a line across her stomach.

Cursing the women, she sobbed and tried to brace for the next application. The women continued to beat her with electricity for a prolonged period, applying their strokes anywhere they wished because there could be no physical damage done to her.

Sweating and screaming, crying and gibbering, Mina

was hauled through her initiation, hating every second of it, despising her bondage and her own foolish perversity that had placed her in it for life.

The flagellating voltage stopped and Mina sighed, the loss of such distress suddenly flipping the event like a coin, turning it completely around so that now she was sighing, expectant of more, hungry for it.

The last thing she expected was the flood of water that started to pour into her suit. Squirming against the chaotic flood that churned between her skin and the artificial shell, Mina's legs shuddering from the turbulence around her loins. Gurgling upon the deep gag, she relished the feel of the retraction of the rinse, and a howling soft gale started to lift the rubber from her skin to the tinniest degree, permitting her to be dried.

She felt movement in the pipe pouring down into her stomach as she was automatically fed, unable to even taste that which was being forced into her.

'Did you enjoy that, slaves?' asked Charybdis into their ears, and Mina nodded as best she could, unknowing of what Melissa's opinion was.

'There is so much more to show you. The conductors across your body have a tremendous range, and we shall be testing them all. And when I have you suspended next to my bed so you can watch me sleep, or pleasure one of your less restrained sisters, I'll leave some random programmes running, to flick pleasure, pain, or both into you, at any time, for any duration. You both belong only to me. You'll stay in those prisons for the next twelve months, and during that time I'll throw a deluge of sensuality upon you. I'll cook your sanity with pleasure and pain, make you scream for it, crave it like nothing you've ever known. By the time this year is up, you'll be begging me to leave you in those suits, locked inside latex for the rest of your lives, suffering together for my amusement.' He smiled imperiously.

'Oh, and did I forget to mention that you'll also be receiving gene therapy via your food?' he went on, running his hands down the succulent rubber-encased forms, tracing the contours of the females sealed deep beneath.

'Have you heard of p21? I'm sure Mina has.' He smiled, chuckling as she stiffened and struggled with new effort. He couldn't have! It wasn't possible!

'P21 is a specific master gene that was unearthed a decade ago by my labs, and only this year by a Chicago institute. You see, genes in a ten-year-old and a ninety-year-old operate the same, its only p21 that tells them to deteriorate, creating the ravages of old age – arthritis, Alzheimer's, all the ailments that can rob a person of their life prematurely. Where normal medicine struggles to even figure out p21, my labs have been working on perfecting the means to shut this little monster up all this time. Two years ago we succeeded. In effect, we own the fountain of youth, which prompted the Korin, Turan merger. You see, we want to ensure that it doesn't hit the market and ruin the world by making everyone virtually immortal before we've sorted out factors such as environment and population explosion. Until this time, which probably won't ever come, we'll be keeping this little secret to a very select few, and I've decided to include you both in addition to Scylla and myself. So enjoy the feel of your latex tombs, my pets – you're in them quiet literally for eternity.'

Mina's eyes fluttered shut with delight at hearing such words, knowing now that this fate was going to give her everything she could ever have hoped for. She was a perfect slave – perfectly bound, perfectly controlled, and utterly owned, forever.

The beginning…

More exciting titles available from Chimera

All **Chimera** titles are available from your local bookshop or newsagent, or direct from our mail order department. Please send your order with your credit card details, a cheque or postal order (made payable to *Chimera Publishing Ltd*) to: **Chimera Publishing Ltd., Readers' Services, PO Box 152, Waterlooville, Hants, PO8 9FS**. Or call our **24 hour telephone/fax credit card hotline: +44 (0)23 92 783037** (Visa, Mastercard, Switch, JCB and Solo only).

To order, send: Title, author, ISBN number and price for each book ordered, your full name and address, cheque or postal order for the total amount, and include the following for postage and packing:
UK and BFPO: £1.00 for the first book, and 50p for each additional book to a maximum of £3.50.
Overseas and Eire: £2.00 for the first book, £1.00 for the second and 50p for each additional book.

*Titles £5.99. **All others (latest releases) £6.99**

For a copy of our free catalogue please write to:

Chimera Publishing Ltd
Readers' Services
PO Box 152
Waterlooville
Hants
PO8 9FS

or email us at:
sales@chimerabooks.co.uk

or purchase from our range of superb titles at:
www.chimerabooks.co.uk

Sales and Distribution in the USA and Canada

Client Distribution Services, Inc
193 Edwards Drive
Jackson
TN 38301
USA
(800) 343 4499

Sales and Distribution in Australia

Dennis Jones & Associates Pty Ltd
19a Michellan Ct
Bayswater
Victoria
Australia 3153